The Masquerader

by

Katherine Cecil Thurston

The Echo Library 2006

Published by

The Echo Library

Echo Library
131 High St.
Teddington
Middlesex TW11 8HH

www.echo-library.com

Please report serious faults in the text to complaints@echo-library.com

ISBN 1-40681-190-4

THE MASQUERADER

I

Two incidents, widely different in character yet bound together by results, marked the night of January the twenty-third. On that night the blackest fog within a four years' memory fell upon certain portions of London, and also on that night came the first announcement of the border risings against the Persian government in the province of Khorasan the announcement that, speculated upon, even smiled at, at the time, assumed such significance in the light of after events.

At eight o'clock the news spread through the House of Commons; but at nine men in the inner lobbies were gossiping, not so much upon how far Russia, while ostensibly upholding the Shah, had pulled the strings by which the insurgents danced, as upon the manner in which the 'St. Geotge's Gazette', the Tory evening newspaper, had seized upon the incident and shaken it in the faces of the government.

More than once before, Lakely—the owner and editor of the 'St. George's'—had stepped outside the decorous circle of tradition and taken a plunge into modern journalism, but to-night he essayed deeper waters than before, and under an almost sensational heading declared that in this apparently innocent border rising we had less an outcome of mere racial antagonism than a first faint index of a long-cherished Russian scheme, growing to a gradual maturity under the "drift" policy of the present British government.

The effect produced by this pronouncement, if strong, was varied. Members of the Opposition saw, or thought they saw, a reflection of it in the smiling unconcern on the Ministerial benches; and the government had an uneasy sense that behind the newly kindled interest on the other side of the House lay some mysterious scenting of battle from afar off. But though these impressions ran like electricity through the atmosphere, nothing tangible marked their passage, and the ordinary business of the House proceeded until half-past eleven, when an adjournment was moved.

The first man to hurry from his place was John Chilcote, member for East Wark. He passed out of the House quickly, with the half-furtive quickness that marks a self-absorbed man; and as he passed the policeman standing stolidly under the arched door-way of the big court-yard he swerved a little, as if startled out of his thoughts. He realized his swerve almost before it was accomplished, and pulled himself together with nervous irritability.

"Foggy night, constables," he said, with elaborate carelessness.

"Foggy night, sir, and thickening up west," responded the man.

"Ah, indeed!" Chilcote's answer was absent. The constable's cheery voice jarred on him, and for the second time he was conscious of senseless irritation.

Without a further glance at the man, he slipped out into the court-yard and turned towards the main gate.

At the gate-way two cab lamps showed through the mist of shifting fog like the eyes of a great cat, and the familiar "Hansom, sir?" came to him indistinctly.

He paused by force of custom; and, stepping forward, had almost touched the open door when a new impulse caused him to draw back.

"No," he said, hurriedly. "No. I'll walk."

The cabman muttered, lashed his horse, and with a clatter of hoofs and harness wheeled away; while Chilcote, still with uncertain hastiness, crossed the road in the direction of Whitehall.

About the Abbey the fog had partially lifted, and in the railed garden that faces the Houses of Parliament the statues were visible in a spectral way. But Chilcote's glance was unstable and indifferent; he skirted the railings heedlessly, and, crossing the road with the speed of long familiarity, gained Whitehall on the lefthand side.

There the fog had dropped, and, looking upward towards Trafalgar Square, it seemed that the chain of lamps extended little farther than the Horse Guards, and that beyond lay nothing.

Unconscious of this capricious alternation between darkness and light, Chilcote continued his course. To a close observer the manner of his going had both interest and suggestion; for though he walked on, apparently self-engrossed, yet at every dozen steps he started at some sound or some touch, like a man whose nervous system is painfully overstrung.

Maintaining his haste, he went deliberately forward, oblivious of the fact that at each step the curtain of darkness about him became closer, damper, more tangible; that at each second the passers-by jostled each other with greater frequency. Then, abruptly, with a sudden realization of what had happened, he stood quite still. Without anticipation or preparation he had walked full into the thickness of the fog—a thickness so dense that, as by an enchanter's wand, the figures of a moment before melted, the street lamps were sucked up into the night.

His first feeling was a sense of panic at the sudden isolation, his second a thrill of nervous apprehension at the oblivion that had allowed him to be so entrapped. The second feeling outweighed the first. He moved forward, then paused again, uncertain of himself. Finally, with the consciousness that inaction was unbearable, he moved on once more, his eyes wide open, one hand thrust out as a protection and guide.

The fog had closed in behind him as heavily as in front, shutting off all possibility of retreat; all about him in the darkness was a confusion of voices—cheerful, dubious, alarmed, or angry; now and then a sleeve brushed his or a hand touched him tentatively. It was a strange moment, a moment of possibilities, to which the crunching wheels, the oaths and laughter from the blocked traffic of the road-way, made a continuous accompaniment.

Keeping well to the left, Chilcote still beat on; there was a persistence in his movements that almost amounted to fear —a fear born of the solitude filled with innumerable sounds. For a space he groped about him without result, then his fingers touched the cold surface of a shuttered shop-front, and a thrill of reassurance passed through him. With renewed haste, and clinging to his landmark as a blind man might, he started forward with fresh impetus.

For a dozen paces he moved rapidly and unevenly, then the natural result occurred. He collided with a man coming in the opposite direction.

The shock was abrupt. Both men swore simultaneously, then both laughed. The whole thing was casual, but Chilcote was in that state of mind when even the commonplace becomes abnormal. The other man's exclamation, the other man's laugh, struck on his nerves; coming out of the darkness, they sounded like a repetition of his own.

Nine out of every ten men in London, given the same social position and the same education, might reasonably be expected to express annoyance or amusement in the same manner, possibly in the same tone of voice; and Chilcote remembered this almost at the moment of his nervous jar.

"Beastly fog!" he said, aloud. "I'm trying to find Grosvenor Square, but the chances seem rather small."

The other laughed again, and again the laugh upset Chilcote. He wondered uncomfortably if he was becoming a prey to illusions. But the stranger spoke before the question had solved itself.

"I'm afraid they are small," he said. "It would be almost hard to find one's way to the devil on a night like this."

Chilcote made a murmur of amusement and drew back against the shop.

"Yes. We can see now where the blind man scores in the matter of salvation. This is almost a repetition of the fog of six years ago. Were you out in that?"

It was a habit of his to jump from one sentence to another, a habit that had grown of late.

"No." The stranger had also groped his way to the shopfront. "No, I was out of England six years ago."

"You were lucky." Chilcote turned up the collar of his coat. "It was an atrocious fog, as black as this, but more universal. I remember it well. It was the night Lexington made his great sugar speech. Some of us were found on Lambeth Bridge at three in the morning, having left the House at twelve."

Chilcote seldom indulged in reminiscences, but this conversation with an unseen companion was more like a soliloquy than a dialogue. He was almost surprised into an exclamation when the other caught up his words.

"Ah! The sugar speech!" he said. "Odd that I should have been looking it up only yesterday. What a magnificent dressing-up of a dry subject it was! What a career Lexington promised in those days!"

Chilcote changed his position.

"You are interested in the muddle down at Westminster?" he asked, sarcastically.

"I—?" It was the turn of the stranger to draw back a step. "Oh, I read my newspaper with the other five million, that is all. I am an outsider." His voice sounded curt; the warmth that admiration had brought into it a moment before had frozen abruptly.

"An outsider!" Chilcote repeated. "What an enviable word!"

"Possibly, to those who are well inside the ring. But let us go back to Lexington. What a pinnacle the man reached, and what a drop he had! It has always seemed to me an extraordinary instance of the human leaven running through us all. What was the real cause of his collapse?" he asked, suddenly. "Was it drugs or drink? I have often wished to get at the truth."

Again Chilcote changed his attitude.

"Is truth ever worth getting at?" he asked, irrelevantly.

"In the case of a public man—yes. He exchanges his privacy for the interest of the masses. If he gives the masses the details of his success, why not the details of his failure? But was it drink that sucked him under?"

"No." Chilcote's response came after a pause.

"Drugs?"

Again Chilcote hesitated. And at the moment of his indecision a woman brushed past him, laughing boisterously. The sound jarred him.

"Was it drugs?" the stranger went on easily. "I have always had a theory that it was."

"Yes. It was morphia." The answer came before Chilcote had realized it. The woman's laugh at the stranger's quiet persistence had contrived to draw it from him. Instantly he had spoken he looked about him quickly, like one who has for a moment forgotten a necessary vigilance.

There was silence while the stranger thought over the information just given him. Then he spoke again, with a new touch of vehemence.

"So I imagined," he said. "Though, on my soul, I never really credited it. To have gained so much, and to have thrown it away for a common vice!" He made an exclamation of disgust.

Chilcote gave an unsteady laugh. "You judge hardly." he said.

The other repeated his sound of contempt. "Justly so. No man has the right to squander what another would give his soul for. It lessens the general respect for power."

"You are a believer in power?" The tone was sarcastic, but the sarcasm sounded thin.

"Yes. All power is the outcome of individuality, either past or present. I find no sentiment for the man who plays with it."

The quiet contempt of the tone stung Chilcote.

"Do you imagine that Lexington made no fight?" he asked, impulsively. "Can't you picture the man's struggle while the vice that had been slave gradually became master?" He stopped to take breath, and in the cold pause that followed it seemed to him that the other made a murmur of incredulity.

"Perhaps you think of morphia as a pleasure?" he added. "Think of it, instead, as a tyrant—that tortures the mind if held to, and the body if cast off." Urged by the darkness and the silence of his companion, the rein of his speech had loosened. In that moment he was not Chilcote the member for East Wark, whose moods and silences were proverbial, but Chilcote the man whose mind craved the relief of speech.

"You talk as the world talks—out of ignorance and self-righteousness," he went on. "Before you condemn Lexington you should put yourself in his place—"

"As you do?" the other laughed.

Unsuspecting and inoffensive as the laugh was, it startled Chilcote. With a sudden alarm he pulled himself up.

"I—?" He tried to echo the laugh, but the attempt fell flat. "Oh, I merely speak from—from De Quincey. But I believe this fog is shifting—I really believe it is shifting. Can you oblige me with a light? I had almost forgotten that a man may still smoke though he has been deprived of sight." He spoke fast and disjointedly. He was overwhelmed by the idea that he had let himself go, and possessed by the wish to obliterate the consequences. As he talked he fumbled; for his cigarette-case.

His bead was bent as he searched for it nervously. Without looking up, he was conscious that the cloud of fog that held him prisoner was lifting, rolling away, closing back again, preparatory to final disappearance. Having found the case, he put a cigarette between his lips and raised his hand at the moment that the stranger drew a match across his box.

For a second each stared blankly at the other's face, suddenly made visible by the lifting of the fog. The match in the stranger's hand burned down till it scorched his fingers, and, feeling the pain, he laughed and let it drop.

"Of all odd things!" he said. Then he broke off. The circumstance was too novel for ordinary remark.

By one of those rare occurrences, those chances that seem too wild for real life and yet belong to no other sphere, the two faces so strangely hidden and strangely revealed were identical, feature for feature. It seemed to each man that he looked not at the face of another, but at his own face reflected in a flawless looking-glass.

Of the two, the stranger was the first to regain self-possession. Seeing Chilcote's bewilderment, he came to his rescue with brusque tactfulness.

"The position is decidedly odd," he said. "But after all, why should we be so surprised? Nature can't be eternally original; she must dry up sometimes, and when she gets a good model why shouldn't she use it twice?" He drew back, surveying Chilcote whimsically. "But, pardon me, you are still waiting for that light!"

Chilcote still held the cigarette between his lips. The paper had become dry, and he moistened it as he leaned towards his companion.

"Don't mind me," he said. "I'm rather—rather unstrung to-night, and this thing gave me a jar. To be candid, my imagination took head in the fog, and I got to fancy I was talking to myself—"

"And pulled up to find the fancy in some way real?"

"Yes. Something like that."

Both were silent for a moment. Chilcote pulled hard at his cigarette, then, remembering his obligations, he turned quickly to the other.

"Won't you smoke?" he asked.

The stranger accepted a cigarette from the case held out to him; and as he did so the extraordinary likeness to himself struck Chilcote with added force. Involuntarily he put out his hand and touched the other's arm.

"It's my nerves!" he said, in explanation. "They make me want to feel that you are substantial. Nerves play such beastly tricks!" He laughed awkwardly.

The other glanced up. His expression on the moment was slightly surprised, slightly contemptuous, but he changed it instantly to conventional interest. "I am afraid I am not an authority on nerves," he said.

But Chilcote was preoccupied. His thoughts had turned into another channel.

"How old are you?" he asked, suddenly.

The other did not answer immediately. "My age?" he said at last, slowly. "Oh, I believe I shall be thirty-six to-morrow—to be quite accurate."

Chilcote lifted his head quickly.

"Why do you use that tone?" he asked. "I am six months older than you, and I only wish it was six years. Six years nearer oblivion—"

Again a slight incredulous contempt crossed the other's eyes. "Oblivion?" he said. "Where are your ambitions?"

"They don't exist."

"Don't exist? Yet you voice your country? I concluded that much in the fog."

Chilcote laughed sarcastically.

"When one has voiced one's country for six years one gets hoarse—it's a natural consequence."

The other smiled. "Ah, discontent!" he said. "The modern canker. But we must both be getting under way. Good-night! Shall we shake hands—to prove that we are genuinely material?"

Chilcote had been standing unusually still, following the stranger's words—caught by his self-reliance and impressed by his personality. Now, as he ceased to speak, he moved quickly forward, impelled by a nervous curiosity.

"Why should we just hail each other and pass—like the proverbial ships?" he said, impulsively. "If Nature was careless enough to let the reproduction meet the original, she must abide the consequences."

The other laughed, but his laugh was short. "Oh, I don't know. Our roads lie differently. You would get nothing out of me, and I—" He stopped and again laughed shortly. "No," he said; "I'd be content to pass, if I were you. The unsuccessful man is seldom a profitable study. Shall we say good-night?"

He took Chilcote's hand for an instant; then, crossing the footpath, he passed into the road-way towards the Strand.

It was done in a moment; but with his going a sense of loss fell upon Chilcote. He stood for a space, newly conscious of unfamiliar faces and unfamiliar voices in the stream of passersby; then, suddenly mastered by an impulse, he wheeled rapidly and darted after the tall, lean figure so ridiculously like his own.

Half-way across Trafalgar Square he overtook the stranger. He had paused on one of the small stone islands that break the current of traffic, and was waiting for an opportunity to cross the street. In the glare of light from the lamp above his head, Chilcote saw for the first time that, under a remarkable neatness of appearance, his clothes were well worn—almost shabby. The discovery struck him with something stronger than surprise. The idea of poverty seemed incongruous is connection with the reliance, the reserve, the personality of the man. With a certain embarrassed haste he stepped forward and touched his arm.

"Look here," he said, as the other turned quietly. "I have followed you to exchange cards. It can't injure either of us, and I—I have a wish to know my other self." He laughed nervously as he drew out his card-case.

The stranger watched him in silence. There was the same faint contempt, but also there was a reluctant interest in his glance, as it passed from the fingers fumbling with the case to the pale face with the square jaw, straight mouth, and level eyebrows drawn low over the gray eyes. When at last the card was held out to him he took it without remark and slipped it into his pocket.

Chilcote looked at him eagerly. "Now the exchange?" he said.

For a second the stranger did not respond. Then, almost unexpectedly, he smiled.

"After all, if it amuses you—" he said; and, searching in his waistcoat pocket, he drew out the required card.

"It will leave you quite unenlightened," he added. "The name of a failure never spells anything." With another smile, partly amused, partly ironical, he stepped from the little island and disappeared into the throng of traffic.

Chilcote stood for an instant gazing at the point where he had vanished; then, turning to the lamp, he lifted the card and read the name it bore: "Mr. John Loder, 13 Clifford's Inn."

II

On the morning following the night of fog Chilcote woke at nine. He woke at the moment that his man Allsopp tiptoed across the room and laid the salver with his early cup of tea on the table beside the bed.

For several seconds he lay with his eyes shut; the effort of opening them on a fresh day—the intimate certainty of what he would see on opening them—seemed to weight his lids. The heavy, half-closed curtains; the blinds severely drawn; the great room with its splendid furniture, its sober coloring, its scent of damp London winter; above all, Allsopp, silent, respectful, and respectable—were things to dread.

A full minute passed while he still feigned sleep. He heard Allsopp stir discreetly, then the inevitable information broke the silence:

"Nine o'clock, sir!"

He opened his eyes, murmured something, and closed them again.

The man moved to the window, quietly pulled back the curtains and half drew the blind.

"Better night, sir, I hope?" he ventured, softly.

Chilcote had drawn the bedclothes over his face to screen himself from the daylight, murky though it was.

"Yes," he responded. "Those beastly nightmares didn't trouble me, for once." He shivered a little as at some recollection. "But don't talk—don't remind me of them. I hate a man who has no originality." He spoke sharply. At times he showed an almost childish irritation over trivial things.

Allsopp took the remark in silence. Crossing the wide room, he began to lay out his master's clothes. The action affected Chilcote to fresh annoyance.

"Confound it!" he said. "I'm sick of that routine: I can see you laying out my winding-sheet the day of my burial. Leave those things. Come back in half an hour."

Allsopp allowed himself one glance at his master's figure huddled in the great bed; then, laying aside the coat he was holding, he moved to the door. With his fingers on the handle he paused.

"Will you breakfast in your own room, sir—or down-stairs?"

Chilcote drew the clothes more tightly round his shoulders. "Oh, anywhere—nowhere!" he said. "I don't care."

Allsopp softly withdrew.

Left to himself, Chilcote sat up in bed and lifted the salver to his knees. The sudden movement jarred him physically; he drew a handkerchief from under the pillow and wiped his forehead; then he held his hand to the light and studied it. The hand looked sallow and unsteady. With a nervous gesture he thrust the salver back upon the table and slid out of bed.

Moving hastily across the room, he stopped before one of the tall wardrobes and swung the door open; then after a furtive glance around the room he thrust his hand into the recesses of a shelf and fumbled there.

The thing he sought was evidently not hard to find. for almost at once he withdrew his hand and moved from the wardrobe to a table beside the fireplace, carrying a small glass tube filled with tabloids.

On the table were a decanter, a siphon, and a water-jug. Mixing some whiskey, he uncorked the tube, again he glanced apprehensively towards the door, then with a very nervous hand dropped two tabloids into the glass.

While they dissolved he stood with his hand on the table and his eyes fixed on the floor, evidently restraining his impatience. Instantly they had disappeared he seized the glass and drained it at a draught, replaced the bottle in the wardrobe, and, shivering slightly in the raw air, slipped back into bed.

When Allsopp returned he was sitting up, a cigarette between his lips, the teacup standing empty on the salver. The nervous irritability had gone from his manner. He no longer moved jerkily, his eyes looked brighter, his pale skin more healthy.

"Ah, Allsopp," he said, "there are some moments in life, after all. It isn't all blank wall."

"I ordered breakfast in the small morning-room, sir," said Allsopp, without a change of expression.

Chilcote breakfasted at ten. His appetite, always fickle, was particularly uncertain in the early hours. He helped himself to some fish, but sent away his plate untouched; then, having drunk two cups of tea, he pushed back his chair, lighted a fresh cigarette, and shook out the morning's newspaper.

Twice he shook it out and twice turned it, but the reluctance to fix his mind upon it made him dally.

The effect of the morphia tabloids was still apparent in the greater steadiness of his hand and eye, the regained quiet of his susceptibilities, but the respite was temporary and lethargic. The early days—the days of six years ago, when these tabloids meant an even sweep of thought, lucidity of brain, a balance of judgment in thought and effort—were days of the past. As he had said of Lexington and his vice, the slave had become master.

As he folded the paper in a last attempt at interest, the door opened and his secretary came a step or two into the room.

"Good-morning, sir!" he said. "Forgive me for being so untimely."

He was a fresh-mannered, bright-eyed boy of twenty-three. His breezy alertness, his deference, as to a man who had attained what he aspired to, amused and depressed Chilcote by turns.

"Good-morning, Blessington. What is it now?" He sighed through habit, and, putting up his hand, warded off a ray of sun that had forced itself through the misty atmosphere as if by mistake.

The boy smiled. "It's that business of the Wark timber contract, sir," he said. "You promised you'd look into it to-day; you know you've shelved it for a week already, and Craig, Burnage are rather clamoring for an answer." He moved forward and laid the papers he was carrying on the table beside Chilcote. "I'm sorry to be such a nuisance," he added. "I hope your nerves aren't worrying you to-day?"

Chilcote was toying with the papers. At the word nerves he glanced up suspiciously. But Blessington's ingenuous face satisfied him.

"No," he said. "I settled my nerves last night with—with a bromide. I knew that fog would upset me unless I took precautions."

"I'm glad of that, sir—though I'd avoid bromides. Bad habit to set up. But this Wark business—I'd like to get it under way, if you have no objection."

Chilcote passed his fingers over the papers. "Were you out in that fog last night, Blessington?"

"No, sir. I supped with some people at the Savoy, and we just missed it. It was very partial, I believe."

"So I believe."

Blessington put his hand to his neat tie and pulled it. He was extremely polite, but he had an inordinate sense of duty.

"Forgive me, sir," he said, "but about that contract—I know I'm a frightful bore."

"Oh, the contract!" Chilcote looked about him absently. "By-the-way, did you see anything of my wife yesterday? What did she do last night?"

"Mrs. Chilcote gave me tea yesterday afternoon. She told me she was dining at Lady Sabinet's, and looking in at one or two places later." He eyed his papers in Chilcote's listless hand.

Chilcote smiled satirically. "Eve is very true to society," he said. "I couldn't dine at the Sabinets' if it was to make me premier. They have a butler who is an institution—a sort of heirloom in the family. He is fat, and breathes audibly. Last time I lunched there he haunted me for a whole night."

Blessington laughed gayly. "Mrs. Chilcote doesn't see ghosts, sir," he said; "but if I may suggest—"

Chilcote tapped his fingers on the table.

"No. Eve doesn't see ghosts. We rather miss sympathy there."

Blessington governed his impatience. He stood still for some seconds, then glanced down at his pointed boot.

"If you will be lenient to my persistency, sir, I would like to remind you—"

Chilcote lifted his head with a flash of irritability.

"Confound it, Blessington!" he exclaimed. "Am I never to be left in peace? Am I never to sit down to a meal without having work thrust upon me? Work—work—perpetually work? I have heard no other word in the last six years. I declare there are times"—he rose suddenly from his seat and turned to the window—"there are times when I feel that for sixpence I'd chuck it all—the whole beastly round—"

Startled by his vehemence, Blessington wheeled towards him.

"Not your political career, sir?"

There was a moment in which Chilcote hesitated, a moment in which the desire that had filled his mind for months rose to his lips and hung there; then the question, the incredulity in Blessington's face, chilled it and it fell back into silence.

"I—I didn't say that," he murmured. "You young men jump to conclusions, Blessington."

"Forgive me, sir. I never meant to imply retirement. Why, Rickshaw, Vale, Cressham, and the whole Wark crowd would be about your ears like flies if such a thing were even breathed —now more than ever, since these Persian rumors. By-the-way, is there anything real in this border business? The 'St. George's' came out rather strong last night."

Chilcote had moved back to the table. His face was pale from his outburst and his fingers toyed restlessly with the open newspaper.

"I haven't seen the 'St. George's'," he said, hastily. "Lakely is always ready to shake the red rag where Russia is concerned; whether we are to enter the arena is another matter. But what about Craig, Burnage? I think you mentioned something of a contract."

"Oh, don't worry about that, sir." Blessington had caught the twitching at the corners of Chilcote's mouth, the nervous sharpness of his voice. "I can put Craig, Burnage off. If they have an answer by Thursday it will be time enough." He began to collect his papers, but Chilcote stopped him.

"Wait," he said, veering suddenly. "Wait. I'll see to it now. I'll feel more myself when I've done something. I'll come with you to the study."

He walked hastily across the room; then, with his hand on the door, he paused.

"You go first, Blessington," he said. "I'll—I'll follow you in ten minutes. I must glance through the newspapers first."

Blessington looked uncertain. "You won't forget, sir?"

"Forget? Of course not."

Still doubtfully, Blessington left the room and closed the door.

Once alone, Chilcote walked slowly back to the table, drew up his chair, and sat down with his eyes on the white cloth, the paper lying unheeded beside him.

Time passed. A servant came into the room to remove the breakfast. Chilcote moved slightly when necessary, but otherwise retained his attitude. The servant, having finished his task, replenished the fire and left the room. Chilcote still sat on.

At last, feeling numbed, he rose and crossed to the fireplace. The clock on the mantel-piece stared him in the face. He looked at it, started slightly, then drew out his watch. Watch and clock corresponded. Each marked twelve o'clock. With a nervous motion he leaned forward and pressed the electric bell long and hard.

Instantly a servant answered.

"Is Mr. Blessington in the study?" Chilcote asked.

"He was there, sir, five minutes back."

Chilcote looked relieved.

"All right! Tell him I have gone out—had to go out. Something important. You understand?"

"I understand, sir."

But before the words had been properly spoken Chilcote had passed the man and walked into the hall.

III

Leaving his house, Chilcote walked forward quickly and aimlessly. With the sting of the outer air the recollection of last night's adventure came back upon him. Since the hour of his waking it had hung about with vague persistence, but now in the clear light of day it seemed to stand out with a fuller peculiarity.

The thing was preposterous, nevertheless it was genuine. He was wearing the overcoat he had worn, the night before, and, acting on impulse, he thrust his hand into the pocket and drew out the stranger's card.

"Mr. John Loder!" He read the name over as he walked along, and it mechanically repeated itself in his brain—falling into measure with his steps. Who was John Loder? What was he? The questions tantalized him till his pace unconsciously increased. The thought that two men so absurdly alike could inhabit the same, city and remain unknown to each other faced him as a problem: it tangled with his personal worries and aggravated them. There seemed to be almost a danger in such an extraordinary likeness. He began to regret his impetuosity in thrusting his card upon the man. Then, again, how he had let himself go on the subject of Lexington! How narrowly he had escaped compromise! He turned hot and cold at the recollection of what he had said and what he might have said. Then for the first time he paused in his walk and looked about him.

On leaving Grosvenor Square he had turned westward, moving rapidly till the Marble Arch was reached; there, still oblivious to his surroundings, he had crossed the roadway to the Edgware Road, passing along it to the labyrinth of shabby streets that lie behind Paddington. Now, as he glanced about him, he saw with some surprise how far he had come.

The damp remnants of the fog still hung about the house-tops in a filmy veil; there were no glimpses of green to break the monotony of tone; all was quiet, dingy, neglected. But to Chilcote the shabbiness was restful, the subdued atmosphere a satisfaction. Among these sad houses, these passers-by, each filled with his own concerns, he experienced a sense of respite and relief. In the fashionable streets that bounded his own horizon, if a man paused in his walk to work out an idea he instantly drew a crowd of inquisitive or contemptuous eyes; here, if a man halted for half an hour it was nobody's business but his own.

Enjoying this thought, he wandered on for close upon an hour, moving from one street to another with steps that were listless or rapid, as inclination prompted; then, still acting with vagrant aimlessness, he stopped in his wanderings and entered a small eating-house.

The place was low-ceiled and dirty, the air hot and steaming with the smell of food, but Chilcote passed through the door and moved to one of the tables with no expression of disgust, and with far less furtive watchfulness than he used in his own house. By a curious mental twist he felt greater freedom, larger opportunities in drab surroundings such as these than in the broad issues and weighty responsibilities of his own life. Choosing a corner seat, he called for coffee; and there, protected by shadow and wrapped in cigarette smoke, he set about imagining himself some vagrant unit who had slipped his moorings and was blissfully adrift.

The imagination was pleasant while it lasted, but with him nothing was permanent. Of late the greater part of his sufferings had been comprised in the irritable fickleness of all his aims—the distaste for and impossibility of sustained effort in any direction. He had barely lighted a second cigarette when the old restlessness fell upon him; he stirred nervously in his seat, and the cigarette was scarcely burned out when he rose, paid his small bill, and left the shop.

Outside on the pavement he halted, pulled out his watch, and saw that two hours stretched in front before any appointment claimed his attention. He wondered vaguely where he might go to—what he might do in those two hours? In the last few minutes a distaste for solitude had risen in his mind, giving the close street a loneliness that had escaped him before.

As he stood wavering a cab passed slowly down the street. The sight of a well-dressed man roused the cabman; flicking his whip, he passed Chilcote close, feigning to pull up.

The cab suggested civilization. Chilcote's mind veered suddenly and he raised his hand. The vehicle stopped and he climbed in.

"Where, sir?" The cabman peered down through the roof-door.

Chilcote raised his head. "Oh, anywhere near Pall Mall," he said. Then, as the horse started forward, he put up his hand and shook the trap-door. "Wait!" he called. "I've changed my mind. Drive to Cadogan Gardens—No. 33."

The distance to Cadogan Gardens was covered quickly. Chilcote had hardly realized that his destination was reached when the cab pulled up. Jumping out, he paid the fare and walked quickly to the hall-door of No. 33.

"Is Lady Astrupp at home?" he asked, sharply, as the door swung back in answer to his knock.

The servant drew back deferentially. "Her ladyship has almost finished lunch, sir," he said.

For answer Chilcote stepped through the door-way and walked half-way across the hall.

"All right," he said. "But don't disturb her on my account. I'll wait in the white room till she has finished." And, without taking further notice of the servant, he began to mount the stairs.

In the room where he had chosen to wait a pleasant wood-fire brightened the dull January afternoon and softened the thick, white curtains, the gilt furniture, and the Venetian vases filled with white roses. Moving straight forward, Chilcote paused by the grate and stretched his hands to the blaze; then, with his usual instability, he turned and passed to a couch that stood a yard or two away.

On the couch, tucked away between a novel and a crystal gazing-ball, was a white Persian kitten, fast asleep. Chilcote picked up the ball and held it between his eyes and the fire; then he laughed superciliously, tossed it back into its place, and caught the kitten's tail. The little animal stirred, stretched itself, and began to purr. At the same moment the door of the room opened.

Chilcote turned round. "I particularly said you were not to be disturbed," he began. "Have I merited displeasure?" He spoke fast, with the uneasy tone that so often underran his words.

Lady Astrupp took his hand with a confiding gesture and smiled.

"Never displeasure," she said, lingeringly, and again she smiled. The smile might have struck a close observer as faintly, artificial. But what man in Chilcote's frame of mind has time to be observant where women are concerned? The manner of the smile was very sweet and almost caressing —and that sufficed.

"What have you been doing?" she asked, after a moment. "I thought I was quite forgotten." She moved across to the couch, picked up the kitten, and kissed it. "Isn't this sweet?" she added.

She looked very graceful as she turned, holding the little animal up. She was a woman of twenty-seven, but she looked a girl. The outline of her face was pure, the pale gold of her hair almost ethereal, and her tall, slight figure still suggested the suppleness, the possibility of future development, that belongs to youth. She wore a lace-colored gown that harmonized with the room and with the delicacy of her skin.

"Now sit down and rest—or walk about the room. I sha'n't mind which." She nestled into the couch and picked up the crystal ball.

"What is the toy for?" Chilcote looked at her from the mantel-piece, against which he was resting. He had never defined the precise attraction that Lillian Astrupp held for him. Her shallowness soothed him; her inconsequent egotism helped him to forget himself. She never asked him how he was, she never expected impossibilities. She let him come and go and act as he pleased, never demanding reasons. Like the kitten, she was charming and graceful and easily amused; it was possible that, also like the kitten, she could scratch and be spiteful on occasion, but that did not weigh with him. He sometimes expressed a vague envy of the late Lord Astrupp; but, even had circumstances permitted, it is doubtful whether he would have chosen to be his successor. Lillian as a friend was delightful, but Lillian as a wife would have been a different consideration.

"What is the toy for?" he asked again.

She looked up slowly. "How cruel of you, Jack! It is my very latest hobby."

It was part of her attraction that she was never without a craze. Each new one was as fleeting as the last, but to each she brought the same delightfully insincere enthusiasm, the same picturesque devotion. Each was a pose, but she posed so sweetly that nobody lost patience.

"You mustn't laugh!" she protested, letting the kitten slip to the ground. "I've had lessons at five guineas each from the most fascinating person—a professional; and I'm becoming quite an adept. Of course I haven't been much beyond the milky appearance yet, but the milky appearance is everything, you know; the rest will come. I am trying to persuade Blanche to let me have a pavilion at her party in March, and gaze for all you dull political people." Again she smiled.

Chilcote smiled as well. "How is it done?" he asked, momentarily amused.

"Oh, the doing is quite delicious. You sit at a table with the ball in front of you; then you take the subject's hands, spread them out on the table, and stroke them very softly while you gaze into the crystal; that gets up the sympathy, you know." She looked up innocently. "Shall I show you?"

Chilcote moved a small table nearer to the couch and spread his hands upon it, palms downward. "Like this, eh?" he said. Then a ridiculous nervousness seized him and he moved away. "Some other day," he said, quickly. "You can show me some other day. I'm not very fit this afternoon."

If Lillian felt any disappointment, she showed none. "Poor old thing!" she said, softly. "Try to sit here by me and we won't bother about anything." She made a place for him beside her, and as he dropped into it she took his hand and patted it sympathetically.

The touch was soothing, and he bore it patiently enough. After a moment she lifted the hand with a little exclamation of reproof.

"You degenerate person! You have ceased to manicure. What has become of my excellent training?"

Chilcote laughed. "Run to seed," he said, lightly. Then his expression and tone changed. "When a man gets to my age," he added, "little social luxuries don't seem worth while; the social necessities are irksome enough. Personally, I envy the beggar in the street—exempt from shaving, exempt from washing—"

Lillian raised her delicate eyebrows. The sentiment was beyond her perception.

"But manicuring," she said, reproachfully, "when you have such nice hands. It was your hands and your eyes, you know, that first appealed to me." She sighed gently, with a touch of sentimental remembrance. "And I thought it so strong of you not to wear rings—it must be such a temptation." She looked down at her own fingers, glittering with jewels.

But the momentary pleasure of her touch was gone. Chilcote drew away his hand and picked up the book that lay between them.

"Other Men's Shoes!" he read. "A novel, of course?"

She smiled. "Of course. Such a fantastic story. Two men changing identities."

Chilcote rose and walked back to the mantel-piece.

"Changing identities?" he said, with a touch of interest.

"Yes. One man is an artist, the other a millionaire; one wants to know what fame is like, the other wants to know how it feels to be really sinfully rich. So they exchange experiences for a month." She laughed.

Chilcote laughed as well. "But how?" he asked.

"Oh, I told you the idea was absurd. Fancy two people so much alike that neither their friends nor their servants see any difference! Such a thing couldn't be, could it?"

Chilcote looked down at the fire. "No," he said, doubtfully. "No. I suppose not."

"Of course not. There are likenesses, but not freak likenesses like that."

Chilcote's head was bent as she spoke, but at the last words he lifted it.

"By Jove! I don't know about that!" he said. "Not so very long ago I saw two men so much alike that I—I—" He stopped.

Lillian smiled.

He colored quickly. "You doubt me?" he asked.

"My dear Jack!" Her voice was delicately reproachful.

"Then you think that my—my imagination has been playing me tricks?"

"My dear boy! Nothing of the kind. Come back to your place and tell me the whole tale?" She smiled again, and patted the couch invitingly.

But Chilcote's balance had been upset. For the first time he saw Lillian as one of the watchful, suspecting crowd before which he was constantly on guard. Acting on the sensation, he moved suddenly towards the door.

"I—I have an appointment at the House," he said, quickly. "I'll look in another day when—when I'm better company. I know I'm a bear to-day. My nerves, you know." He came back to the couch and took her hand; then he touched her cheek for an instant with his fingers.

"Good-bye," he said. "Take care of yourself—and the kitten," he added, with forced gayety, as he crossed the room.

That afternoon Chilcote's nervous condition reached its height. All day he had avoided the climax, but no evasion can be eternal, and this he realized as he sat in his place on the Opposition benches during the half-hour of wintry twilight that precedes the turning-on of the lights. He realized it in that half-hour, but the application of the knowledge followed later, when the time came for him to question the government on some point relating to a proposed additional dry-dock at Talkley, the naval base. Then for the first time he knew that the sufferings of the past months could have a visible as well as a hidden side—could disorganize his daily routine as they had already demoralized his will and character.

The thing came upon him with extraordinary lack of preparation. He sat through the twilight with tolerable calm, his nervousness showing only in the occasional lifting of his hand to his collar and the frequent changing of his position; but when the lights were turned on, and he leaned back in his seat with closed eyes, he became conscious of a curious impression—a disturbing idea that through his closed lids he could see the faces on the opposite side of the House, see the rows of eyes, sleepy, interested, or vigilant. Never before had the sensation presented itself, but, once set up, it ran through all his susceptibilities. By an absurd freak of fancy those varying eyes seemed to pierce through his lids, almost through his eyeballs. The cold perspiration that was his daily horror broke out on his forehead; and at the same moment Fraide, his leader, turned, leaned over the back of his seat, and touched his knee.

Chilcote started and opened his eyes. "I—I believe I was dozing," he said, confusedly.

Fraide smiled his dry, kindly smile. "A fatal admission for a member of the Opposition," he said. "But I was looking for you earlier in the day, Chilcote. There is something behind this Persian affair. I believe it to be a mere first move on Russia's part. You big trading people will find it worth watching."

Chilcote shrugged his shoulders. "Oh, I don't know," he said. "I scarcely believe in it. Lakely put a match to the powder in the 'St. George's', but 'twill only be a noise and a puff of smoke."

But Fraide did not smile. "What is the feeling down at Wark?" he asked. "Has it awakened any interest?"

"At Wark? Oh, I—I don't quite know. I have been a little out of touch with Wark in the last few weeks. A man has so many private affairs to look to—" He was uneasy under his chief's scrutiny.

Fraide's lips parted as if to make reply, but with a certain dignified reticence he closed them again and turned away.

Chilcote leaned back in his place and furtively passed his hand over his forehead. His mind was possessed by one consideration—the consideration of himself. He glanced down the crowded, lighted House to the big glass doors; he glanced about him at his colleagues, indifferent or interested; then surreptitiously his fingers strayed to his waistcoat-pocket.

Usually he carried his morphia tabloids with him, but to-day by a lapse of memory he had left them at home. He knew this, nevertheless he continued to search, while the need of the drug rushed through him with a sense of physical sickness. He lost hold on the business of the House; unconsciously he half rose from his seat.

The man next him looked up. "Hold your ground, Chilcote," he said. "Rayforth is drying up."

With a wave of relief Chilcote dropped back into his place. Whatever the confusion in his mind, it was evidently not obvious in his face.

Rayforth resumed his seat, there was the usual slight stir and pause, then Salett, the member for Salchester, rose.

With Salett's first words Chilcote's hand again sought his pocket, and again his eyes strayed towards the doors, but Fraide's erect head and stiff back just in front of him held him quiet. With an effort he pulled out his notes and smoothed them nervously; but though his gaze was fixed on the pages, not a line of Blessington's clear writing reached his mind. He glanced at the face of the Speaker, then at the faces on the Treasury Bench, then once more he leaned back in his seat.

The man beside him saw the movement. "Funking the drydock?" he whispered, jestingly.

"No"—Chilcote turned to him suddenly—"but I feel beastly —have felt beastly for weeks."

The other looked at him more closely. "Anything wrong?" he asked. It was a novel experience to be confided in by Chilcote.

"Oh, it's the grind-the infernal grind." As he said it, it seemed to him suddenly that his strength gave way. He forgot his companion, his position, everything except the urgent instinct that filled mind and body. Scarcely knowing what he did, he rose and leaned forward to whisper in Fraide's ear.

Fraide was seen to turn, his thin face interested and concerned, then he was seen to nod once or twice in acquiescence, and a moment later Chilcote stepped quietly out of his place.

One or two men spoke to him as he hurried from the House, but he shook them off almost uncivilly, and, making for the nearest exit, hailed a cab.

The drive to Grosvenor Square was a misery. Time after time he changed from one corner of the cab to the other, his acute internal pains prolonged by every delay and increased by every motion. At last, weak in all his limbs, he stepped from the vehicle at his own door.

Entering the house, he instantly mounted the stairs and passed to his own rooms. Opening the bedroom door, he peered in cautiously, then pushed the door wide. The light had been switched on, but the room was empty. With a nervous excitement scarcely to be kept in check, he entered, shut and locked the door, then moved to the wardrobe, and, opening it, drew the tube of tabloids from the shelf.

His hand shook violently as he carried the tube to the table. The strain of the day, the anxiety of the past hours, with their final failure, had found sudden expression. Mixing a larger dose than any he had before allowed himself, he swallowed it hastily, and, walking across the room, threw himself, fully dressed, upon the bed.

IV

To those whose sphere lies in the west of London, Fleet Street is little more than a name, and Clifford's Inn a mere dead letter. Yet Clifford's Inn lies as safely stowed away in the shadow of the Law Courts as any grave under a country church wall; it is as green of grass, as gray of stone, as irresponsive to the passing footstep.

Facing the railed-in grass-plot of its little court stood the house in which John Loder had his rooms. Taken at a first glance, the house had the deserted air of an office, inhabited only in the early hours; but, as night fell, lights would be seen to show out, first on one floor, then on another—faint, human beacons unconsciously signalling each other. The rooms Loder inhabited were on the highest floor; and from their windows one might gaze philosophically on the tree-tops, forgetting the uneven pavement and the worn railing that hemmed them round. In the landing outside the rooms his name appeared above his door, but the paint had been soiled by time, and the letters for the most part reduced to shadows; so that, taken in conjunction with the gaunt staircase and bare walls, the place had a cheerless look.

Inside, however, the effect was somewhat mitigated. The room on the right hand, as one entered the small passage that served as hall, was of fair size, though low-ceiled. The paint of the wall-panelling, like the name above the outer door, had long ago been worn to a dirty and nondescript hue, and the floor was innocent of carpet; yet in the middle of the room stood a fine old Cromwell table, and on the plain deal book-shelves and along the mantel-piece were some valuable books—political and historical. There were no curtains on the windows, and a common reading-lamp with a green shade stood on a desk. It was the room of a man with few hobbies and no pleasures—who existed because he was alive, and worked because he must.

Three nights after the great fog John Loder sat by his desk in the light of the green-shaded lamp. The remains of a very frugal supper stood on the centre-table, and in the grate a small and economical-looking fire was burning.

Having written for close on two hours, he pushed back his chair and stretched his cramped fingers; then he yawned, rose, and slowly walked across the room. Reaching the mantel-piece, he took a pipe from the pipe-rack and some tobacco from the jar that stood behind the books. His face looked tired and a little worn, as is common with men who have worked long at an uncongenial task. Shredding the tobacco between his hands, he slowly filled the pipe, then lighted it from the fire with a spill of twisted paper.

Almost at the moment that he applied the light the sound of steps mounting the uncarpeted stairs outside caught his attention, and he raised his head to listen.

Presently the steps halted and he heard a match struck. The stranger was evidently uncertain of his whereabouts. Then the steps moved forward again and paused.

An expression of surprise crossed Loder's face, and he laid down his pipe. As the visitor knocked, he walked quietly across the room and opened the door.

The passage outside was dark, and the new-comer drew back before the light from the room.

"Mr. Loder—?" he began, interrogatively. Then all at once he laughed in embarrassed apology. "Forgive me," he said. "The light rather dazzled me. I didn't realize who it was."

Loder recognized the voice as belonging to his acquaintance of the fog.

"Oh, it's you!" he said. "Won't you come in?" His voice was a little cold. This sudden resurrection left him surprised —and not quite pleasantly surprised. He walked back to the fireplace, followed by his guest.

The guest seemed nervous and agitated. "I must apologize for the hour of my visit," he said. "My—my time is not quite my own."

Loder waved his hand. "Whose time is his own?" he said.

Chilcote, encouraged by the remark, drew nearer to the fire. Until this moment he had refrained from looking directly at his host; now, however, he raised his eyes, and, despite his preparation, he recoiled unavoidably before the extraordinary resemblance. Seen here, in the casual surroundings of a badly furnished and crudely lighted room, it was even more astounding than it had been in the mystery of the fog.

"Forgive me," he said again. "It is physical—purely physical. I am bowled over against my will."

Loder smiled. The slight contempt that Chilcote had first inspired rose again, and with it a second feeling less easily defined. The man seemed so unstable, so incapable, yet so grotesquely suggestive to himself.

"The likeness is rather overwhelming," he said; "but not heavy enough to sink under. Come nearer the fire. What brought you here? Curiosity?" There was a wooden arm-chair by the fireplace. He indicated it with a wave of the hand; then turned and took up his smouldering pipe.

Chilcote, watching him furtively, obeyed the gesture and sat down.

"It is extraordinary!" he said, as if unable to dismiss the subject. "It—it is quite extraordinary!"

The other glanced round. "Let's drop it," he said. "It's so confoundedly obvious." Then his tone changed. "Won't you smoke?" he asked.

"Thanks." Chilcote began to fumble for his cigarettes.

But his host forestalled him. Taking a box from the mantel-piece, he held it out.

"My one extravagance!" he said, ironically. "My resources bind me to one; and I think I have made a wise selection. It is about the only vice we haven't to pay for six times over." He glanced sharply at the face so absurdly like his own, then, lighting a fresh spill, offered his guest a light.

Chilcote moistened his cigarette and leaned forward. In the flare of the paper his face looked set and anxious, but Loder saw that the lips did not twitch as they had done on the previous occasion that he had given him a light, and a look of comprehension crossed his eyes.

"What will you drink? Or, rather, will you have a whiskey? I keep nothing else. Hospitality is one of the debarred luxuries."

Chilcote shook his head. "I seldom drink. But don't let that deter you."

Loder smiled. "I have one drink in the twenty-four hours —generally at two o'clock, when my night's work is done. A solitary man has to look where he is going."

"You work till two?"

"Two—or three."

Chilcote's eyes wandered to the desk. "You write?" he asked.

The other nodded curtly.

"Books?" Chilcote's tone was anxious.

Loder laughed, and the bitter note showed in his voice.

"No—not books," he said.

Chilcote leaned back in his chair and passed his hand across his face. The strong wave of satisfaction that the words woke in him was difficult to conceal.

"What is your work?"

Loder turned aside. "You must not ask that," he said, shortly. "When a man has only one capacity, and the capacity has no outlet, he is apt to run to seed in a wrong direction. I cultivate weeds—at abominable labor and a very small reward." He stood with his back to the fire, facing his visitor; his attitude was a curious blending of pride, defiance, and despondency.

Chilcote leaned forward again. "Why speak of yourself like that? You are a man of intelligence and education." He spoke questioningly, anxiously.

"Intelligence and education!" Loder laughed shortly. "London is cemented with intelligence. And education! What is education? The court dress necessary to presentation, the wig and gown necessary to the barrister. But do the wig and gown necessarily mean briefs? Or the court dress royal favor? Education is the accessory; it is influence that is essential. You should know that."

Chilcote moved restlessly in his seat. "You talk bitterly," he said.

The other looked up. "I think bitterly, which is worse. I am one of the unlucky beggars who, in the expectation of money, has been denied a profession—even a trade, to which to cling in time of shipwreck; and who, when disaster comes, drift out to sea. I warned you the other night to steer clear of me. I come under the head of flotsam!"

Chilcote's face lighted. "You came a cropper?" he asked.

"No. It was some one else who came the cropper—I only dealt in results."

"Big results?"

"A drop from a probable eighty thousand pounds to a certain eight hundred."

Chilcote glanced up. "How did you take it?" he asked.

"I? Oh, I was twenty-five then. I had a good many hopes and a lot of pride; but there is no place for either in a working world."

"But your people?"

"My last relation died with the fortune."

"Your friends?"

Loder laid down his pipe. "I told you I was twenty-five," he said, with the tinge of humor that sometimes crossed his manner. "Doesn't that explain things? I had never taken favors in prosperity; a change of fortune was not likely to alter my ways. As I have said, I was twenty-five." He smiled. "When I realized my position I sold all my belongings with the exception of a table and a few books—which I stored. I put on a walking-suit and let my beard grow; then, with my entire capital in my pocket, I left England without saying good-bye to any one."

"For how long?"

"Oh, for six years. I wandered half over Europe and through a good part of Asia in the time."

"And then?"

"Then? Oh, I shaved off the beard and came back to London!" He looked at Chilcote, partly contemptuous, partly amused at his curiosity.

But Chilcote sat staring in silence. The domination of the other's personality and the futility of his achievements baffled him.

Loder saw his bewilderment. "You wonder what the devil I came into the world for," he said. "I sometimes wonder the same myself."

At his words a change passed over Chilcote. He half rose, then dropped back into his seat.

"You have no friends?" he said. "Your life is worth nothing to you?"

Loder raised his head. "I thought I had conveyed that impression."

"You are an absolutely free man."

"No man is free who works for his bread. If things had been different I might have been in such shoes as yours, sauntering in legislative byways; my hopes turned that way once. But hopes, like more substantial things, belong to the past—" He stopped abruptly and looked at his companion.

The change in Chilcote had become more acute; he sat fingering his cigarette, his brows drawn down, his lips set nervously in a conflict of emotions. For a space he stayed very still, avoiding Loder's eyes; then, as if decision had suddenly come to him, he turned and met his gaze.

"How if there was a future," he said, "as well as a past?"

V

For the space of a minute there was silence in the room, then outside in the still night three clocks simultaneously chimed eleven, and their announcement was taken up and echoed by half a dozen others, loud and faint, hoarse and resonant; for all through the hours of darkness the neighborhood of Fleet Street is alive with chimes.

Chilcote, startled by the jangle, rose from his seat; then, as if driven by an uncontrollable impulse, he spoke again.

"You probably think I am mad—" he began.

Loder took his pipe out of his mouth. "I am not so presumptuous," he said, quietly.

For a space the other eyed him silently, as if trying to gauge his thoughts; then once more he broke into speech.

"Look here," he said. "I came to-night to make a proposition. When I have made it you'll first of all jeer at it—as I jeered when I made it to myself; then you'll see its possibilities—as I did; then,"—he paused and glanced round the room nervously—"then you'll accept it—as I did." In the uneasy haste of his speech his words broke off almost unintelligibly.

Involuntarily Loder lifted his head to retort, but Chilcote put up his hand. His face was set with the obstinate determination that weak men sometime exhibit.

"Before I begin I want to say that I am not druuk—that I am neither mad nor drunk." He looked fully at his companion with his restless glance. "I am quite sane—quite reasonable."

Again Loder essayed to speak, but again he put up his hand.

"No. Hear me out. You told me something of your story. I'll tell you something of mine. You'll be the first person, man or woman, that I have confided in for ten years. You say you have been treated shabbily. I have treated myself shabbily —which is harder to reconcile. I had every chance—and I chucked every chance away."

There was a strained pause, then again Loder lifted his head.

"Morphia?" he said, very quietly.

Chilcote wheeled round with a scared gesture. "How did you know that?" he asked, sharply.

The other smiled. "It wasn't guessing—it wasn't even deduction. You told me, or as good as told me, in the fog —when we talked of Lexington. You were unstrung that night, and I—Well, perhaps one gets over-observant from living alone." He smiled again.

Chilcote collapsed into his former seat and passed his handkerchief across his forehead.

Loder watched him for a space; then he spoke. "Why don't you pull up?" he said. "You are a young man still. Why don't you drop the thing before it gets too late?" His face was unsympathetic, and below the question in his voice lay a note of hard ness.

Chilcote returned his glance. The suggestion of reproof had accentuated his pallor. Under his excitement he looked ill and worn.

"You might talk till doomsday, but every word would be wasted," he said, irritably. "I'm past praying for, by something like six years."

"Then why come here?" Loder was pulling hard on his pipe. "I'm not a dealer in sympathy."

"I don't require sympathy." Chilcote rose again. He was still agitated, but the agitation was quieter. "I want a much more expensive thing than sympathy—and I am willing to pay for it."

The other turned and looked at him. "I have no possession in the world that would be worth a fiver to you," he said, coldly. "You're either under a delusion or you're wasting my time."

Chilcote laughed nervously. "Wait," he said. "Wait. I only ask you to wait. First let me sketch you my position —it won't take many words:

"My grandfather was a Chilcote of Westmoreland; he was one of the first of his day and his class to recognize that there was a future in trade, so, breaking his own little twig from the family tree, he went south to Wark and entered a ship-owning firm. In thirty years' time he died, the owner of one of the biggest trades in England, having married the daughter of his chief. My father was twenty-four and still at Oxford when he inherited. Almost his first act was to reverse my grandfather's early move by going north and piecing together the family friendship. He married his first cousin; and then, with the Chilcote prestige revived and the shipping money to back it, he entered on his ambition, which was to represent East Wark in the Conservative interest. It was a big fight, but he won —as much by personal influence as by any other. He was an aristocrat, but he was a keen business-man as well. The combination carries weight with your lower classes. He never did much in the House, but he was a power to his party in Wark. They still use his name there to conjure with."

Loder leaned forward interestedly.

"Robert Chilcote?" he said. "I have heard of him. One of those fine, unostentatious figures—strong in action, a little narrow in outlook, perhaps, but essential to a country's staying power. You have every reason to be proud of your father."

Chilcote laughed suddenly. "How easily we sum up, when a matter is impersonal! My father may have been a fine figure, but he shouldn't have left me to climb to his pedestal."

Loder's eyes questioned. In his newly awakened interest he had let his pipe go out.

"Don't you grasp my meaning?" Chilcote went on. "My father died and I was elected for East Wark. You may say that if I had no real inclination for the position I could have kicked. But I tell you I couldn't. Every local interest, political and commercial, hung upon the candidate being a Chilcote. I did what eight men out of ten would have done. I yielded to pressure."

"It was a fine opening!" The words escaped Loder.

"Most prisons have wide gates!" Chilcote laughed again unpleasantly. "That was six years ago. I had started on the morphia tack four years earlier, but up to my father's death I had it under my thumb—or believed I had; and in the realization of my new responsibilities and the excitement of the political fight I almost put it aside. For several months after I entered Parliament I worked. I believe I made one speech that marked me as a coming man." He laughed derisively. "I even married—"

"Married?"

"Yes. A girl of nineteen—the ward of a great statesman. It was a brilliant marriage—politically as well as socially. But it didn't work. I was born without the capacity for love. First the social life palled on me; then my work grew irksome. There was only one factor to make life endurable—morphia. Before six months were out I had fully admitted that."

"But your wife?"

"Oh, my wife knew nothing—knows nothing. It is the political business, the beastly routine of the political life, that is wearing me out." He stopped nervously, then hurried on, again. "I tell you it's hell to see the same faces, to sit in the same seat day in, day out, knowing all the time that you must hold yourself in hand, must keep your grip on the reins—"

"It is always possible to apply for the Chiltern Hundreds."

"To retire? Possible to retire?" Chilcote broke into a loud, sarcastic laugh. "You don't know what the local pressure of a place like Wark stands for. Twenty times I have been within an ace of chucking the whole thing. Once last year I wrote privately to Vale, one of our big men there, and hinted that my health was bad. Two hours after he had read my letter he was in my study. Had I been in Greenland the result would have been the same. No. Resignation is a meaningless word to a man like me."

Loder looked down. "I see," he said, slowly, "I see."

"Then you see everything—the difficulty, the isolation of the position. Five years ago—three—even two years ago—I was able to endure it; now it gets more unbearable with every month. The day is bound to come when—when"—he paused, hesitating nervously—"when it will be physically impossible for me to be at my post."

Loder remained silent.

"Physically impossible," Chilcote repeated, excitedly. "Until lately I was able to calculate—to count upon myself to some extent; but yesterday I received a shock—yesterday I discovered that—that"—again he hesitated painfully—"that I have passed the stage when one may calculate."

The situation was growing more embarrassing. To hide its awkwardness, Loder moved back to the grate and rebuilt the fire, which had fallen low.

Chilcote, still excited by his unusual vehemence, followed him, taking up a position by the mantelpiece.

"Well?" he said, looking down.

Very slowly Loder rose from his task. "Well?" he reiterated.

"Have you nothing to say?"

"Nothing, except that your story is unique, and that I suppose I am flattered by your confidence." His voice was intentionally brusque.

Chilcote paid no attention to the voice. Taking a step forward, he laid his fingers on the lapel of Loder's coat.

"I have passed the stage where I can count upon myself," he said, "and I want to count upon somebody else. I want to keep my place in the world's eyes and yet be free—"

Loder drew back involuntarily, contempt struggling with bewilderment in his expression.

Chilcote lifted his head. "By an extraordinary chance," he said, "you can do for me what no other man in creation could do. It was suggested to me unconsciously by the story of a book—a book in which men change identities. I saw nothing in it at the time, but this morning, as I lay in bed, sick with yesterday's fiasco, it came back to me—it rushed over my mind in an inspiration. It will save me—and make you. I'm not insulting you, though you'd like to think so."

Without remark Loder freed himself from the other's touch and walked back to his desk. His anger, his pride, and, against his will, his excitement were all aroused.

He sat down, leaned his elbow on the desk and took his face between his hands. The man behind him undoubtedly talked madness; but after five years of dreary sanity madness had a fascination. Against all reason it stirred and roused him. For one instant his pride and his anger faltered before it, then common-sense flowed back again and adjusted the balance.

"You propose," he said, slowly, "that for a consideration of money I should trade on the likeness between us—and become your dummy, when you are otherwise engaged?"

Chilcote colored. "You are unpleasantly blunt," he said.

"But I have caught your meaning?"

"In the rough, yes."

Loder nodded curtly. "Then take my advice and go home," he said. "You're unhinged."

The other returned his glance, and as their eyes met Loder was reluctantly compelled to admit that, though the face was disturbed, it had no traces of insanity.

"I make you a proposal," Chilcote repeated, nervously but with distinctness. "Do you accept?"

For an instant Loder was at a loss to find a reply sufficiently final. Chilcote broke in upon the pause.

"After all," he urged, "what I ask of you is a simple thing. Merely to carry through my routine duties for a week or two occasionally when I find my endurance giving way—when a respite becomes essential. The work would be nothing to a man in your state of mind, the pay anything you like to name." In his eagerness he had followed Loder to the desk. "Won't you give me an answer? I told you I am neither mad nor drunk."

Loder pushed back the scattered papers that lay under his arm.

"Only a lunatic would propose such a scheme." he said, brusquely and without feeling.

"Why?"

The other's lips parted for a quick retort; then in a surprising way the retort seemed to fail him. "Oh, because the thing isn't feasible, isn't practicable from any point of view."

Chilcote stepped closer. "Why?" he insisted.

"Because it couldn't work, man! Couldn't hold for a dozen hours."

Chilcote put out his hand and touched his arm. "But why?" he urged. "Why? Give me one unanswerable reason."

Loder shook off the hand and laughed, but below his laugh lay a suggestion of the other's excitement. Again the scene stirred him against his sounder judgment; though his reply, when it came, was firm enough.

"As for reasons—" he said. "There are a hundred, if I had time to name them. Take it, for the sake of supposition, that I were to accept your offer. I should take my place in your house at—let us say at dinnertime. Your man gets me into your evening-clothes, and there, at the very start, you have the first suspicion set up. He has probably known you for years—known you until every turn of your appearance, voice, and manner is far more familiar to him than it is to you. There are no eyes like a servant's."

"I have thought of that. My servant and my secretary can both be changed. I will do the thing thoroughly."

Loder glanced at him in surprise. The madness had more method than he had believed. Then, as he still looked, a fresh idea struck him, and he laughed.

"You have entirely forgotten one thing," he said. "You can hardly dismiss your wife."

"My wife doesn't count."

Again Loder laughed. "I'm afraid I scarcely agree. The complications would be slightly—slightly—" He paused.

Chilcote's latent irritability broke out suddenly. "Look here," he said, "this isn't a chaffing matter, It may be moonshine to you, but it's reality to me."

Again Loder took his face between his hands.

"Don't ridicule the idea. I'm in dead earnest."

Loder said nothing.

"Think—think it over before you refuse."

For a moment Loder remained motionless; then h rose suddenly, pushing back his chair.

"Tush, man! You don't know what you say. The fact of your being married bars it. Can't you see that?"

Again Chilcote caught his arm.

"You misunderstand," he said. "You mistake the position. I tell you my wife and I are nothing to each other. She goes her way; I go mine. We have our own friends, our own rooms. Marriage, actual marriage, doesn't enter the question. We meet occasionally at meals, and at other people's houses; sometimes we go out together for the sake of appearances; beyond that, nothing. If you take up my life, nobody in it will trouble you less than Eve—I can promise that." He laughed unsteadily.

Loder's face remained unmoved.

"Even granting that," he said, "the thing is still impossible."

"Why?"

"There is the House. The position there would be untenable. A man is known there as he is known in his own club." He drew away from Chilcote's touch.

"Very possibly. Very possibly." Chilcote laughed quickly and excitedly. "But what club is without its eccentric member? I am glad you spoke of that. I am glad you raised that point. It was a long time ago that I hit upon a reputation for moods as a shield for—for other things, and, the more useful it has become, the more I have let it grow. I tell you you might go down to the House to-morrow and spend the whole day without speaking to, even nodding to, a single man, and as long as you were I to outward appearances no one would raise an eyebrow. In the same way you might vote in my place ask a question, make a speech if you wanted to—"

At the word speech Loder turned involuntarily For a fleeting second the coldness of his manner dropped and his face changed.

Chilcote, with his nervous quickness of perception, saw the alteration, and a new look crossed his own face.

"Why not?" he said, quickly. "You once had ambitions in that direction. Why not renew the ambitions?"

"And drop back from the mountains into the gutter?" Loder smiled and slowly shook his head.

"Better to live for one day than to exist for a hundred!" Chilcote's voice trembled with anxiety. For the third time he extended his hand and touched the other.

This time Loder did not shake off the detaining; hand; he scarcely seemed to feel its pressure.

"Look here." Chilcote's fingers tightened. "A little while ago you talked of influence. Here you can step into a position built by influence. You might do all you once hoped to do—"

Loder suddenly lifted his head. "Absurd!" he said. "Absurd! Such a scheme was never carried through."

"Precisely why it will succeed. People never suspect until they have a precedent. Will you consider it? At least consider it. Remember, if there is a risk, it is I who am running it. On your own showing, you have no position to jeopardize."

The other laughed curtly.

"Before I go to-night will you promise me to consider it?"

"No."

"Then you will send me your decision by wire to-morrow. I won't take your answer now."

Loder freed his arm abruptly. "Why not?" he asked.

Chilcote smiled nervously. "Because I know men—and men's temptations. We are all very strong till the quick is touched; then we all wince. It's morphia with one man, ambitions with another. In each case it's only a matter of sooner or later." He laughed in his satirical, unstrung way, and held out his hand. "'You have my address," he said. "Au revoir."

Loder pressed the hand and dropped it. "Goodbye," he said, meaningly. Then he crossed the room quietly and held the door open. "Good-bye," he said again as the other passed him.

As he crossed the threshold, Chilcote paused. "Au revoir," he corrected, with emphasis.

Until the last echo of his visitor's steps had died away Loder stood with his hand on the door; then, closing it quietly, he turned and looked round the room. For a considerable space he stood there as if weighing the merits of each object; then very slowly he moved to one of the book-shelves, drew out May's Parliamentary Practice, and, carrying it to the desk, readjusted the lamp.

VI

All the next day Chilcote moved in a fever of excitement. Hot with hope one moment, cold with fever the next, he rushed with restless energy into every task that presented itself—only to drop it as speedily. Twice during the morning he drove to the entrance of Clifford's Inn, but each time his courage failed him and he returned to Grosvenor Square—to learn that the expected message from Loder had not come.

It was a wearing condition of mind; but at worst it was scarcely more than an exaggeration of what his state had been for months, and made but little obvious difference in his bearing or manner.

In the afternoon he took his place in the House, but, though it was his first appearance since his failure of two days ago, he drew but small personal notice. When he chose, his manner could repel advances with extreme effect, and of late men had been prone to draw away from him.

In one of the lobbies he encountered Fraide surrounded by a group of friends. With his usual furtive haste he would have passed on; but, moving away from his party, the old man accosted him. He was always courteously particular in his treatment of Chilcote, as the husband of his ward and godchild.

"Better, Chilcote?" he said, holding out his hand.

At the sound of the low, rather formal tones, so characteristic of the old statesman, a hundred memories rose to Chilcote's mind, a hundred hours, distasteful in the living and unbearable in the recollection; and with them the new flash of hope, the new possibility of freedom. In a sudden rush of confidence he turned to his leader.

"I believe I've found a remedy for my nerves," he said. "I —I believe I'm going to be anew man." He laughed with a touch of excitement,

Fraide pressed his fingers kindly, "That is right," he said. "That is right. I called at Grosvenor Square this morning, but Eve told me your illness of the other day was not serious. She was very busy this morning—she could only spare me a quarter of an hour. She is indefatigable over the social side of your prospects. Chilcote. You owe her a large debt. A popular wife means a great deal to a politician."

The steady eyes of his companion disturbed Chilcote.

He drew away his hand.

"Eve is unique," he said, vaguely.

Fraide smiled. "That is right," he said again. "Admiration is too largely excluded from modern marriages." And with a courteous excuse he rejoined his friends.

It was dinner-time before Chilcote could desert the House, but the moment departure was possible he hurried to Grosvenor Square.

As he entered the house, the hall was empty. He swore irritably under his breath and pressed the nearest bell. Since his momentary exaltation in Fraide's presence, his spirits had steadily fallen, until now they hung at the lowest ebb.

As he waited in unconcealed impatience for an answer to his summons, he caught sight of his man Allsopp at the head of the stairs.

"Come here!" he called, pleased to find some one upon whom to vent his irritation. "Has that wire come for me?"

"No, sir. I inquired five minutes back."

"Inquire again."

"Yes, sir." Allsopp disappeared.

A second after his disappearance the bell of the hall door whizzed loudly.

Chilcote started. All sudden sounds, like all strong lights, affected him. He half moved to the door, then stopped himself with a short exclamation. At the same instant Allsopp reappeared.

Chilcote turned on him excitedly.

"What the devil's the meaning of this?" he said. "A battery of servants in the house and nobody to open the hall door!"

Allsopp looked embarrassed. "Crapham is coming directly, sir. He only left the hall to ask Jeffries—"

Chilcote turned. "Confound Crapham!" he exclaimed. "Go and open the door yourself."

Allsopp hesitated, his dignity struggling with his obedience. As he waited, the bell sounded again.

"Did you hear me?" Chilcote said.

"Yes, sir." Allsopp crossed the hall.

As the door was opened Chilcote passed his handkerchief from one hand to the other in the tension of hope and fear; then, as the sound of his own name in the shrill tones of a telegraph-boy reached his ears, he let the handkerchief drop to the ground.

Allsopp took the yellow envelope and carried it to his master.

"A telegram, sir," he said. "And the boy wishes to know if there is an answer." Picking up Chilcote's handkerchief, he turned aside with elaborate dignity.

Chilcote's hands were so unsteady that he could scarcely insert his finger under the flap of the envelope. Tearing off a corner, he wrenched the covering apart and smoothed out the flimsy pink paper.

The message was very simple, consisting of but seven words:

"Shall expect you at eleven to-night.-LODER."

He read it two or three times, then he looked up. "No answer," he said, mechanically; and to his own ears the relief in his voice sounded harsh and unnatural.

Exactly as the clocks chimed eleven Chilcote mounted the stairs to Loder's rooms. But this time there was more of haste than of uncertainty in his steps, and, reaching the landing, he crossed it in a couple of strides and knocked feverishly on the door.

It opened at once, and Loder stood before him.

The occasion was peculiar. For a moment neither spoke; each involuntarily looked at the other with new eyes and under changed conditions. Each had assumed a fresh stand-point in the other's thought. The passing astonishment, the half-impersonal curiosity that had previously tinged their relationship, was cast aside, never to be reassumed. In each, the other saw himself —and something more.

As usual, Loder was the first to recover himself.

"I was expecting you," he said. "Won't you come in?"

The words were almost the same as his words of the night before, but his voice had a different ring; just as his face, when he drew back into the room, had a different expression—a suggestion of decision and energy that had been lacking before. Chilcote caught the difference as he crossed the threshold, and for a bare second a flicker of something like jealousy touched him. But the sensation was fleeting.

"I have to thank you!" he said, holding out his hand. He was too well bred to show by a hint that he understood the drop in the other's principles. But Loder broke down the artifice.

"Let's be straight with each other, since everybody else has to be deceived," he said, taking the other's hand. "You have nothing to thank me for, and you know it. It's a touch of the old Adam. You tempted me, and I fell." He laughed, but below the laugh ran a note of something like triumph—the curious triumph of a man who has known the tyranny of strength and suddenly appreciates the freedom of a weakness.

"You fully realize the thing you have proposed?" he added, in a different tone. "It's not too late to retract, even now."

Chilcote opened his lips, paused, then laughed in imitation of his companion; but the laugh sounded forced.

"My dear fellow," he said at last, "I never retract."

"Never?"

"No."

"Then the bargain's sealed."

Loder walked slowly across the room, and, taking up his position by the mantel-piece, looked at his companion. The similarity between them as they faced each other seemed abnormal, defying even the closest scrutiny. And yet, so mysterious is Nature even in her lapses, they were subtly, indefinably different. Chilcote was Loder deprived of one essential: Loder, Chilcote with that essential bestowed. The difference lay neither in feature, in coloring, nor in height, but in that baffling, illusive inner illumination that some call individuality, and others soul.

Something of this idea, misted and tangled by nervous imagination, crossed Chilcote's mind in that moment of scrutiny, but he shrank from it apprehensively.

"I—I came to discuss details," he said, quickly, crossing the space that divided him from his host. "Shall we—? Are you—?" He paused uneasily.

"I'm entirely in your hands." Loder spoke with abrupt decision. Moving to the table, he indicated a chair, and drew another forward for himself.

Both men sat down.

Chilcote leaned forward, resting elbows on the table. "There will be several things to consider—" he began, nervously, looking across at the other.

"Quite so." Loder glanced back appreciatively. "I thought about those things the better part of last night. To begin with, I must study your handwriting. I guarantee to get it right, but it will take a month."

"A month!"

"Well, perhaps three weeks. We mustn't make a mess of things."

Chilcote shifted his position.

"Three weeks!" he repeated. "Couldn't you—?"

"No; I couldn't." Loder spoke authoritatively. "I might never want to put pen to paper, but, on the other hand, I might have to sign a check one day." He laughed. "Have you ever thought of that?—that I might have to, or want to, sign a check?"

"No. I confess that escaped me."

"You risk your fortune that you, may keep the place it bought for you?" Loder laughed again. "How do you know that I am not a blackguard?" he added. "How do you know that I won't clear out one day and leave you high and dry? What is to prevent John Chilcote from realizing forty or fifty thousand pounds and then making himself scarce?"

"You won't do that," Chilcote said, with unusual decision. "I told you your weakness last night; and it wasn't money. Money isn't the rock you'll split over."

"Then you think I'll split upon some rock? But that's beyond the question. To get to business again. You'll risk my studying your signature?"

Chilcote nodded.

"Right! Now item two." Loder counted on his: fingers. "I must know the names and faces of your men friends as far as I can. Your woman friends don't count. While I'm you, you will be adamant." He laughed again pleasantly. "But the men are essential—the backbone of the whole business."

"I have no men friends. I don't trust the idea of friendship."

"Acquaintances, then."

Chilcote looked up sharply. "I think we score there," he said. "I have a reputation for absent-mindedness that will carry you anywhere. They tell me I can look through the most substantial man in the House as if he were gossamer, though I may have lunched with him the same day."

Loder smiled. "By Jove!" he exclaimed. "Fate Must have been constructing this before either of us was born. It dovetails ridiculously. But I must know your colleagues—even if it's only to cut them. You'll have to take me to the House."

"Impossible!"

"Not at all!" Again the tone of authority fell to Loder. "I can pull my hat over my eyes and turn up my coat-collar. Nobody will notice me. We can choose the fall of the afternoon. I promise you 'twill be all right."

"Suppose the likeness should leak out? It's a risk."

Loder laughed confidently. "Tush, man! Risk is the salt of life. I must see you at your post, and I must see the men you work with." He rose, walked across the room, and took his pipe from the rack. "When I go in for a thing, I like to go in over head and ears," he added, as he opened his tobacco-jar.

His pipe filled, he resumed his seat, resting his elbows on the table in unconscious imitation of Chilcote.

"Got a match?" he said, laconically, holding out his hand.

In response Chilcote drew his match-box from his pocket and struck a light. As their hands touched, an exclamation escaped him.

"By Jove!" he said, with a fretful mixture of disappointment and surprise. "I hadn't noticed that!" His eyes were fixed in annoyed interest on Loder's extended hand.

Loder, following his glance, smiled. "Odd that we should both have overlooked it! It clean escaped my mind. It's rather an ugly scar." He lifted his hand till the light fell more fully on it. Above the second joint of the third finger ran a jagged furrow, the reminder of a wound that had once laid bare the bone.

Chilcote leaned forward. "How did you come by it?" he asked.

The other shrugged his shoulders. "Oh, that's ancient history."

"The results are present-day enough. It's very awkward! Very annoying!" Chilcote's spirits, at all times overeasily played upon, were damped by this obstacle.

Loder, still looking at his hand, didn't seem to hear. "There's only one thing to be done," he said. "Each wear two rings on the third finger of the left hand. Two rings ought to cover it." He made a speculative measurement with the stem of his pipe.

Chilcote still looked irritable and disturbed. "I detest rings. I never wear rings."

Loder raised his eyes calmly. "Neither do I," he said. "But there's no reason for bigotry."

But Chilcote's irritability was started. He pushed back his chair. "I don't like the idea," he said.

The other eyed him amusedly. "What a queer beggar you are!" he said. "You waive the danger of a man signing your checks and shy at wearing a piece of jewelry. I'll have a fair share of individuality to study."

Chilcote moved restlessly. "Everybody knows I detest jewelry."

"Everybody knows you are capricious. It's got to be the rings or nothing, so far as I make out."

Chilcote again altered his position, avoiding the other's eyes. At last, after a struggle with himself, he looked up.

"I suppose you're right!" he said. "Have it your own way." It was the first small, tangible concession to the stronger will.

Loder took his victory quietly. "Good!" he said. "Then it's all straight sailing?"

"Except for the matter of the—the remuneration." Chilcote hazarded the word uncertainly.

There was a faint pause, then Loder laughed brusquely. "My pay?"

The other was embarrassed. "I didn't want to put it quite like that."

"But that was what you thought. Why are you never honest —even with yourself?"

Chilcote drew his chair closer to the table. He did not attend to the other's remark, but his fingers strayed to his waistcoat pocket and fumbled there.

Loder saw the gesture. "Look here," he said, "you are overtaxing yourself. The affair of the pay isn't pressing; we'll shelve it to another night. You look tired out."

Chilcote lifted his eyes with a relieved glance. "Thanks. I do feel a bit fagged. If I may, I'll have that whiskey that I refused last night."

"Why, certainly." Loder rose at once and crossed to a cupboard in the wall. In silence he brought out whiskey, glasses, and a siphon of soda-water. "Say when!" he said, lifting the whiskey.

"Now. And I'll have plain water instead of soda, if it's all the same."

"Oh, quite." Loder recrossed the room. Instantly his back was turned, Chilcote drew a couple of tabloids from his pocket and dropped them into his glass. As the other came slowly back he laughed nervously.

"Thanks. See to your own drink now; I can manage this." He took the jug unceremoniously, and, carefully guarding his glass from the light, poured in the water with excited haste.

"What shall we drink to?" he said.

Loder methodically mixed his own drink and lifted the glass. "Oh, to the career of John Chilcote!" he answered.

For an instant the other hesitated. There was something prophetic in the sound of the toast. But he shook the feeling off and held up his glass.

"To the career of John Chilcote!" he said, with another unsteady laugh.

VII

It was a little less than three weeks since Chilcote and Loder had drunk their toast, and again Loder was seated at his desk.

His head was bent and his hand moved carefully as he traced line after line of meaningless words on a sheet of foolscap. Having covered the page with writing, he rose, moved to the centre-table, and compared his task with an open letter that lay there. The comparison seemed to please him; he straightened his shoulders and threw back his head in an attitude of critical satisfaction. So absorbed was he that, when a step sounded on the stairs outside, he did not notice it, and only raised his head when the door was thrown open unceremoniously. Even then his interest was momentary.

"Hullo!" he said, his eyes returning to their scrutiny of his task.

Chilcote shut the door and came hastily across the room. He looked ill and harassed. As he reached Loder he put out his hand nervously and touched his arm.

Loder looked up. "What is it?" he asked. "Any new development?"

Chilcote tried to smile. "Yes," he said, huskily; "it's come."

Loder freed his arm. "What? The end of the world?"

"No. The end of me." The words came jerkily, the strain that had enforced them showing in every syllable.

Still Loder was uncomprehending; he could not, or would not, understand.

Again Chilcote caught and jerked at his sleeve. "Don't you see? Can't you see?"

"No."

Chilcote dropped the sleeve and passed his handkerchief across his forehead. "It's come," he repeated. "Don't you understand? I want you." He drew away, then stepped back again anxiously. "I know I'm taking you unawares," he said. "But it's not my fault. On my soul, it's not! The thing seems to spring at me and grip me—" He stopped, sinking weakly into a chair.

For a moment Loder stood erect and immovable—then, almost with reluctance, his glance turned to the figure beside him.

"You want me to take your place to-night—without preparation?" His voice was distinct and firm, but it was free from contempt.

"Yes; yes, I do." Chilcote spoke without looking up.

"That you may spend the night in morphia—this and other nights?"

Chilcote lifted a flushed, unsettled face. "You have no right to preach. You accepted the bargain."

Loder raised his head quickly. "I never—" he began; then both his face and voice altered. "You are quite right," he said, coldly. "You won't have to complain again."

Chilcote stirred uncomfortably. "My dear chap," he said, "I meant no offence. It's merely—"

"Your nerves. I know. But come to business. What am I to do?"

Chilcote rose excitedly. "Yes, business. Let's come to business. It's rough on you, taking you short like this. But you have an erratic person to deal with. I've had a horrible day—a horrible day." His face had paled again, and in the green lamplight it possessed a grayish hue. Involuntarily Loder turned away.

Chilcote watched him as he passed to the desk and began mechanically sorting papers. "A horrible day!" he repeated. "So bad that I daren't face the night. You have read De Quincey?" he asked, with a sudden change of tone.

"Yes."

"Then read him again and you'll understand. I have all the horrors—without any art. I have no 'Ladies of Sorrow,' but I have worse monsters than his 'crocodile'." He laughed unpleasantly.

Loder turned. "Why in the devil's name—" he began; then again he halted. Something in Chilcote's drawn, excited face checked him. The strange sense of predestination that we sometimes see in the eyes of another struck cold upon him, chilling his last attempt at remonstrance. "What do you want me to do?" he substituted, in an ordinary voice.

The words steadied Chilcote. He laughed a little. The laugh was still shaky, but it was pitched in a lower key.

"You—you're quite right to pull me up. We have no time to waste. It must be one o'clock." He pulled out his watch, then walked to the window and stood looking down into the shadowy court. "How quiet you are here!" he said. Then abruptly a new thought struck him and he wheeled back into the room. "Loder," he said, quickly—"Loder, I have an idea! While you are me, why shouldn't I be you? Why shouldn't I be John Loder instead of the vagrant we contemplated? It covers everything—it explains everything. It's magnificent! I'm amazed we never thought of it before."

Loder was still beside the desk. "I thought of it," he said, without looking back.

"And didn't suggest it?"

"No."

"Why?"

Loder said nothing and the other colored.

"Jealous of your reputation?" he said, satirically.

"I have none to be jealous of."

Chilcote laughed disagreeably. "Then you aren't so for gone in philosophy as I thought. You have a niche in your own good opinion."

Again Loder was silent; then he smiled. "You have an oddly correct perception at times," he said. "I suppose I have had a lame sort of pride in keeping my name clean. But pride like that is out of fashion—and I've got to float with the tide." He laughed, the short laugh that Chilcote had heard once or twice before, and, crossing the room, he stood beside his visitor. "After all," he said, "what business have I with pride, straight or lame? Have my identity, if you want it. When all defences have been broken down one barrier won't save the town." Laughing again, he laid his hand on the other's arm. "Come," he said, "give your orders. I capitulate."

An hour later the two men passed from Loder's bed room, where the final arrangements had been completed, back into the sitting-room. Loder came first, in faultless evening-dress. His hair was carefully brushed, the clothes he wore fitted him perfectly. To any glance, critical or casual, he was the man who had mounted the stairs and entered the rooms earlier in the evening. Chilcote's manner of walking and poise of the head seemed to have descended upon him with Chilcote's clothes. He came into the room hastily and passed to the desk.

"I have no private papers," he said, "so I have nothing to lock up. Everything can stand as it is. A woman named Robins comes in the mornings to clean up and light the fire; otherwise you must shift for yourself. Nobody will disturb you. Quiet, dead quiet, is about the one thing you can count on."

Chilcote, half halting in the doorway, made an attempt to laugh. Of the two, he was noticeably the more embarrassed. In Loder's well-worn, well-brushed tweed suit he felt stranded on his own personality, bereft for the moment of the familiar accessories that helped to cloak deficiencies and keep the wheel of conventionality comfortably rolling. He stood unpleasantly conscious of himself, unable to shape his sensations even in thought. He glanced at the fire, at the table, finally at the chair on which he had thrown his overcoat before entering the bedroom. At the sight of the coat his gaze brightened, the aimlessness forsook him, and he gave an exclamation of relief.

"By Jove!" he said. "I clean forgot."

"What?" Loder looked round.

"The rings." He crossed to the coat and thrust his hand into the pocket. "The duplicates only arrived this afternoon. The nick of time, eh?" He spoke fast, his fingers searching busily. Occupation of any kind came as a boon.

Loder slowly followed him, and as the box was brought to light he leaned forward interestedly.

"As I told you, one is the copy of an old signet-ring, the other a plain band—a plain gold band like a wedding-ring." Chilcote laughed as he placed the four rings side by side on his palm. "I could think of nothing else that would be wide —and not ostentatious. You know how I detest display."

Loder touched the rings. "You have good taste," he said. "Let's see if they serve their purpose?" He picked them up and carried them to the lamp.

Chilcote followed him. "That was an ugly wound," he said, his curiosity reawakening as Loder extended his finger. "How did you come by it?"

The other smiled. "It's a memento," he said.

"Of bravery?"

"No. Quite the reverse." He looked again at his hand, then glanced back at Chilcote. "No," he repeated, with an unusual impulse of confidence. "It serves to remind me that I am not exempt—that I have been fooled like other men."

"That implies a woman?"

"Yes." Again Loder looked at the scar on his finger. "I seldom recall the thing, it's so absolutely past. But I rather like to remember it to-night. I rather want you to know that I've been through the fire. It's a sort of guarantee."

Chilcote made a hasty gesture, but the other interrupted it.

"Oh, I know you trust me. But you're giving me a risky post. I want you to see that women are out of my line—quite out of it."

"But, my dear chap—"

Loder went on without heeding. "This thing happened eight years ago at Santasalare," he said, "a little place between Luna and Pistoria—a mere handful of houses wedged between two hills. A regular relic of old Italy crumbling away under flowers and sunshine, with nothing to suggest the present century except the occasional passing of a train round the base of one of the hills. I had literally stumbled upon the place on a long tramp south from Switzerland, and had been tempted into a stay at the little inn. The night after my arrival something unusual occurred. There was an accident to the train at the point where it skirted the village.

"There was a small excitement; all the inhabitants were anxious to help, and I took my share. As a matter of fact, the smash was not disastrous; the passengers were hurt and frightened, but nobody was killed."

He paused and looked at his companion, but, seeing him interested, went on:

"Among these passengers was an English lady. Of all concerned in the business, she was the least upset. When I came upon her she was sitting on the shattered door of one of the carriages, calmly rearranging her hat. On seeing me she looked up with the most charming smile imaginable.

"'I have just been waiting for somebody like you,' she said. 'My stupid maid has got herself smashed up somewhere in the second-class carriages, and I have nobody to help me to find my dog.'

"Of course, that first speech ought to have enlightened me, but it didn't. I only saw the smile and heard the voice; I knew nothing of whether they were deep or shallow. So I found the maid and found the dog. The first expressed gratitude; the other didn't. I extricated him with enormous difficulty from the wreck of the luggage-van, and this was how he marked his appreciation." He held out his hand and nodded towards the scar.

Chilcote glanced up. "So that's the explanation?"

"Yes. I tried to conceal the thing when I restored the dog, but I was bleeding abominably and I failed. Then the whole business was changed. It was I who needed seeing to, my new friend insisted; I who should be looked after, and not she. She forgot the dog in the newer interest of my wounded finger. The maid, who was practically unhurt, was sent on to engage rooms at the little inn, and she and I followed slowly.

"That walk impressed me. There was an attractive mistiness of atmosphere in the warm night, a sensation more than attractive in being made much of by a woman of one's own class and country after five years' wandering." He laughed with a touch of irony. "But I won't take up your time with details. You know the progress of an ordinary love affair. Throw in a few more flowers and a little more sunshine than is usual, a man who is practically a hermit and a woman who knows the world by heart, and you have the whole thing.

"She insisted on staying in Santasalare for three days in order to keep my finger bandaged; she ended by staying three weeks in the hope of smashing up my life.

"On coming to the hotel she had given no name; and in our first explanations to each other she led me to conclude her an unmarried girl. It was at the end of the three weeks that I learned that she was not a free agent, as I had innocently imagined, but possessed a husband whom she had left ill with malaria at Florence or Rome.

"The news disconcerted me, and I took no pains to hide it. After that the end came abruptly. In her eyes I had become a fool with middle-class principles; in my eyes—But there is no need for that. She left Santasalare the same night in a great confusion of trunks and hat-boxes; and next morning I strapped on my knapsack and turned my face to the south."

"And women don't count ever after?" Chilcote smiled, beguiled out of himself.

Loder laughed. "That's what I've been trying to convey. Once bitten, twice shy!" He laughed again and slipped the two rings over his finger with an air of finality.

"Now, shall I start? This is the latch-key?" He drew a key from the pocket of Chilcote's evening-clothes. "When I get to Grosvenor Square I am to find your house, go straight in, mount the stairs, and there on my right hand will be the door of your—I mean my own—private rooms. I think I've got it all by heart. I feel inspired; I feel that I can't go wrong." He handed the two remaining rings to Chilcote and picked up the overcoat.

"I'll stick on till I get a wire—," he said. "Then I'll come back and we'll reverse again." He slipped on the coat and moved back towards the table. Now that the decisive moment had come, it embarrassed him.

Scarcely knowing how to bring it to an end, he held out his hand.

Chilcote took it, paling a little. "'Twill be all right!" he said, with a sudden return of nervousness. "'Twill be all right! And I've made it plain about—about the remuneration? A hundred a week—besides all expenses."

Loder smiled again. "My pay? Oh yes, you've made it clear as day. Shall we say good-night now?"

"Yes. Good-night."

There was a strange, distant note in Chilcote's voice, but the other did not pretend to hear it. He pressed the hand he was holding, though the cold dampness of it repelled him.

"Good-night," he said again.

"Good-night."

They stood for a moment, awkwardly looking at each other, then Loder quietly disengaged his hand, crossed the room, and passed through the door.

Chilcote, left standing alone in the middle of the room, listened while the last sound of the other's footsteps was audible on the uncarpeted stairs; then, with a furtive, hurried gesture, he caught up the green-shaded lamp and passed into Loder's bedroom.

VIII

To all men come portentous moments, difficult moments, triumphant moments. Loder had had his examples of all three, but no moment in his career ever equalled in strangeness of sensation that in which, dressed in another man's clothes, he fitted the latchkey for the first time into the door of the other man's house.

The act was quietly done. The key fitted the lock smoothly and his fingers turned it without hesitation, though his heart, usually extremely steady, beat sharply for a second. The hall loomed massive and sombre despite the modernity of electric lights. It was darkly and expensively decorated in black and brown; a frieze of wrought bronze, representing peacocks with outspread tails, ornamented the walls; the banisters were of heavy iron-work, and the somewhat formidable fireplace was of the same dark metal.

Loder looked about him, then advanced, his heart again beating quickly as his hand touched the cold banister and he began his ascent of the stairs. But at each step his confidence strengthened, his feet became more firm; until, at the head of the stairs, as if to disprove his assurance, his pulses played him false once more, this time to a more serious tune. From the farther end of a well-lighted corridor a maid was coming straight in his direction.

For one short second all things seemed to whiz about him; the certainty of detection overpowered his mind. The indisputable knowledge that he was John Loder and no other, despite all armor of effrontery and dress, so dominated him that all other considerations shrank before it. It wanted but one word, one simple word of denunciation, and the whole scheme was shattered. In the dismay of the moment, he almost wished that the word might be spoken and the suspense ended.

But the maid came on in silence, and so incredible was the silence that Loder moved onward, too. He came within a yard of her, and still she did not speak; then, as he passed her, she drew back respectfully against the wall.

The strain, so astonishingly short, had been immense, but with its slackening came a strong reaction. The expected humiliation seethed suddenly to a desire to dare fate. Pausing quickly, he turned and called the woman back.

The spot where he had halted was vividly bright, the ceiling light being directly above his head; and as she came towards him he raised his face deliberately and waited.

She looked at him without surprise or interest. "Yes, sir?" she said.

"Is your mistress in?" he asked. He could think of no other question, but it served his purpose as a test of his voice.

Still the woman showed no surprise. "She's not in sir," she answered. "But she's expected in half an hour."

"In half an hour? All right! That's all I wanted." With a movement of decision Loder walked back to the stair-head, turned to the right, and opened the door of Chilcote's rooms.

The door opened on a short, wide passage; on one side stood the study, on the other the bed, bath, and dressing-rooms. With a blind sense of knowledge and unfamiliarity, bred of much description on Chilcote's part, he put his hand on the study door and, still exalted by the omen of his first success, turned the handle.

Inside the room there was firelight and lamplight and a studious air of peace. The realization of this and a slow incredulity at Chilcote's voluntary renunciation were his first impressions; then his attention was needed for more imminent things.

As he entered, the new secretary was returning a volume to its place on the book-shelves. At sight of him, he pushed it hastily into position and turned round.

"I was making a few notes on the political position of Khorasan," he said, glancing with slight apprehensiveness at the other's face. He was a small, shy man, with few social attainments but an extraordinary amount of learning—the antithesis of the alert Blessington, whom he had replaced.

Loder bore his scrutiny without flinching. Indeed, it struck him suddenly that there was a fund of interest, almost of excitement, in the encountering of each new pair of eyes. At the thought he moved forward to the desk.

"Thank you, Greening," he said. "A very useful bit of work."

The secretary glanced up, slightly puzzled. His endurance had been severely taxed in the fourteen days that he had filled his new post.

"I'm glad you think so, sir," he said, hesitatingly. "You rather pooh-poohed the matter this morning, if you remember."

Loder was taking off his coat, but stopped in the operation.

"This morning?" he said. "Oh, did I? Did I?" Then, struck by the opportunity the words gave him, he turned towards the secretary. "You've got to get used to me, Greening," he said. "You haven't quite grasped me yet, I can see. I'm a man of moods, you know. Up to the present you've seen my slack side, my jarred side, but I have quite another when I care to show it. I'm a sort of Jekyll-and-Hyde affair." Again he laughed, and Greening echoed the sound diffidently. Chilcote had evidently discouraged familiarity.

Loder eyed him with abrupt understanding. He recognized the loneliness in the anxious, conciliatory manner.

"You're tired," he said, kindly. "Go to bed. I've got some thinking to do. Good-night." He held out his hand.

Greening took it, still half distrustful of this fresh side to so complex a man.

"Good-night, sir," he said. "To-morrow, if you approve, I shall go on with my notes. I hope you will have a restful night."

For a second Loder's eyebrows went up, but he recovered himself instantly.

"Ah, thanks, Greening," he said. "Thanks. I think your hope will be fulfilled."

He watched the little secretary move softly and apologetically to the door; then he walked to the fire, and, resting his elbows on the mantel-piece, he took his face in his hands.

For a space he stood absolutely quiet, then his hands dropped to his sides and he turned slowly round. In that short space he had balanced things and found his bearings. The slight nervousness shown in his brusque sentences and overconfident manner faded out, and he faced facts steadily.

With the return of his calmness he took a long survey of the room. His glance brightened appreciatively as it travelled from the walls lined with well-bound books to the lamps modulated to the proper light; from the lamps to the desk fitted with every requirement. Nothing was lacking. All he had once possessed, all he had since dreamed of, was here, but on a greater scale. To enjoy the luxuries of life a man must go long without them. Loder had lived severely— so severely that until three weeks ago he had believed bimself exempt from the temptations of humanity. Then the voice of the world had spoken, and within him another voice had answered, with a tone so clamorous and insistent that it had outcried his surprised and incredulous wonder at its existence and its claims. That had been the voice of suppressed ambition; and now as he stood in the new atmosphere a newer voice lifted itself. The joy of material things rose suddenly, overbalancing the last remnant of the philosophy he had reared. He saw all things in a fresh light—the soft carpets, the soft lights, the numberless pleasant, unnecessary things that color the passing landscape and oil the wheels of life. This was power—power made manifest. The choice bindings of one's books, the quiet harmony of one's surroundings, the gratifying deference of one's dependants—these were the visible, the outward signs, the things he had forgotten.

Crossing the room slowly, he lifted and looked at the different papers on the desk. They had a substantial feeling, an importance, an air of value. They were like the solemn keys to so many vexed problems. Beside the papers were a heap of letters neatly arranged and as yet unopened. He turned them over one by one. They were all thick, and interesting to look at. He smiled as he recalled his own scanty mail: envelopes long and bulky or narrow and thin—unwelcome manuscripts or very welcome checks. Having sorted the letters, he hesitated. It was his task to open them, but he had never in his life opened an envelope addressed to another man.

He stood uncertain, weighing them in his hand.

Then all at once a look of attention and surprise crossed his face, and he raised his head. Some one had unmistakably paused outside the door which Greening had left ajar.

There was a moment of apparent doubt, then a stir of skirts, a quick, uncertain knock, and the intruder entered.

For a couple of seconds she stood in the doorway; then, as Loder made no effort to speak, she moved into the room. She had apparently but just returned from some entertainment, for, though she had drawn off her long gloves, she was still wearing an evening cloak of lace and fur.

That she was Chilcote's wife Loder instinctively realized the moment she entered the room. But a disconcerting confusion of ideas was all that followed the knowledge. He stood by the desk, silent and awkward, trying to fit his expectations to his knowledge. Then, faced by the hopelessness of the task, he turned abruptly and looked at her again.

She had taken off her cloak and was standing by the fire. The compulsion of moving through life alone had set its seal upon her in a certain self-possession, a certain confidence of pose; yet her figure, as Loder then saw it, backgrounded by the dark books and gowned in pale blue, had a suggestion of youthfulness that seemed a contradiction. The remembrance of Chilcote's epithets "cold" and "unsympathetic" came back to him with something like astonishment. He felt no uncertainty, no dread of discovery and humiliation in her presence as he had felt in the maid's; yet there was something in her face that made him infinitely more uncomfortable. A look he could find no name for—a friendliness that studiously covered another feeling, whether question, distrust, or actual dislike he could not say. With a strange sensation of awkwardness he sorted Chilcote's letters, waiting for her to speak.

As if divining his thought, she turned towards him. "I'm afraid I rather intrude," she said. "If you are busy—"

His sense of courtesy was touched; he had begun life with a high opinion of women, and the words shook up an echo of the old sentiment.

"Don't think that," he said, hastily. "I was only looking through—my letters. You mustn't rate yourself below letters." He was conscious that his tone was hurried, that his words were a little jagged; but Eve did not appear to notice. Unlike Greening, she took the new manner without surprise. She had known Chilcote for six years.

"I dined with the Fraides to-night," she said. "Mr. Fraide sent you a message."

Unconsciously Loder smiled. There was humor in the thought of a message to him from the great Fraide. To hide his amusement he wheeled one of the big lounge-chairs forward.

"Indeed," he said. "Won't you sit down?"

They were near together now, and he saw her face more fully. Again he was taken aback. Chilcote had spoken of her as successful and intelligent, but never as beautiful. Yet her beauty was a rare and uncommon fact. Her hair was black —not a glossy black, but the dusky black that is softer than any brown; her eyes were large and of a peculiarly pure blue; and her eyelashes were black, beautifully curved and of remarkable thickness.

"Won't you sit down?" he said again, cutting short his thoughts with some confusion.

"Thank you." She gravely accepted the proffered chair. But he saw that without any ostentation she drew her skirts aside as she passed him. The action displeased him unaccountably.

"Well," he said, shortly, "what had Fraide to say?" He walked to the mantel-piece with his customary movement and stood watching her. The instinct towards hiding his face had left him. Her instant and uninterested acceptance of him almost nettled him; his own half-contemptuous impression of Chilcote came to him unpleasantly, and with it the first desire to assert his own individuality. Stung by the conflicting emotions, he felt in Chilcote's pockets for something to smoke.

Eve saw and interpreted the action. "Are these your cigarettes?" She leaned towards a small table and took up a box made of lizard-skin.

"Thanks." He took the box from her, and as it passed from one to the other he saw her glance at his rings. The glance was momentary; her lips parted to express question or surprise, then closed again without comment. More than any spoken words, the incident showed him the gulf that separated husband and wife.

"Well?" he said again, "what about Fraide?"

At his words she sat straighter and looked at him more directly, as if bracing herself to a task.

"Mr. Fraide is—is as interested as ever in you," she began.

"Or in you?" Loder made the interruption precisely as he felt Chilcote would have made it. Then instantly he wished the words back.

Eve's warm skin colored more deeply; for a second the inscrutable underlying expression that puzzled him showed in her eyes, then she sank back into a corner of the chair.

"Why do you make such a point of sneering at my friends?" she asked, quietly. "I overlook it when you are nervous." She halted slightly on the word. "But you are not nervous tonight."

Loder, to his great humiliation, reddened. Except for an occasional outburst on the part of Mrs. Robins, his charwoman, he had not merited a woman's displeasure for years.

"The sneer was unintentional," he said.

For the first time Eve showed a personal interest. She looked at him in a puzzled way. "If your apology was meant," she said, hesitatingly, "I should be glad to accept it."

Loder, uncertain of how to take the words, moved back to the desk. He carried an unlighted cigarette between his fingers.

There was an interval in which neither spoke. Then, at last, conscious of its awkwardness, Eve rose. With one hand on the back of her chair, she looked at him.

"Mr. Fraide thinks it's such a pity that"—she stopped to choose her words—"that you should lose hold on things—lose interest in things, as you are doing. He has been thinking a good deal about you in the last three weeks—ever since the day of your—your illness in the House; and it seems to him," —again she broke off, watching Loder's averted head—"it seems to him that if you made one real effort now, even now, to shake off your restlessness, that your—your health might improve. He thinks that the present crisis would be"—she hesitated—" would give you a tremendous opportunity. Your trade interests, bound up as they are with Persia, would give any opinion you might hold a double weight." Almost unconsciously a touch of warmth crept into her words.

"Mr. Fraide talked very seriously about the beginning of your career. He said that if only the spirit of your first days could come back—" Her tone grew quicker, as though she feared ridicule in Loder's silence. "He asked me to use my influence. I know that I have little—none, perhaps—but I couldn't tell him that, and so—so I promised."

"And have kept the promise?" Loder spoke at random. Her manner and her words had both affected him. There was a sensation of unreality in his brain.

"Yes," she answered. "I always want to do—what I can."

As she spoke a sudden realization of the effort she was making struck upon him, and with it his scorn of Chilcote rose in renewed force.

"My intention—" he began, turning to her. Then the futility of any declaration silenced him. "I shall think over what you say," he added, after a minute's wait. "I suppose I can't say more than that."

Their eyes met and she smiled a little.

"I don't believe I expected as much," she said. "I think I'll go now. You have been wonderfully patient." Again she smiled slightly, at the same time extending her hand. The gesture was quite friendly, but in Loder's eyes it held relief as well as friendliness; and when their hands met he noticed that her fingers barely brushed his.

He picked up her cloak and carried it across the room. As he held the door open, he laid it quietly across her arm.

"I'll think over what you've said," he repeated.

Again she glanced at him as if suspecting sarcasm then, partly reassured, she paused. "You will always despise your opportunities, and I suppose I shall always envy them," she said. "That's the way with men and women. Good-night!" With another faint smile she passed out into the corridor.

Loder waited until he heard the outer door close, then he crossed the room thoughtfully and dropped into the chair that she had vacated. He sat for a time looking at the hand her fingers had touched; then he lifted his head with a characteristic movement.

"By Jove!" he said, aloud, "how cordially she detests tests him!"

IX

Loder slept soundly and dreamlessly in Chilcote's canopied bed. To him the big room with its severe magnificence suggested nothing of the gloom and solitude that it held in its owner's eyes. The ponderous furniture, the high ceiling, the heavy curtains, unchanged since the days of Chilcote's grandfather, all hinted at a far-reaching ownership that stirred him. The ownership was mythical in his regard, and the possessions a mirage, but they filled the day. And, surely, sufficient for the day—

That was his frame of mind as he opened his eyes on the following morning, and lay appreciative of his comfort, of the surrounding space, even of the light that filtered through the curtain chinks, suggestive of a world recreated. With day, all things seem possible to a healthy man. He stretched his arms luxuriously, delighting in the glossy smoothness of the sheets.

What was it Chilcote had said? Better live for a day than exist for a lifetime! That was true; and life had begun. At thirty-six he was to know it for the first time.

He smiled, but without irony. Man is at his best at thirty-six, he mused. He has retained his enthusiasms and shed his exuberances; he has learned what to pick up and what to pass by; he no longer imagines that to drain a cup one must taste the dregs. He closed his eyes and stretched again, not his arms only, but his whole body. The pleasure of his mental state insisted on a physical expression. Then, sitting up in bed, he pressed the electric bell.

Chilcote's new valet responded.

"Pull those curtains, Renwick!" he said. "What's the time?" He had passed the ordeal of Renwick's eyes the night before.

The man was slow, even a little stupid. He drew back the curtains carefully, then looked at the small clock on the dressing-table. "Eight o'clock, sir. I didn't expect the bell so early, sir."

Loder felt reproved, and a pause followed.

"May I bring your cup of tea, sir?"

"No. Not just yet. I'll have a bath first."

Renwick showed ponderous uncertainty. "Warm, sir?" he hazarded.

"No. Cold."

Still perplexed, the man left the room.

Loder smiled to himself. The chances of discovery in that quarter were not large. He was inclined to think that Chilcote had even overstepped necessity in the matter of his valet's dullness.

He breakfasted alone, following Chilcote's habit, and after breakfast found his way to the study.

As he entered, Greening rose with the same conciliatory haste that he had shown the night before.

Loder nodded to him. "Early at work?" he said, pleasantly.

The little man showed instant, almost ridiculous relief. "Good-morning, sir," he said; "you too are early. I rather feared your nerves troubled you after I left last night, for I found your letters still unopened this morning. But I am glad to see you look so well."

Loder promptly turned his back to the light. "Oh, last night's letters!" he said. "To tell you the truth, Greening, my wife"—his hesitation was very slight—"my wife looked me up after you left, and we gossiped. I clean forgot the post." He smiled in an explanatory way as he moved to the desk and picked up the letters.

With Greening's eyes upon him, there was no time for scruples. With very creditable coolness he began opening the envelopes one by one. The letters were unimportant, and he passed them one after another to the secretary, experiencing a slight thrill of authority as each left his hand. Again the fact that power is visible in little things came to his mind.

"Give me my engagement-book, Greening," he said, when the letters had been disposed of.

The book that Greening handed him was neat in shape and bound, like Chilcote's cigarette-case, in lizard-skin.

As Loder took it, the gold monogram "J.C." winked at him in the bright morning light. The incident moved his sense of humor. He and the book were cooperators in the fraud, it seemed. He felt an inclination to wink back. Nevertheless, he opened it with proper gravity and skimmed the pages.

The page devoted to the day was almost full. On every other line were jottings in Chilcote's irregular hand, and twice among the entries appeared a prominent cross in blue pencilling. Loder's interest quickened as his eye caught the mark. It had been agreed between them that only engagements essential to Chilcote's public life need be carried through during his absence, and these, to save confusion, were to be crossed in blue pencil. The rest, for the most part social claims, were to be left to circumstance and Loder's inclination, Chilcote's erratic memory always accounting for the breaking of trivial promises.

But Loder in his new energy was anxious for obligations; the desire for fresh and greater tests grew with indulgence. He scanned the two lines with eagerness. The first was an interview with Cresham, one of Chilcote's supporters in Wark; the other an engagement to lunch with Fraide. At the idea of the former his interest quickened, but at thought of the latter it quailed momentarily. Had the entry been a royal command it would have affected him infinitely less. For a space his assurance faltered; then, by coincidence, the recollection of Eve and Eve's words of last night came back to him, and his mind was filled with a new sensation.

Because of Chilcote, he was despised by Chilcote's wife! There was no denying that in all the pleasant excitement of the adventure that knowledge had rankled. It came to him now linked with remembrance of the slight, reluctant touch of her fingers, the faintly evasive dislike underlying her glance. It was a trivial thing, but it touched his pride as a man. That was how he put it to himself. It wasn't that he valued this woman's opinion—any woman's opinion; it was merely that it touched his pride. He turned again to the window and gazed out, the engagement book still between his hands. What if he compelled her respect? What if by his own personality cloaked under Chilcote's identity he forced her to admit his capability? It was a matter of pride, after all—scarcely even of pride; self-respect was a better word.

Satisfied by his own reasoning, he turned back into the room.

"See to those letters, Greening," he said. "And for the rest of the morning's work you might go on with your Khorasan notes. I believe we'll all want every inch of knowledge we can get in that quarter before we're much older. I'll see you again later." With a reassuring nod he crossed the room and passed through the door.

He lunched with Fraide at his club, and afterwards walked with him to Westminster. The walk and lunch were both memorable. In that hour he learned many things that had been sealed to him before. He tasted his first draught of real elation, his first drop of real discomfiture. He saw for the first time how a great man may condescend—how unostentatiously, how fully, how delightfully. He felt what tact and kindness perfectly combined may accomplish, and he burned inwardly with a sense of duplicity that crushed and elated him alternately. He was John Loder, friendless, penniless, with no present and no future, yet he walked down Whitehall in the full light of day with one of the greatest statesmen England has known.

Some strangers were being shown over the Terrace when he and Fraide reached the House, and, noticing the open door, the old man paused.

"I never refuse fresh air," he said. "Shall we take another breath of it before settling down?" He took Loder's arm and drew him forward. As they passed through the door-way the pressure of his fingers tightened. "I shall reckon to-day among my pleasantest memories, Chilcote," he said, gravely. "I can't explain the feeling, but I seem to have touched Eve's husband—the real you, more closely this morning than I ever did before. It has been a genuine happiness." He looked up with the eyes that, through all his years of action and responsibility, had remained so bright.

But Loder paled suddenly, and his glance turned to the river-wide, mysterious, secret. Unconsciously Fraide had stripped the illusion. It was not John Loder who walked here; it was Chilcote—Chilcote with his position, his constituency —his wife. He half extricated his arm, but Fraide held it.

"No," he said. "Don't draw away from me. You have always been too ready to do that. It is not often I have a pleasant truth to tell. I won't be deprived of the enjoyment."

"Can the truth ever be pleasant, sir?" Involuntarily Loder echoed Chilcote.

Fraide looked up. He was half a head shorter than his companion, though his dignity concealed the fact. "Chilcote," he said, seriously, "give up cynicism! It is the trade-mark of failure, and I do not like it in my friends."

Loder said nothing. The quiet insight of the reproof, its mitigating kindness, touched him sharply. In that moment he saw the rails down which he had sent his little car of existence spinning, and the sight daunted him. The track was steeper, the gauge narrower, than he had guessed; there were curves and sidings upon which he had not reckoned. He turned his head and met Fraide's glance.

"Don't count too much on me, sir," he said, slowly. "I might disappoint you again." His voice broke off on the last word, for the sound of other voices and of laughter came to them across the Terrace as a group of two women and three men passed through the open door. At a glance he realized that the slighter of the two women was Eve.

Seeing them, she disengaged herself from her party and came quickly forward. He saw her cheeks flush and her eyes brighten pleasantly as they rested on his companion; but he noticed also that after her first cursory glance she avoided his own direction.

As she came towards them, Fraide drew away his hand in readiness to greet her.

"Here comes my godchild!" he said. "I often wish, Chilcote, that I could do away with the prefix." He added the last words in an undertone as he reached them; then he responded warmly to her smile.

"What!" he said. "Turning the Terrace into the Garden of Eden in January! We cannot allow this."

Eve laughed. "Blame Lady Sarah!" she said. "We met at lunch, and she carried me off. Needless to say I hadn't to ask where."

They both laughed, and Loder joined, a little uncertainly. He had yet to learn that the devotion of Fraide and his wife was a long-standing jest in their particular set.

At the sound of his tardy laugh Eve turned to him. "I hope I didn't rob you of all sleep last night," she said. "I caught him in his den," she explained, turning to Fraide, "and invaded it most courageously. I believe we talked till two."

Again Loder noticed bow quickly she looked from him to Fraide. The knowledge roused his self-assertion.

"I had an excellent night," he said. "Do I look as if I hadn't slept?"

Somewhat slowly and reluctantly Eve looked back. "No," she said, truthfully, and with a faint surprise that to Loder seemed the first genuine emotion she had shown regarding him. "No, I don't think I ever saw you look so well." She was quite unconscious and very charming as she made the admission. It struck Loder that her coloring of hair and eyes gained by daylight—were brightened and vivified by their setting of sombre river and sombre stone.

Fraide smiled at her affectionately; then looked at Loder. "Chilcote has got anew lease of nerves, Eve," he said, quietly. "And I—believe—I have got a new henchman. But I see my wife beckoning to me. I must have a word with her before she flits away. May I be excused?" He made a courteous gesture of apology; then smiled at Eve.

She looked after him as he moved away. "I sometimes wonder what I should do if anything were to happen to the Fraides," she said, a little wistfully. Then almost at once she laughed, as if regretting her impulsiveness. "You heard what he said," she went on, in a different voice. "Am I really to congratulate you?"

The change of tone stung Loder unaccountably. "Will you always disbelieve in me?" he asked.

Without answering, she walked slowly across the deserted Terrace and, pausing by the parapet, laid her hand on the stonework. Still in silence she looked out across the river.

Loder had followed closely. Again her aloofness seemed a challenge. "Will you always disbelieve in me?" he repeated.

At last she looked up at him, slowly.

"Have you ever given me cause to believe!" she asked, in a quiet voice.

To this truth he found no answer, though the subdued incredulity nettled him afresh.

Prompted to a further effort, he spoke again. "Patience is necessary with every person and every circumstance," he said. "We've all got to wait and see."

She did not lower her gaze as he spoke; and there seemed to him something disconcerting in the clear, candid blue of her eyes. With a sudden dread of her next words, he moved forward and laid his hand beside hers on the parapet.

"Patience is needed for every one," he repeated, quickly. "Sometimes a man is like a bit of wreckage; he drifts till some force stronger than himself gets in his way and stops him." He looked again at her face. He scarcely knew what he was saying; he only felt that he was a man in an egregiously false position, trying stupidly to justify himself. "Don't you believe that flotsam can sometimes be washed ashore?" he asked.

High above them Big Ben chimed the hour.

Eve raised her head. It almost seemed to him that he could see her answer trembling on her lips; then the voice of Lady Sarah Fraide came cheerfully from behind them.

"Eve!" she called. "Eve! We must fly. It's absolutely three o'clock!"

X

In the days that followed Fraide's marked adoption of him Loder behaved with a discretion that spoke well for his qualities. Many a man placed in the same responsible, and yet strangely irresponsible, position might have been excused if, for the time at least, he gave himself a loose rein. But Loder kept free of the temptation.

Like all other experiments, his showed unlooked-for features when put to a working test. Its expected difficulties smoothed themselves away, while others, scarcely anticipated, came into prominence. Most notable of all, the physical likeness between himself and Chilcote, the bedrock of the whole scheme, which had been counted upon to offer most danger, worked without a hitch. He stood literally amazed before the sweeping credulity that met him on every hand. Men who had known Chilcote from his youth, servants who had been in his employment for years, joined issue in the unquestioning acceptance. At times the ease of the deception bewildered him; there were moments when he realized that, should circumstances force him to a declaration of the truth, he would not be believed. Human nature prefers its own eyesight to the testimony of any man.

But in face of this astonishing success he steered a steady course. In the first exhilaration of Fraide's favor, in the first egotistical wish to break down Eve's scepticism, he might possibly have plunged into the vortex of action, let it be in what direction it might; but fortunately for himself, for Chilcote, and for their scheme, he was liable to strenuous second thoughts—those wise and necessary curbs that go further to the steadying of the universe than the universe guesses. Sitting in the quiet of the House, on the same day that he had spoken with Eve on the Terrace, he had weighed possibilities slowly and cautiously. Impressed to the full by the atmosphere of the place that in his eyes could never lack character, however dull its momentary business, however prosy the voice that filled it, he had sifted impulse from expedience, as only a man who has lived within himself can sift and distinguish. And at the close of that first day his programme bad been formed. There must be no rush, no headlong plunge, he had decided; things must work round. It was his first expedition into the new country, and it lay with fate to say whether it would be his last.

He had been leaning back in his seat, his eyes on the ministers opposite, his arms folded in imitation of Chilcote's most natural attitude, when this final speculation had come to him; and as it came his lips had tightened for a moment and his face become hard and cold. It is an unpleasant thing when a man first unconsciously reckons on the weakness of another, and the look that expresses the idea is not good to see. He had stirred uneasily; then his lips had closed again. He was tenacious by nature, and by nature intolerant of weakness. At the first suggestion of reckoning upon Chilcote's lapses, his mind had drawn back in disgust; but as the thought came again the disgust had lessened.

In a week—two weeks, perhaps—Chilcote would reclaim his place. Then would begin the routine of the affair. Chilcote, fresh from indulgence and freedom, would find his obligations a thousand times more irksome than before; he would struggle for a time; then—

A shadowy smile had touched Loder's lips as the idea formed itself.

Then would come the inevitable recall; then in earnest he might venture to put his hand to the plough. He never indulged in day-dreams, but something in the nature of a vision had flashed over his mind in that instant. He had seen himself standing in that same building, seen the rows of faces first bored, then hesitatingly transformed under his personal domination, under the one great power he knew himself to possess—the power of eloquence. The strength of the suggestion had been almost painful. Men who have attained self-repression are occasionally open to a perilous onrush of feeling. Believing that they know themselves, they walk boldly forward towards the high-road and the pitfall alike.

These had been Loder's disconnected ideas and speculations on the first day of his new life. At four o'clock on the ninth day he was pacing with quiet confidence up and down Chilcote's study, his mind pleasantly busy and his cigar comfortably alight, when he paused in, his walk and frowned, interrupted by the entrance of a servant.

The man came softly into the room, drew a small table towards the fire, and proceeded to lay an extremely fine and unserviceable-looking cloth.

Loder watched him in silence. He had grown to find silence a very useful commodity. To wait and let things develop was the attitude he oftenest assumed. But on this occasion he was perplexed. He had not rung for tea, and in any case a cup on a salver satisfied his wants. He looked critically at the fragile cloth.

Presently the servant departed, and solemnly reentered carrying a silver tray, with cups, a teapot, and cakes. Having adjusted them to his satisfaction, he turned to Loder.

"Mrs. Chilcote will be with you in five minutes, sir," he said.

He waited for some response, but Loder gave none. Again he had found the advantages of silence, but this time it was silence of a compulsory kind. He had nothing to say.

The man, finding him irresponsive, retired; and, left to himself, Loder stared at the array of feminine trifles; then, turning abruptly, he moved to the centre of the room.

Since the day they had talked on the Terrace, he had only seen Eve thrice, and always in the presence e others. Since the night of his first coming, she has not invaded his domain, and he wondered what this new departure might mean.

His thought of her had been less vivid in the last few days; for, though still using steady discretion, he had been drawn gradually nearer the fascinating whirlpool of new interests and new work. Shut his eyes as he might, there was no denying that this moment, so personally vital to him, was politically vital to the whole country; and that by a curious coincidence Chilcote's position well-nigh forced him to take an active interest in the situation. Again and again the suggestion had arisen that—should the smouldering fire in Persia break into a flame, Chilcote's commercial interests would facilitate, would practically compel, his standing in in the campaign against the government.

The little incident of the tea-table, recalling the social side of his obligations, had aroused the realization of greater things. As he stood meditatively in the middle of the room he saw suddenly how absorbed he had become in these greater things. How, in the swing of congenial interests, he had been borne insensibly forward—his capacities expanding, his intelligence asserting itself. He had so undeniably found his sphere that the idea of usurpation had receded gently as by natural laws, until his own personality had begun to color the day's work.

As this knowledge came, he wondered quickly if it held a solution of the present little comedy; if Eve had seen what others, he knew, had observed—that Chilcote was showing a grasp of things that he had not exhibited for years. Then, as a sound of skirts came softly down the corridor, he squared his shoulders with his habitual abrupt gesture and threw his cigar into the fire.

Eve entered the room much as she had done on her former visit, but with one difference. In passing Loder she quietly held out her hand.

He took it as quietly. "Why am I so honored?" he said.

She laughed a little and looked across at the fire. "How like a man! You always want to begin with reasons. Let's have tea first and explanations after." She moved forward towards the table, and he followed. As he did so, it struck him that her dress seemed in peculiar harmony with the day and the room, though beyond that he could not follow its details. As she paused beside the table he drew forward a chair with a faint touch of awkwardness.

She thanked him and sat down.

He watched her in silence as she poured out the tea, and the thought crossed his mind that it was incredibly long since he had seen a woman preside over a meal. The deftness of her fingers filled him with an unfamiliar, half-inquisitive wonder. So interesting was the sensation that, when she held his cup towards him, he didn't immediately see it.

"Don't you want any?" She smiled a little.

He started, embarrassed by his own tardiness. "I'm afraid I'm dull," he said. "I've been so—"

"So keen a worker in the last week?"

For a moment he felt relieved. Then, as a fresh silence fell, his sense of awkwardness returned. He sipped his tea and ate a biscuit. He found himself wishing, for almost the first time, for some of the small society talk that came so pleasantly to other men. He felt that the position was ridiculous. He glanced at Eve's averted head, and laid his empty cup upon the table.

Almost at once she turned, and their eyes met.

"John," she said, "do you guess at all why I wanted to have tea with you?"

He looked down at her. "No," he said, honestly and without embellishment.

The curtness of the answer might have displeased another woman. Eve seemed to take no offence.

"I had a talk with the Fraides to-day," she said "A long talk. Mr. Fraide said great things of you—things I wouldn't have believed from anybody but Mr. Fraide." She altered her position and looked from Loder's face back into the fire.

He took a step forward. "What things?" he said. He was almost ashamed of the sudden, inordinate satisfaction that welled up at her words.

"Oh, I mustn't tell you!" She laughed a little. "But you have surprised him." She paused, sipped her tea, then looked up again with a change of expression.

"John," she said, more seriously, "there is one point that sticks a little. Will this great change last?" Her voice was direct and even—wonderfully direct for a woman, Loder thought. It came to him with a certain force that beneath her remarkable charm might possibly lie a remarkable character. It was not a possibility that had occurred to him before, and it caused him to look at her a second time. In the new light he saw her beauty differently, and it interested him differently. Heretofore he had been inclined to class women under three heads—idols, amusements, or encumbrances; now it crossed his mind that a woman might possibly fill another place—the place of a companion.

"You are very sceptical," he said, still looking down at her.

She did not return his glance. "I think I have been made sceptical," she said.

As she spoke the image of Chilcote shot through his mind. Chilcote, irritable, vicious, unstable, and a quick compassion for this woman so inevitably shackled to him followed it.

Eve, unconscious of what was passing in his mind, went on with her subject.

"When we were married," she said, gently, "I had such a great interest in things, such a great belief in life. I had lived in politics, and I was marrying one of the coming men—everybody said you were one of the coming men—I scarcely felt there was anything left to ask for. You didn't make very ardent love," she smiled, "but I think I had forgotten about love. I wanted nothing so much as to be like Lady Sarah—married to a great man." She paused, then went on more hurriedly: "For a while things went right; then slowly things, went wrong. You got your—your nerves."

Loder changed his position with something of abruptness.

She misconstrued the action.

"Please don't think I want to be disagreeable," she said, hastily. "I don't. I'm only trying to make you understand why—why I lost heart."

"I think I know," Loder's voice broke in involuntarily. "Things got worse—then still worse. You found interference useless. At last you ceased to have a husband."

"Until a week ago." She glanced up quickly. Absorbed in her own feelings, she had seen nothing extraordinary in his words.

But at hers, Loder changed color.

"It's the most incredible thing in the world," she said. "It's quite incredible, and yet I can't deny it. Against all my reason, all my experience, all my inclination I seem to feel in the last week something of what I felt at first." She stopped with an embarrassed laugh. "It seems that, as if by magic, life has been picked up where I dropped it six years ago." Again she stopped and laughed.

Loder was keenly uncomfortable, but he could think of nothing to say.

"It seemed to begin that night I dined with the Fraides," she went on. "Mr. Fraide talked so wisely and so kindly about many things. He recalled all we had hoped for in you; and —and he blamed me a little." She paused and laid her cup aside. "He said that when people have made what they call their last effort, they should always make just one effort more. He promised that if I could once persuade you to take an interest in your work, he would do the rest. He said all that, and a thousand other kinder things—and I sat and listened. But all the time I thought of nothing but their uselessness. Before I left I promised to do my best —but my thought was still the same. It was stronger than ever when I forced myself to come up here—" She paused again, and glanced at Loder's averted head. "But I came, and then—as if by conquering myself I had compelled a reward, you seemed—you somehow seemed different. It sounds ridiculous, I know." Her voice was half amused, half deprecating. "It wasn't a difference in your face, though I knew directly that you were free from— nerves." Again she hesitated over the word. "It was a difference in yourself, in the things you said, more than in the way you said them." Once more she paused and laughed a little.

Loder's discomfort grew.

"But it didn't affect me then." She spoke more slowly. "I wouldn't admit it then. And the next day when we talked on the Terrace I still refused to admit it—though I felt it more strongly than before. But I have watched you since that day, and I know there is a change. Mr. Fraide feels the same, and he is never mistaken. I know it's only nine or ten days, but I've hardly seen you in the same mood for nine or ten hours in the last three years." She stopped, and the silence was expressive. It seemed to plead for confirmation of her instinct.

Still Loder could find no response.

After waiting for a moment, she leaned forward in her chair and looked up at him.

"John," she said, "is it going to last? That's what I came to ask. I don't want to believe till I'm sure; I don't want to risk a new disappointment." Loder felt the earnestness of her gaze, though he avoided meeting it.

"I couldn't have said this to you a week ago, but to-day I can. I don't pretend to explain why—the feeling is too inexplicable. I only know that I can say it now, and that I couldn't a week ago. Will you understand—and answer?"

Still Loder remained mute. His position was horribly incongruous. What could he say? What dared he say?

Confused by his silence, Eve rose.

"If it's only a phase, don't try to hide it," she said. "But if it's going to last—if by any possibility it's going to last—" She hesitated and looked up.

She was quite close to him. He would have been less than man had he been unconscious of the subtle contact of her glance, the nearness of her presence— and no one had ever hinted that manhood was lacking in him. It was a moment of temptation. His own energy, his own intentions, seemed so near; Chilcote and Chilcote's claims so distant and unreal. After all, his life, his ambitions, his determinations, were his own. He lifted his eyes and looked at her.

"You want me to tell you that I will go on?" he said.

Her eyes brightened; she took a step forward. "Yes," she said, "I want it more than anything in the world."

There was a wait. The declaration that would satisfy her came to Loder's lips, but he delayed it. The delay, was fateful. While he stood silent the door opened and the servant who had brought in the tea reappeared.

He crossed the room and handed Loder a telegram. "Any answer, sir?" he said.

Eve moved back to her chair. There was a flush on her cheeks and her eyes were still alertly bright.

Loder tore the telegram open, read it, then threw it Into the fire.

"No answer!" he said, laconically.

At the brusqueness of his voice, Eve looked up. "Disagreeable news?" she said, as the servant departed.

He didn't look at her. He was watching the telegram withering in the centre of the fire.

"No," he said at last, in a strained voice. "No. Only news that I—that I had forgotten to expect."

XI

There was a silence—an uneasy break—after Loder spoke. The episode of the telegram was, to all appearances, ordinary enough, calling forth Eve's question and his own reply as a natural sequence; yet in the pause that followed it each was conscious of a jar, each was aware that in some subtle way the thread of sympathy had been dropped, though to one the cause was inexplicable and to the other only too plain.

Loder watched the ghost of his message grow whiter and thinner, then dissolve into airy fragments and flutter up the chimney. As the last morsel wavered out of sight, he turned and looked at his companion.

"You almost made me commit myself," he said. In the desire to hide his feelings his tone was short.

Eve returned his glance with a quiet regard, but he scarcely saw it. He had a stupefied sense of disaster; a feeling of bitter self-commiseration that for the moment outweighed all other considerations. Almost at the moment of justification the good of life had crumbled in his fingers, the soil given beneath his feet, and with an absence of logic, a lack of justice unusual in him, he let resentment against Chilcote sweep suddenly over his mind.

Eve, still watching him, saw the darkening of his expression, and with a quiet movement rose from her chair.

"Lady Sarah has a theatre-party to-night, and I am dining with her," she said. "It is an early dinner, so I must think about dressing. I'm sorry you think I tried to draw you into anything. I must have explained myself badly." She laughed a little, to cover the slight discomfiture that her tone betrayed, and as she laughed she moved across the room towards the door.

Loder, engrossed in the check to his own schemes, incensed at the suddenness of Chilcote's recall, and still more incensed at his own folly in not having anticipated it, was oblivious for the moment of both her movement and her words. Then, quite abruptly, they obtruded themselves upon him, breaking through his egotism with something of the sharpness of pain following a blow. Turning quickly from the fireplace, he faced the shadowy room across which she had passed, but simultaneously with his turning she gained the door.

The knowledge that she was gone struck him with a sense of double loss. "Wait!" he called, suddenly moving forward. But almost at once he paused, chilled by the solitude of the room.

"Eve!" he said, using her name unconsciously for the first time.

But the corridor, as well as the room, was empty; he was too late. He stood irresolute; then he laughed shortly, turned, and passed back towards the fireplace.

The blow had fallen, the inevitable come to pass, and nothing remained but to take the fact with as good a grace as possible. Chilcote's telegram had summoned him to Clifford's Inn at seven o'clock, and it was now well on towards six. He pulled out his watch—Chilcote's watch he realized, with a touch of grim humor as he stooped to examine the dial by the light of the fire; then, as if the humor had verged to another feeling, he stood straight again and felt for the electric button in the wall. His fingers touched it, and simultaneously the room was lighted.

The abrupt alteration from shadow to light came almost as a shock. The feminine arrangement of the tea-table seemed incongruous beside the sober books and the desk laden with papers—incongruous as his own presence in the place. The thought was unpleasant, and he turned aside as if to avoid it; but at the movement his eyes fell on Chilcote's cigarette-box with its gleaming monogram, and the whimsical suggestion of his first morning rose again. The idea that the inanimate objects in the room knew him for what he was—recognized the interloper where human eyes saw the rightful possessor—returned to his mind. Through all his disgust and chagrin a smile forced itself to his lips, and, crossing the room for the second time, he passed into Chilcote's bedroom.

There the massive furniture and sombre atmosphere fitted better with his mood than the energy and action which the study always suggested. Walking directly to the great bed, he sat on its side and for several minutes stared straight in front of him, apparently seeing nothing; then at last the apathy passed from him, as his previous anger against Chilcote had passed. He stood up slowly, drawing his long limbs together, and recrossed the room, passing along the corridor and through the door communicating with the rest of the house. Five minutes later he was in the open air and walking steadily eastward, his hat drawn forward and his overcoat buttoned up.

As he traversed the streets he allowed himself no thought, Once, as he waited in Trafalgar Square to find a passage between the vehicles, the remembrance of Chilcote's voice coming out of the fog on their first night made itself prominent, but he rejected it quickly, guarding himself from even an involuntary glance at the place of their meeting. The Strand, with its unceasing life, came to him as something almost unfamiliar. Since his identification with the new life no business had drawn him east of Charing Cross, and his first sight of the narrower stream of traffic struck him as garish and unpleasant. As the impression came he accelerated his steps, moved by the wish to make regret and retrospection alike impossible by a contact with actual forces.

Still walking hastily, he entered Clifford's Inn, but there almost unconsciously his feet halted. There was something in the quiet immutability of the place that sobered energy, both mental and physical. A sense of changelessness—the changelessness of inanimate things, that rises in such solemn contrast to the variableness of mere human nature, which a new environment, a new outlook, sometimes even a new presence, has power to upheave and remould. He paused; then with slower and steadier steps crossed the little court and mounted the familiar stairs of his own house.

As he turned the handle of his own door some one stirred inside the sitting-room. Still under the influence of the stones and trees that he had just left, he moved directly towards the sound, and, without waiting for permission, entered the room. After the darkness of the passage it seemed well alight, for, besides the lamp with its green shade, a large fire burned in the grate and helped to dispel the shadows.

As he entered the room Chilcote rose and came forward, his figure thrown into strong relief by the double light. He was dressed in a shabby tweed suit; his face looked pale and set with a slightly nervous tension, but besides the look and a certain added restlessness of glance there was no visible change. Reaching Loder, he held out his hand.

"Well?" he said, quickly.

The other looked at him questioningly.

"Well? Well? How has it gone?"

"The scheme? Oh, excellently!" Loder's manner was abrupt. Turning from the restless curiosity in Chilcote's eyes, he moved a little way across the room and began to draw off his coat. Then, as if struck by the incivility of the action, he looked back again. "The scheme has gone extraordinarily," he said. "I could almost say absurdly. There are some things, Chilcote, that fairly bowl a man over."

A great relief tinged Chilcote's face. "Good!" he exclaimed. "Tell me all about it."

But Loder was reticent. The moment was not propitious. It was as if a hungry man had dreamed a great banquet and had awakened to his starvation. He was chary of imparting his visions.

"There's nothing to tell," he said, shortly. "All that you'll want to know is here in black and white. I don't think you'll find I have slipped anything; it's a clear business record." From an inner pocket he drew out a bulky note-book, and, recrossing the room, laid it open on the table. It was a correct, even a minute, record of every action that had been accomplished in Chilcote's name. "I don't think you'll find any loose ends," he said, as he turned back the pages. "I had you and your position in my mind all through." He paused and glanced up from the book. "You have a position that absolutely insists upon attention," he added, in a different voice.

At the new tone Chilcote looked up as well. "No moral lectures!" he said, with a nervous laugh. "I was anxious to know if you had pulled it off—and you have reassured me. That's enough. I was in a funk this afternoon to know how things were going-one of those sudden, unreasonable funks. But now that I see you"—he cut himself short and laughed once more "now that I see you, I'm hanged if I don't want to—to prolong your engagement."

Loder glanced at him, then glanced away. He felt a quick shame at the eagerness that rose at the words—a surprised contempt at his own readiness to anticipate the man's weakness. But almost as speedily as he had turned away he looked back again.

"Tush, man!" he said, with his old, intolerant manner. "You're dreaming. You've had your holiday and school's begun again. You must remember you are dining with the Charringtons to-night. Young Charrington's coming of age— quite a big business. Come along! I want my clothes." He laughed, and, moving closer to Chilcote, slapped him on the shoulder.

Chilcote started; then, suddenly becoming imbued with the other's manner, he echoed the laugh.

"By Jove!" he said, "you're right! You're quite right! A man must keep his feet in their own groove." Raising his hand, he began to fumble with his tie.

But Loder kept the same position. "You'll find the check-book in its usual drawer," he said. "I've made one entry of a hundred pounds—pay for the first week. The rest can stand over until—" He paused abruptly.

Chilcote shifted his position. "Don't talk about that. It upsets me to anticipate. I can make out a check to-morrow payable to John Loder."

"No. That can wait. The name of Loder is better out of the book. We can't be too careful." Loder spoke with unusual impetuosity. Already a slight, unreasonable jealousy was coloring his thoughts. Already he grudged the idea of Chilcote with his unstable glance and restless fingers opening the drawers and sorting the papers that for one stupendous fortnight had been his without question. Turning aside, he changed the subject brusquely.

"Come into the bedroom," he said. "It's half-past seven if it's a minute, and the Charringtons' show is at nine." Without waiting for a reply, he walked across the room and held the door open.

There was no silence while they exchanged clothes. Loder talked continuously, sometimes in short, curt sentences, sometimes with ironic touches of humor; he talked until Chilcote, strangely affected by contact with another personality after his weeks of solitude, fell under his influence—his excitement rising, his imagination stirring at the novelty of change. At last, garbed once more in the clothes of his own world, he passed from the bedroom back into the sitting-room, and there halted, waiting for his companion.

Almost directly Loder followed. He came into the room quietly, and, moving at once to the table, picked up the note-book.

"I'm not going to preach," he began, "so you needn't shut me up. But I'll say just one thing—a thing that will get said. Try and keep your hold! Remember your responsibilities—and keep your hold!" He spoke energetically, looking earnestly into Chilcote's eyes. He did not realize it, but he was pleading for his own career.

Chilcote paled a little, as he always did in face of a reality. Then he extended his hand.

"My dear fellow," he said, with a touch of hauteur, "a man can generally be trusted to look after his own life."

Extricating his hand almost immediately, he turned towards the door and without a word of farewell passed into the little hall, leaving Loder alone in the sitting-room.

XII

On the night of Chilcote's return to his own, Loder tasted the lees of life poignantly for the first time. Before their curious compact had been entered upon he had been, if not content, at least apathetic; but with action the apathy had been dispersed, never again to regain its old position.

He realized with bitter certainty that his was no real home-coming. On entering Chilcote's house he had experienced none of the unfamiliarity, none of the unsettled awkwardness, that assailed him now. There he had almost seemed the exile returning after many hardships; here, in the atmosphere made common by years, he felt an alien. It was illustrative of the man's character that sentimentalities found no place in his nature. Sentiments were not lacking, though they lay out of sight, but sentimentalities he altogether denied.

Left alone in the sitting-room after Chilcote's departure, his first sensation was one of physical discomfort and unfamiliarity. His own clothes, with their worn looseness, brought no sense of friendliness such as some men find in an old garment. Lounging, and the clothes that suggested lounging, had no appeal for him. In his eyes the garb that implies responsibility was symbolic and even inspiring.

And, as with clothes, so with his actual surroundings. Each detail of his room was familiar, but not one had ever become intimately close. He had used the place for years, but he had used it as he might use a hotel; and whatever of his household gods had come with him remained, like himself, on sufferance. His entrance into Chilcote's surroundings had been altogether different. Unknown to himself, he had been in the position of a young artist who, having roughly modelled in clay, is brought into the studio of a sculptor. To his outward vision everything is new, but his inner sight leaps to instant understanding. Amid all the strangeness he recognizes the one essential—the workshop, the atmosphere, the home.

On this first night of return Loder comprehended something of his position; and, comprehending, he faced the problem and fought with it.

He had made his bargain and must pay his share. Weighing this, he had looked about his room with a quiet gaze. Then at last, as if finding the object really sought for, his eyes had come round to the mantel-piece and rested on the pipe-rack. The pipes stood precisely as he had left them. He had looked at them for a long time, then an ironic expression that was almost a smile had touched his lips, and, crossing the room, he had taken the oldest and blackest from its place and slowly filled it with tobacco.

With the first indrawn breath of smoke his attitude had unbent. Without conscious determination, he had chosen the one factor capable of easing his mood. A cigarette is for the trivial moments of life; a cigar for its fulfilments, its pleasant, comfortable retrospections; but in real distress—in the solving of question, the fighting of difficulty—a pipe is man's eternal solace,

So he had passed the first night of his return to the actualities of life. Next day his mind was somewhat settled and outward aid was not so essential; but though facts faced him more solidly, they were nevertheless very drab in shade. The necessity for work, that blessed antidote to ennui, no longer forced him to endeavor. He was no longer penniless; but the money, he possessed brought with it no desires. When a man has lived from hand to mouth for years, and suddenly finds himself with a hundred pounds in his pocket, the result is sometimes curious. He finds with a vague sense of surprise that he has forgotten how to spend. That extravagance, like other artificial passions, requires cultivation.

This he realized even more fully on the days that followed the night of his first return; and with it was born a new bitterness. The man who has friends and no money may find life difficult; but the man who has money and no friend to rejoice in his fortune or benefit by his generosity is aloof indeed. With the leaven of incredulity that works in all strong natures, Loder distrusted the professional beggar —therefore the charity that bestows easily and promiscuously was denied him; and of other channels of generosity he was too self-contained to have learned the secret.

When depression falls upon a man of usually even temperament it descends with a double weight. The mercurial nature has a hundred counterbalancing devices to rid itself of gloom—a sudden lifting of spirit, a memory of other moods lived through, other blacknesses dispersed by time; but the man of level nature has none of these. Depression, when it comes, is indeed depression; no phase of mind to be superseded by another phase, but a slackening of all the chords of life.

It was through such a depression as this that he labored during three weeks, while no summons and no hint of remembrance came from Chilcote. His position was peculiarly difficult. He found no action in the present, and towards the future he dared not trust himself to look. He had slipped the old moorings that familiarity had rendered endurable; but having slipped them, he had found no substitute. Such was his case on the last night of the three weeks, and such his frame of mind as he crossed Fleet Street from Clifford's Inn to Middle Temple Lane.

It was scarcely seven o'clock, but already the dusk was falling; the greater press of vehicles had ceased, and the light of the street lamps gleamed back from the spaces of dry and polished roadway, worn smooth as a mirror by wheels and hoofs. Something of the solitude of night that sits so ill on the strenuous city street was making itself felt, though the throngs of people on the pathway still streamed eastward and westward and the taverns made a busy trade.

Having crossed the roadway, Loder paused for a moment to survey the scene. But humanity in the abstract made small appeal to him, and his glance wandered from the passers-by to the buildings massed like clouds against the dark sky. As his gaze moved slowly from one to the other a clock near at hand struck seven, and an instant later the chorus was taken up by a dozen clamorous tongues. Usually he scarcely heard, and never heeded, these innumerable chimes; but this evening their effect was strange. Coming out of the darkness, they seemed to possess a personal note, a human declaration. The impression was fantastic, but it was strong; with a species of revolt against life and his own personality, he turned slowly and moved forward in the direction of Ludgate Hill.

For a space he continued his course, then, reaching Bouverie Street, he turned sharply to the right and made his way down the slight incline that leads to the Embankment. There he paused and drew a long breath. The sense of space and darkness soothed him. Pulling his cap over his eyes, he crossed to the river and walked on in the direction of Westminster Bridge.

As he walked the great mass, of water by his side looked dense and smooth as oil with its sweeping width and network of reflected light. On its farther bank rose the tall buildings, the chimneys, the flaring lights that suggest another and an alien London; close at hand stretched the solid stone parapet, giving assurance of protection.

All these things he saw with his mental eyes, but with his mental eyes only, for his physical gaze was fixed ahead where the Houses of Parliament loomed out of the dusk. From the great building his eyes never wavered until the Embankment was traversed and Westminster Bridge reached. Then he paused, resting his arms on the coping of the bridge.

In the tense quietude of the darkness the place looked vast and inspiring. The shadowy Terrace, the silent river, the rows of lighted windows, each was significant. Slowly and comprehensively his glance passed from one to the other. He was no sentimentalist and no dreamer; his act was simply the act of a man whose interests, robbed of their natural outlet, turn instinctively towards the forms and symbols of the work that is denied them. His scrutiny was steady— even cold. He was raised to no exaltation by the vastness of the building, nor was he chilled by any dwarfing of himself. He looked at it long and thoughtfully; then, again moving slowly, he turned and retraced his steps.

His mind was full as he walked back, still oblivious of the stone parapet of the Embankment, the bare trees, and the flaring lights of the advertisements across the water. Turning to the left, he regained Fleet Street and made for his own habitation with the quiet accuracy that some men exhibit in moments of absorption.

He crossed Clifford's Inn with the same slow, almost listless step; then, as his own doorway came into view, he stopped. Some one was standing in its recess.

For a moment he wondered if his fancy were playing him a trick; then his reason sprang to certainty with so fierce a leap that for an instant his mind recoiled. For we more often stand aghast at the strength of our own feelings than before the enormity of our neighbor's actions.

"Is that you, Chilcote?" he said, below his breath.

At the sound of his voice the other wheeled round. "Hallo!" he said. "I thought you were the ghost of some old inhabitant. I suppose I am very unexpected?"

Loder took the hand that he extended and pressed the fingers unconsciously. The sight of this man was like the finding of an oasis at the point where the desert is sandiest, deadliest, most unbearable.

"Yes, you are—unexpected," he answered.

Chilcote looked at him, then looked out into the court. "I'm done up," he said. "I'm right at the end of the tether." He laughed as he said it, but in the dim light of the hall Loder thought his face looked ill and harassed despite the flush that the excitement of the meeting had brought to it. Taking his arm, he drew him towards the stairs.

"So the rope has run out, eh?" he said, in imitation of the other's tone. But under the quiet of his manner his own nerves were throbbing with the peculiar alertness of anticipation; a sudden sense of mastery over life, that lifted him above surroundings and above persons—a sense of stature, mental and physical, from which he surveyed the world. He felt as if fate, in the moment of utter darkness, had given him a sign.

As they crossed the hall, Chilcote had drawn away and was already mounting the stairs. And as Loder followed, it came sharply to his mind that here, in the slipshod freedom of a door that was always open and stairs that were innocent of covering, lay his companion's panion's real niche—unrecognized in outward avowal, but acknowledged by the inward, keener sense that manifests the individual.

In silence they mounted the stairs, but on the first landing Chilcote paused and looked back, surveying Loder from the superior height of two steps.

"I did very well at first," he said. "I did very well—I almost followed your example, for a week or so. I found myself on a sort of pinnacle—and I clung on. But in the last ten days I've—I've rather lapsed."

"Why?" Loder avoided looking at his face; he kept his eyes fixed determinately on the spot where his own hand gripped the banister.

"Why?" Chilcote repeated. "Oh, the prehistoric tale—weakness stronger than strength. I'm-I'm sorry to come down on you like this, but it's the social side that bowls me over. It's the social side I can't stick."

"The social side? But I thought—"

"Don't think. I never think; it entails such a constant upsetting of principles and theories. We did arrange for business only, but one can't set up barriers. Society pushes itself everywhere nowadays—into business most of all. I don't want you for theatre-parties or dinners. But a big reception with a political flavor is different. A man has to be seen at these things; he needn't say anything or do anything, but it's bad form if he fails to show up."

Loder raised his head. "You must explain," he said, abruptly.

Chilcote started slightly at the sudden demand.

"I—I suppose I'm rather irrelevant," he said, quickly. "Fact is, there's a reception at the Bramfells' to-night. You know Blanche Bramfell—Viscountess Bramfell, sister to Lillian Astrupp." His words conveyed nothing to Loder, but he did not consider that. All explanations were irksome to him and he invariably chafed to be done with them.

"And you've got to put in an appearance—for party reasons?" Loder broke in.

Chilcote showed relief. "Yes. Old Fraide makes rather a point of it—so does Eve." He said the last words carelessly; then, as if their sound recalled something, his expression changed. A touch of satirical amusement touched his lips and he laughed.

"By-the-way, Loder," he said, "my wife was actually tolerant of me for nine or ten days after my return. I thought your representation was to be quite impersonal? I'm not jealous," he laughed. "I'm not jealous, I assure you; but the burned child shouldn't grow absentminded."

At his tone and his laugh Loder's blood stirred; with a sudden, unexpected impulse his hand tightened on the banister, and, looking up, he caught sight of the face above him—his own face, it seemed, alight with malicious interest. At the sight a strange sensation seized him; his grip on the banister loosened, and, pushing past Chilcote, he hurriedly mounted the stairs.

Outside his own door the other overtook him.

"Loder!" he said. "Loder! I meant no harm. A man must have a laugh sometimes."

But Loder was facing the door and did not turn round.

A sudden fear shook Chilcote. "Loder!" he exclaimed again, "you wouldn't desert me? I can't go back to-night. I can't go back."

Still Loder remained immovable.

Alarmed by his silence, Chilcote stepped closer to him.

"Loder! Loder, you won't desert me?" He caught hastily at his arm.

With a quick repulsion Loder shook him off; then almost as quickly he turned round.

"What fools we all are!" he said, abruptly. "We, only differ in degree. Come in, and let us change our clothes."

XIII

The best moments of a man's life are the moments when, strong in himself, he feels that the world lies before him. Gratified ambition may be the summer, but anticipation is the ardent spring-time of a man's career.

As Loder drove that night frown Fleet Street to Grosvenor Square he realized this—though scarcely with any degree of consciousness—for he was no accomplished self-analyst. But in a wave of feeling too vigorous to be denied he recognized his regained foothold—the step that lifted him at once from the pit to the pinnacle.

In that moment of realization he looked neither backward nor forward. The present was all-sufficing. Difficulties might loom ahead, but difficulties had but one object—the testing and sharpening of a man's strength. In the first deep surge of egotistical feeling he almost rejoiced in Chilcote's weakness. The more Chilcote tangled the threads of his life, the stronger must be the fingers that unravelled them. He was possessed by a great impatience; the joy of action was stirring in his blood.

Leaving the cab, he walked confidently to the door of Chilcote's house and inserted the latch-key. Even in this small act there was a grain of individual satisfaction. Then very quietly he opened the door and crossed the hall.

As he entered, a footman was arranging the fire that burned in the big grate. Seeing the man, he halted.

"Where is your mistress?" he asked, in unconscious repetition of his first question in the same house.

The man looked up. "She has just finished dinner, sir. She dined alone in her own room." He glanced at Loder in the quick, uncertain way that was noticeable in all the servants of the household when they addressed their master. Loder saw the look and wondered what depth of curiosity it betrayed, how much of insight into the domestic life that he must always be content to skim. For an instant the old resentment against Chilcote tinged his exaltation, but he swept it angrily aside. Without further remark he began to mount the stairs.

Gaining the landing, he did not turn as usual to the door that shut off Chilcote's rooms, but moved onward down the corridor towards Eve's private sitting-room. He moved slowly till the door was reached; then he, paused and lifted his hand. There was a moment's wait while his fingers rested on the handle; then a sensation he could not explain—a reticence, a reluctance to intrude upon this one precinct—caused his, fingers to relax. With a slightly embarrassed gesture he drew back slowly and retraced his steps.

Once in Chilcote's bedroom, he walked to the nearest bell and pressed it. Renwick responded, and at sight of him Loder's feelings warmed with the same sense of fitness and familiarity that the great bed and sombre furniture of the room had inspired.

But the man did not come forward as he had expected. He remained close to the door with a hesitation that was unusual in a trained servant. It struck Loder that possibly his stolidity had exasperated Chilcote, and that possibly

Chilcote had been at no pains to conceal the exasperation. The idea caused him to smile involuntarily.

"Come into the room, Renwick," he said. "It's uncomfortable to see you standing there. I want to know if Mrs. Chilcote has sent me any message about to-night."

Renwick studied him furtively as he came forward. "Yes, sir," he said. "Mrs. Chilcote's maid said that the carriage was ordered for ten-fifteen, and she hoped that would suit you." He spoke reluctantly, as if expecting a rebuke.

At the opening sentence Loder had turned aside, but now, as the man finished, he wheeled round again and looked at him closely with his keen, observant eyes.

"Look here," he said. "I can't have you speak to me like that. I may come down on you rather sharply when my—my nerves are bad; but when I'm myself I treat you—well, I treat you decently, at any rate. You'll have to learn to discriminate. Look at me now!" A thrill of risk and of rulership passed through him as he spoke. "Look at me now! Do I look as I looked this morning—or yesterday?"

The man eyed him half stupidly, half timidly.

"Well?" Loder insisted.

"Well, sir," Renwick responded, with some slowness; "you look the same— and you look different. A healthier color, perhaps, sir—and the eye clearer." He grew more confident under Loder's half-humorous, half-insistent gaze. "Now that I look closer, sir—"

Loder laughed. "That's it!" he said. "Now that you look closer. You'll have to grow observant: observation is an excellent quality in a servant. Wheat you come into a room in future, look first of all at me—and take your cue from that. Remember that serving a man with nerves is like serving two masters. Now you can go; and tell Mrs. Chilcote's maid that I shall be quite ready at a quarter-past ten."

"Yes, sir. And after that?"

"Nothing further. I sha'n't want you again to-night." He turned away as he spoke, and moved towards the great fire that was always kept alight in Chilcote's room. But as the man moved towards the door he wheeled back again. "Oh, one thing more, Renwick! Bring me some sandwiches and a whiskey." He remembered for the first time that he had eaten nothing since early afternoon.

At a few minutes after ten Loder left Chilcote's room, resolutely descended the stairs, and took up his position in the hall. Resolution is a strong word to apply to such a proceeding, but something in his bearing, in the attitude of his shoulders and head, instinctively suggested it.

Five or six minutes passed, but he waited without impatience; then at last the sound of a carriage stopping before the house caused him to lift his head, and at the same instant Eve appeared at the head of the staircase.

She stood there for a second, looking down on him, her maid a pace or two behind, holding her cloak. The picture she made struck upon his mind with something of a revelation.

On his first sight of her she had appealed to him as a strange blending of youth and self-possession—a girl with a woman's clearer perception of life; later he had been drawn to study her in other aspects—as a possible comrade and friend; now for the first time he saw her as a power in her own world, a woman to whom no man could deny consideration. She looked taller for the distance between them, and the distinction of her carriage added to the effect. Her black gown was exquisitely soft—as soft as her black hair; above her forehead was a cluster of splendid diamonds shaped like a coronet, and a band of the same stones encircled her neck. Loder realized in a glance that only the most distinguished of women could wear such ornaments and not have her beauty eclipsed. With a touch of the old awkwardness that had before assailed him in her presence, he came slowly forward as she descended the stairs.

"Can I help you with your cloak?" he asked. And as he asked it, something like surprise at his own timidity crossed his mind.

For a second Eve's glance rested on his face. Her expression was quite impassive, but as she lowered her lashes a faint gleam flickered across her eyes; nevertheless, her answer, when it came, was studiously courteous.

"Thank you," she said, "but Marie will do all I want."

Loder looked at her for a moment, then turned aside. He was not hurt by his rebuff; rather, by an interesting sequence of impressions, he was stirred by it. The pride that had refused Chilcote's help, and the self-control that had refused it graciously, moved him to admiration. He understood and appreciated both by the light of person experience.

"The carriage is waiting, sir," Crapham's voice broke in.

Loder nodded, and Eve turned to her maid. "That will do, Marie," she said. "I shall want a cup of chocolate when I get back—probably at one o clock." She drew her cloak about her shoulders and moved towards the door. Then she paused and looked back. "Shall we start?" she asked, quietly.

Loder, still watching her, came forward at once. "Certainly," he said, with unusual gentleness.

He followed her as she crossed the footpath, but made no further offer of help; and when the moment came he quietly took his place beside her in the carriage. His last impression, as the horses wheeled round, was of the open hall door—Crapham in his sombre livery and the maid in her black dress, both silhouetted against the dark background of the hall; then, as the carriage moved forward smoothly and rapidly, he leaned back in his seat and closed his eyes.

During the first few moments of the drive there was silence. To Loder there was a strange, new sensation in this companionship, so close and yet so distant. He was so near to Eve that the slight fragrant scent from her clothes might almost have belonged to his own. The impression was confusing yet vaguely delightful. It was years since he had been so close to a woman of his own class—his own caste. He acknowledged the thought with a curious sense of pleasure. Involuntarily he turned and looked at her.

She was sitting very straight, her fine profile cut clear against the carriage window, her diamonds quivering in the light that flashed by them from the street. For a space the sense of unreality that had pervaded his first entrance into Chilcote's life touched him again, then another and more potent feeling rose to quell it. Almost involuntarily as he looked at her his lips parted.

"May I say something?" he asked.

Eve remained motionless. She did not turn her head, as most women would have done. "Say anything you like," she said, gravely.

"Anything?" He bent a little nearer, filled again by the inordinate wish to dominate.

"Of course."

It seemed to him that her voice sounded forced and a little tired. For a moment he looked through the window at the passing lights; then slowly his gaze returned to her face.

"You look very beautiful to-night," he said. His voice was low and his manner unemotional, but his words had the effect he desired.

She turned her head, and her eyes met his in a glance of curiosity and surprise.

Slight as the triumph was, it thrilled him. The small scene with Chilcote's valet came back to him; his own personality moved him again to a reckless determination to make his own voice heard. Leaning forward, he laid his hand lightly on her arm.

"Eve," he said, quickly—"Eve, do you remember?" Then he paused and withdrew his hand. The horses had slackened speed, then stopped altogether as the carriage fell into line outside Bramfell House.

XIV

Loder entered Lady Bramfell's feeling far more like an actor in a drama than an ordinary man in a peculiar situation. It was the first time he had played Chilcote to a purely social audience, and the first time for many years that he had rubbed shoulders with a well-dressed crowd ostensibly brought together for amusement. As he followed Eve along the corridor that led to the reception-rooms he questioned the reality of the position again and again; then abruptly, at the moment when the sensation of unfamiliarity was strongest, a cheery voice hailed him, and, turning, he saw the square shoulders, light eyes, and pointed mustache of Lakeley, the owner of the 'St. George's Gazette'.

At the sight of the man and the sound of his greeting his doubts and speculations vanished. The essentials of life rose again to the position they had occupied three weeks ago, in the short but strenuous period when his dormant activities had been stirred and he had recognized his true self. He lifted his head unconsciously, the shade of misgiving that had crossed his confidence passing from him as he smiled at Lakeley with a keen, alert pleasure that altered his whole face.

Eve, looking back, saw the expression. It attracted and held her, like a sudden glimpse into a secret room. In all the years of her marriage, in the months of her courtship even, she had never surprised the look on Chilcote's face. The impression came quickly. and with it a strange, warm rush of interest that receded slowly, leaving an odd sense of loneliness. But, at the moment that the feeling came and passed, her attention was claimed in another direction. A slight, fair-haired boy forced his way towards her through the press of people that filled the corridor.

"Mrs. Chilcote!" he exclaimed. "Can I believe my luck in finding you alone?"

Eve laughed. It seemed that there was relief in her laugh. "How absurd you are, Bobby!" she said, kindly. "But you are wrong. My husband is here—I am waiting for him."

Blessington looked round. "Oh!" he said. "Indeed!" Then he relapsed into silence. He was the soul of good-nature, but those who knew him best knew that Chilcote's summary change of secretaries had rankled. Eve, conscious of the little jar, made haste to smooth it away.

"Tell me about yourself," she said. "What have you been doing?"

Blessington looked at her, then smiled again, his buoyancy restored. "Doing?" he said. "Oh, calling every other afternoon at Grosvenor Square—only to find that a certain lady is never at home."

At his tone Eve laughed again. The boy, with his frank and ingenuous nature, had beguiled many a dull hour for her in past days, and she had missed him not a little when his place had been filled by Greening.

"But I mean seriously, Bobby. Has something good turned up?"

Blessington made a wry face "Something is on its way—that's why I am on duty to-right. Old Bramfell and the pater are working it between them. So if

Lady Bramfell or Lady Astrupp happen to drop a fan or a handkerchief this evening, I've got to be here to pick it up. See?"

"As you picked up my fans and handkerchiefs last year—and the year before?" Eve smiled.

Blessington's face suddenly looked grave. "I wish you hadn't said that," he said. Then he paused abruptly. Out of the hum of talk behind them a man's laugh sounded. It was not loud, but it was a laugh that one seldom hears in a London drawing-room —it expressed interest, amusement, and in an inexplicable may it seemed also to express strength.

Eve and Blessington both turned involuntarily.

"By Jove!" said Blessington

Eve said nothing.

Loder was parting with Lakely, and his was the laugh that had attracted them both. The interest excited by his talk was still reflected in his face and bearing as he made his way towards them.

"By Jove!" said Blessington again. "I never realized that Chilcote was so tall."

Again Eve said nothing. But silently and with a more subtle meaning she found herself echoing the words.

Until he was quite close to her, Loder did not seem to see her. Then he stopped quietly.

"I was speaking to Lakely," he said. "He wants me to dine with him one night at Cadogan Gardens."

But Eve was silent, waiting for him to address Blessington. She glanced at him quickly, but though their eyes met he did not catch the meaning that lay in hers. It was a difficult moment. She had known him incredibly, almost unpardonably, absent-minded, but it had invariably been when he was suffering from nerves," as she phrased it to herself. But to-night he was obviously in the possession of unclouded faculties. She colored slightly and glanced under her lashes at Blessington. Had the same idea struck him, she wondered? But he was studiously studying a suit of Chinese armor that stood close by in a niche of the wall.

"Bobby has been keeping me amused while you talked to Mr. Lakely," she said, pointedly.

Directly addressed, Loder turned and looked at Blessington. "How d'you do?" he said, with doubtful cordiality. The name of Bobby conveyed nothing to him.

To his surprise, Eve looked annoyed, and Blessington's fresh-colored face deepened in tone. With a slow, uncomfortable sensation he was aware of having struck a wrong note.

There was a short, unpleasant pause. Then, more by intuition than actual sight, Blessington saw Eve's eyes turn from him to Loder, and with quick tact he saved the situation.

"How d'you do, sir?" he responded, with a smile. "I congratulate you on looking so—so uncommon well. I was just telling Mrs. Chilcote that I hold a commission for Lady Astrupp to-night. I'm a sort of scout at present—reporting on the outposts." He spoke fast and without much meaning, but his boyish voice eased the strain.

Eve thanked him with a smile. "Then we mustn't interfere with a person on active service," she said. "Besides, we have our own duties to get through."

She smiled again, and, touching Loder's arm, indicated the reception-rooms.

When they entered the larger of the two rooms Lady Bramfell was still receiving her guests. She was a tall and angular woman, who, except for a certain beauty of hands and feet and a certain similarity of voice, possessed nothing in common with her sister Lillian. She was speaking to a group of people as they approached, and the first sound of her sweet and rather drawling tones touched Loder with a curious momentary feeling—a vague suggestion of awakened memories. Then the suggestion vanished as she turned and greeted Eve.

"How sweet of you to come!" she murmured. And it seemed to Loder that a more spontaneous smile lighted up her face. Then she extended her hand to him. "And you, too!" she added. "Though I fear we shall bore you dreadfully."

Watching her with interest, he saw the change of expression as her eyes turned from Eve to him, and noticed a colder tone in her voice as she addressed him directly. The observation moved him to self-assertion.

"That's a poor compliment to me," he said "To be bored is surely only a polite way of being inane."

Lady Bramfell smiled. "What!" she exclaimed. "You defending your social reputation?"

Loder laughed a little. "The smaller it is, the more defending it needs," he replied.

Another stream of arrivals swept by them as he spoke; Eve smiled at their hostess and moved across the room, and he perforce followed. As he gained her side, the little court about Lady Bramfell was left well in the rear, the great throng at the farther end of the room was not yet reached, and for the moment they were practically alone.

There was a certain uneasiness in that moment of companionship. It seemed to him that Eve wished to speak, but hesitated. Once or twice she opened and closed the fan that she was carrying, then at last, as if by an effort, she turned and looked at him.

"Why were you so cold to Bobby Blessington?" she asked. "Doesn't it seem discourteous to ignore him as you did?"

Her manner was subdued. It was not the annoyed manner that one uses to a man when he has behaved ill; it was the explanatory tone one might adopt towards an incorrigible child. Loder felt this; but the gist of a remark always came to him first, its mode of expression later. The fact that it was Blessington whom he had encountered—Blessington to whom he had spoken with vague politeness—came to him with a sense of unpleasantness. He was not to blame in the matter, nevertheless he blamed himself. He was annoyed that, he should have made the slip in Eve's presence.

They were moving forward, nearing the press of people in the second room, when Eve spoke, and the fact filled him with an added sense of annoyance.

People smiled and bowed to her from every side; one woman leaned forward as they passed and whispered something in her ear. Again the sensation of futility and vexation filled him; again he realized how palpable was the place she held in the world. Then, as his feelings reached their height and speech seemed forced upon him, a small man with a round face, catching a glimpse of Eve, darted from a circle of people gathered in one of the windows and came quickly towards them.

With an unjust touch of irritation he recognized Lord Bramfell.

Again the sense of Eve's aloofness stung him as their host approached. In another moment she would be lost to him among this throng of strangers— claimed by them as by right.

"Eve—" he said, involuntarily and under his breath.

She half paused and turned towards him. "Yes?" she said; and he wondered if it was his imagination that made the word sound slightly eager.

"About that matter of Blessington—" he began. Then he stopped, Bramfell had reached them.

The little man came up smiling and with an outstretched hand. "There's no penalty for separating husband and wife, is there, Mrs. Chilcote? How are you, Chilcote?" He turned from one to the other with the quick, noiseless manner that always characterized him.

Loder turned aside to hide his vexation, but Eve greeted their host with her usual self-possessed smile.

"You are exempt from all penalties to-night," she said. Then she turned to greet the members of his party who had strolled across from the window in his wake.

As she moved aside Bramfell looked at Loder. "Well, Chilcote, have you dipped into the future yet?" he asked, with a laugh.

Loder echoed the laugh but said nothing. In his uncertainty at the question he reverted to his old resource of silence.

Bramfell raised his eyebrows. "What!" he said. "Don't tell me that my sister-in-law hasn't engaged you as a victim." Then he turned in Eve's direction. "You've heard of our new departure, Mrs. Chilcote?"

Eve looked round from the lively group by which she was surrounded. "Lillian's crystal-gazing? Why, of course!" she said. "She should make a very beautiful seer. We are all quite curious."

Bramfell pursed up his lips. "She has a very beautiful tent at the end of the conservatory. It took five men as many days to rig it up. We couldn't hear ourselves talk, for hammering. My wife said it made her feel quite philanthropic, it reminded her so much of a charity bazaar."

Everybody laughed; and at the same moment Blessington came quickly across the room and joined the group.

"Hallo!" he said. "Anybody seen Witcheston? He's next on my list for the crystal business."

Again the whole party laughed, and Bramfell, stepping forward, touched Blessington's arm in mock seriousness.

"Witcheston is playing bridge, like a sensible man," he said. "Leave him in peace, Bobby."

Blessington made a comical grimace. "But I'm working this on commercial principles," he said. "I keep the list, names and hours complete, and Lady Astrupp gazes, in blissful ignorance as to who her victims are. The whole thing is great—simple and statistical."

"For goodness' sake, Bobby, shut up!" Bramfell's round eyes were twinkling with amusement.

"But my system—"

"Systems! Ah, we all had them when we were as young as you are!"

"And they all had flaws, Bobby," Eve broke in. "We were always finding gaps that had to be filled up. Never mind about Lord Witcheston. Get a substitute; it won't count—if Lillian doesn't know."

Blessington wavered as she spoke. His eyes wandered round the party and again rested on Bramfell.

"Not me, Bobby! Remember, I've breathed crystals—practically lived on them—for the last week. Now, there's Chilcote—" Again his eyes twinkled.

All eyes were turned on Loder, though one or two strayed surreptitiously to Eve. She, seeming sensitive to the position, laughed quickly.

"A very good idea!" she said. "Who wants to see the future, if not a politician?"

Loder glanced from her to Blessington. Then, with a very feminine impulse, she settled the matter beyond dispute.

"Please use your authority, Bobby," she said. "And when you've got him safely under canvas, come back to me. It's years since we've had a talk." She nodded and smiled, then instantly turned to Bramfell with some trivial remark.

For a second Loder waited, then with a movement of resignation he laid his hand on Blessington's arm. "Very well!" he said. "But if my fate is black, witness it was my wife who sent me to it." His faint pause on the word wife, the mention of the word itself in the presence of these people, had a savor of recklessness. The small discomfiture of his earlier slip vanished before it; he experienced a strong reaction of confidence in his luck. With a cool head, a steady step, and a friendly pressure of the fingers on Blessington's arm, he allowed himself to be drawn across the reception-rooms, through the long corridors, and down the broad flight of steps that led to the conservatory.

The conservatory was a feature of the Bramfell townhouse, and to Loder it came as something wonderful and unlooked-for—with its clustering green branches, its slight, unoppressive scents, its temperately pleasant atmosphere. He felt no wish to speak as, still guided by Blessington, he passed down the shadowy paths that in the half-light had the warmth and mystery of a Southern garden. Here and there from the darkness came the whispering of a voice or the sound of a laugh, bringing with them the necessary touch of life. Otherwise the place was still.

Absorbed by the air of solitude, contrasting so remarkably with the noise and crowded glitter left behind in the reception-rooms, he had moved half-way down the long, green aisle before the business in hand came back to him with a sudden sense of annoyance. It seemed so paltry to mar the quiet of the place with the absurdity of a side-show. He turned to Blessington with a touch of abruptness.

"What am I expected to do?" he asked.

Blessington looked up, surprised. "Why, I thought, sir—" he began. Then he instantly altered his tone: "Oh, just enter into the spirit of the thing. Lady Astrupp won't put much strain on your credulity, but she'll make a big call on your solemnity." He laughed.

He had an infectious laugh, and Loder responded to it.

"But what am I to do?" he persisted.

"Oh, nothing. Being the priestess, she, naturally demands acolytes; but she'll let you know that she holds the prior place. The tent is so fixed that she sees nothing beyond your hands; so there's absolutely no delusion." He laughed once more. Then suddenly he lowered his voice and slackened his steps. "Here we are!" he whispered, in pretended awe.

At the end of the path the space widened to the full breadth of the conservatory. The light was dimmer, giving an added impression of distance; away to the left, Loder heard the sound of splashing water, and on his right hand he caught his first glimpse of the tent that was his goal.

It was an artistic little structure—a pavilion formed of silky fabric that showed bronze in the light of an Oriental lamp that hung above its entrance. As they drew closer, a man emerged from it. He stood for a moment in uncertainty, looking about him; then, catching sight of them, he came forward laughing.

"By George!" he exclaimed, "it's as dark as limbo in there! I didn't see you at first. But I say, Blessirigton, it's a beastly shame to have that thunder-cloud barrier shutting off the sorceress. If she gazes at the crystal, mayn't we have something to gaze at, too?"

Blessington laughed. "You want too much, Galltry," he said. "Lady Astrupp understands the value of the unattainable. Come along, sir!" he added to Loder, drawing him forward with an energetic pressure of the arm.

Loder responded, and as he did so a flicker of curiosity touched his mind for the first time. He wondered for an instant who this woman was who aroused so much comment. And with the speculation came the remembrance of how she had assured Chilcote that on one point. at least he was invulnerable. He had spoken then from the height of a past experience—an experience so fully passed that he wondered now if it had been as staple a guarantee as he had then believed. Man's capacity for outliving is astonishingly complete. The long-ago incident in the Italian mountains had faded, like a crayon study in which the tones have merged and gradually lost character. The past had paled before the present—as golden hair might pale before black. The simile came with apparent irrelevance. Then again Blessington pressed his arm.

"Now, sir!" he said, drawing away and lifting the curtain that hung before the entrance of the tent.

Loder looked at the amused, boyish face lighted by the hanging lamp, and smiled pleasantly; then, with a shrug of the shoulders, he entered the pavilion and the curtain fell behind him.

XV

On entering the pavilion, Loder's first feeling was one of annoyed awkwardness at finding himself in almost total darkness. But as his eyes grew accustomed to the gloom, the feeling vanished and the absurdity of the position came to his mind.

The tent was small, heavily draped with silk and smelling of musk. It was divided into two sections by an immovable curtain that hung from the roof to within a few feet of the floor. The only furniture on Loder's side was one low chair, and the only light a faint radiance that, coming from the invisible half of the pavilion; spread across the floor in a pale band. For a short space he stood uncertain, then his hesitation was brought to an end.

"Please sit down," said a low, soft voice.

For a further moment he stood undecided. The voice sounded so unexpectedly near. In the quiet and darkness of the place it seemed to possess a disproportionate weight—almost the weight of a familiar thing. Then, with a sudden, unanalyzed touch of relief, he located the impression. It was the similarity to Lady Bramfell's sweet, slow tones that had stirred his mind. With a sense of satisfaction he drew the chair forward and sat down.

Then, for the first time, he saw that on the other side of the gauze partition, and below it by a few inches, was a small table of polished wood, on which stood an open book, a crystal ball, and a gold dish filled with ink. These were arranged on the side of the table nearest to him, the farther side being out of his range of vision. An amused interest touched him as he made his position more comfortable. Whoever this woman was, she had an eye for stage management, she knew how to marshal her effects. He found himself waiting with some curiosity for the next injunction from behind the curtain.

"The art of crystal-gazing," began the sweet, slow voice after a pause, "is one of the oldest known arts." Loder sat forward. The thought of Lady Bramfell mingled disconcertingly with some other thought more distant and less easy to secure.

"To obtain the best results," went on the seer, "the subject lays his uncovered hands outspread upon a smooth surface." It was evident that the invisible priestess was reading from the open book, for when the word "surface" was reached there was a slight stir that indicated the changing of position; and when. the voice came again it was in a different tone.

"Please lay your hands, palms downward, upon the table."

Loder smiled to himself in the darkness. He pictured Chilcote with his nerves and his impatience going through this ordeal; then in good-humored silence he leaned forward and obeyed the command. His hands rested on the smooth surface of the table in the bar of light from the unseen lamp.

There was a second in which the seer was silent; then he fancied that she raised her head.

"You must take off your rings," she said smoothly. "Any metal interferes with the sympathetic current."

At any other time Loder would have laughed; but the request so casually and graciously made sent all possibility of irony far into the background. The thought of Chilcote and of the one flaw in their otherwise flawless scheme rose to his mind. Instinctively he half withdrew his hands.

"Where is the sympathetic current?" he asked, quietly. His thoughts were busy with the question of whether he would or would not be justified in beating an undignified retreat.

"Between you and me, of course," said the voice, softly. It sounded languid, but very rational. The idea of retreat seemed suddenly theatrical. In this world of low voices and shaded lights people never adopted extreme measures—no occasion made a scene practicable, or even allowable. He leaned back slowly, while he summed up the situation. If by any unlucky chance this woman knew Chilcote to have adopted jewelry and had seen the designs of his rings, the sight of his own scarred finger would suggest question and comment; if, on the other hand, he left the pavilion without excuse, or if, without apparent reason, he refused to remove the rings, he opened up a new difficulty—a fresh road to curiosity. It came upon him with unusual quickness—the obstacles to, and the need for, a speedy decision. He glanced round the tent, then unconsciously he straightened his shoulders. After all, he had stepped into a tight corner, but there was no need to cry out in squeezing his way back. Then he realized that the soft, ingratiating tones were sounding once more.

"It's the passing of my hands over yours, while I look into the crystal, that sets up sympathy"—a slender hand moved swiftly into the light and picked up the ball—"and makes my eyes see the pictures in your mind. Now, will you please take off your rings?"

The very naturalness of the request disarmed him. It was a risk. But, as Chilcote had said, risk was the salt of life!

"I'm afraid you think me very troublesome." The voice came again, delicately low and conciliatory.

For a brief second Loder wondered uncertainly how long or how well Chilcote knew Lady Astrupp; then he dismissed the question. Chilcote had never mentioned her until to-night, and then casually as Lady Bramfell's sister. What a coward he was becoming in throwing the dice with Fate! Without further delay he drew off the rings, slipped them into his pocket, and replaced his hands on the smooth table-top.

Then, at the moment that he replaced them, a peculiar thing occurred.

From the farther side of the dark partition came the quick, rustling stir of a skirt, and the slight scrape of a chair pushed either backward or forward. Then there was silence.

Now, silence can suggest anything, from profound thought to imbecility; but in this case its suggestion was nil. That something had happened, that some change had taken place, was as patent to Loder as the darkness of the curtain or the band of light that crossed the floor, but what had occasioned it, or what it stood for, he made no attempt to decide. He sat bitingly conscious of his hands spread open on the table under the scrutiny of eyes that were invisible to him vividly aware of the awkwardness of his position. He felt with instinctive certainty that a new chord had been struck; but a man seldom acts on instinctive certainties. If the exposure of his hands had struck this fresh note, then any added action would but heighten the dilemma. He sat silent and motionless.

Whether his impassivity had any bearing on the moment he had no way of knowing; but no further movement came from behind the partition. Whatever the emotions that had caused the sharp swish of skirts and the sharp scrape of the chair, they had evidently subsided or been dominated by other feelings.

The next indication of life that came to him was the laying down of the crystal ball. It was laid back upon the table with a slight jerk that indicated a decision come to; and almost simultaneously the seer's voice came to him again. Her tone was lower now than it had been before, and its extreme ease seemed slightly shaken—whether by excitement, surprise, or curiosity, it was impossible to say.

"You will think it strange—" she began. "You will think—" Then she stopped.

There was a pause, as though she waited for some help, but Loder remained mute. In difficulty a silent tongue and a cool head are usually man's best weapons.

His silence was disconcerting. He heard her stir again.

"You will think it strange—" she began once more. Then quite suddenly she checked and controlled her voice. "You must forgive me for what I am going to say," she added, in a completely different tone, "but crystal-gazing is such an illusive thing. Directly you put your hands upon the table I felt that there would be no result; but I wouldn't admit the defeat. Women are such keen anglers that they can never acknowledge that any fish, however big, has slipped the hook." She laughed softly.

At the soand of the laugh Loder shifted his position for the first time. He could not have told why, but it struck him with a slight sense of confusion. A precipitate wish to rise and pass through the doorway into the wider spaces of the conservatory came to him, though he made no attempt to act upon it. He knew that, for some inexplicable reason, this woman behind the screen had lied to him—in the controlling of her speech, in her charge of voice. There had been one moment in which an impulse or an emotion had almost found voice; then training, instinct, or it might have been diplomacy, had conquered, and the moment had passed. There was a riddle in the very atmosphere of the place— and he abominated riddles.

But Lady Astrupp was absorbed in her own concerns. Again she changed her position; and to Loder, listening attentively, it seemed that she leaned forward and examined his hands afresh. The sensation was so acute that he withdrew them involuntarily.

Again there was a confused rustle; the crystal ball rolled from the table, and the seer laughed quickly. Obeying a strenuous impulse, Loder rose.

He had no definite notion of what he expected or what he must avoid. He was only conscious that the pavilion, with its silk draperies, its scent of musk, and its intolerable secrecy, was no longer endurable. He felt cramped and confused in mind and muscle. He stood for a second to straighten his limbs; then he turned, and, moving directly forward, passed through the portiere.

After the dimness of the pavilion the conservatory seemed comparatively bright; but without waiting to grow accustomed to the altered light he moved onward with deliberate haste. The long, green alley, was speedily traversed; in his eyes it no longer possessed greenness, no longer suggested freshness or repose. It was simply a means to the end upon which his mind was set.

As he passed up the flight of steps he drew his rings from his pocket and slipped them on again. Then he stepped into the glare of the thronged corridor.

Some one hailed him as be passed through the crowd, but with Chilcote's most absorbed manner he hurried on. Through the door of the supper-room he caught sight of Blessington and Eve, and then for the first time his expression changed, and he turned directly towards them.

"Eve," he said, "will you excuse me? I have a word to say to Blessington."

She glanced at him in momentary surprise; then she smiled in her quiet, self-possessed way.

"Of course!" she said. "I've been wanting a chat with Millicent Gower, but Bobby has required so much entertaining—" She smiled again, this time at Blessington, and moved away towards a pale girl in green who was standing alone.

Instantly she had turned Loder took Blessington's arm.

"I know you're tremendously busy," he began, in an excellent imitation of Chilcote's hasty manner—" I know you're tremendously busy, but I'm in a fix."

One glance at Blessington's healthy, ingenuous face told him that plain speaking was the method to adopt.

"Indeed, sir?" In a moment Blessington was on the alert.

"Yes. And I—I want your help."

The boy reddened. That Chilcote should appeal to him stirred him to an uneasy feeling of pride and uncertainty.

Loder saw his advantage and pressed it home. "It's come about through this crystal-gazing business. I'm afraid I didn't play my part—rather made an ass of myself; I wouldn't swallow the thing, and—and Lady Astrupp—" He paused, measuring Blessington with a glance. "Well, my dear boy, you—you know what women are!"

Blessington was only twenty-three. He reddened again, and assumed an air of profundity. "I know. sir," he said, with a shake of the head.

Loder's sense of humor was keen, but he kept a grave face. "I knew you'd catch my meaning; but I want you to do something more. If Lady Astrupp should ask you who was in her tent this past ten minutes, I want you—" Again he stopped, looking at his companion's face.

"Yes, sir?"

"I want you to tell an immaterial lie for me."

Blessington returned his glance; then he laughed a little uncomfortably. "But surely, sir—"

"She recognized me, you mean?" Loder's eyes were as keen as steel.
Yes."

"Then you're wrong. She didn't."

Blessington's eyebrows went up.

There was silence. Loder glanced across the room. Eve had parted from the girl in green and was moving towards them, exchanging smiles and greetings as she came.

"My wife is coming back," he said. "Will you do this for me, Blessington? It—it will smooth things—" He spoke quickly, continuing to watch Eve. As he had hoped, Blessington's eyes turned in the same direction. "'Twill smooth matters," he repeated, "smooth them in—in a domestic way that I can't explain."

The shot told. Blessington looked round.

"Right, sir!" he said. "You may leave it to me," And before Loder could speak again he had turned and disappeared into the crowd.

XVI

His business with Blessington over, Loder breathed more freely. If Lady Astrupp had recognized Chilcote by the rings, and had been roused to curiosity, the incident would demand settlement sooner or later—settlement in what proportion he could hazard no guess; if, on the other hand, her obvious change of manner had arisen from any other source he had a hazy idea that a woman's behavior could never be gauged by accepted theories—then he had safeguarded Chilcote's interests and his own by his securing of Blessington's promise. Blessington he knew would be reliable and discreet. With a renewal of confidence—a pleasant feeling that his uneasiness had been groundless—he moved forward to greet Eve.

Her face, with its rich, clear coloring, seemed to his gaze to stand out from the crowd of other faces as from a frame, and a sense of pride touched him. In every eye but his own her beauty belonged to him.

His face looked alive and masterful as she reached his side. "May I monopolize you?" he said, with the quickness of speech borrowed from Chilcote. "We see so little of each other."

Almost as if compelled, her lashes lifted and her eyes met his. Her glance was puzzled, uncertain, slightly confused. There was a deeper color than usual in her cheeks. Loder felt something within his own consciousness stir in response.

"You know you are yielding," he said.

Again she blushed.

He saw the blush, and knew that it was he—his words, his personality—that had called it forth. In Chilcote's actual semblance he had proved his superiority over Chilcote. For the first time he had been given a tacit, personal acknowledgment of his power. Involuntarily he drew nearer to her.

"Let's get out of this crush."

She made no answer except to bend her head; and it came to him that, for all her pride, she liked—and unconsciously yielded to—domination. With a satisfied gesture he turned to make a passage towards the door.

But the passage was more easily desired than made. In the few moments since he had entered the supper-room the press of people had considerably thickened—until a block had formed about the door-way. Drawing Eve with him, he moved forward for a dozen paces, then paused, unable to make further headway.

As they stood there, he looked back at her. "What a study in democracy a crowd always is!" he said.

She responded with a bright, appreciative glance, as if surprised into naturalness. He wondered sharply what she would be like if her enthusiasms were really aroused. Then a stir in the corridor outside caused a movement inside the room; and with a certain display of persistence he was enabled to make a passage to the door.

There again they were compelled to halt. But though tightly wedged into his new position and guarding Eve with one arm, Loder was free to survey the brilliantly thronged corridor over the head of a man a few inches shorter than himself, who stood directly in front of him.

"What are we waiting for?" he asked, good humoredly, addressing the back of the stranger's head.

The man turned, displaying a genial face, a red mustache, and an eye-glass.

"Hullo, Chilcote!" he said. "Hope it's not on your feet I'm standing."

Loder laughed. "No," he said. "And don't change the position. If you were an inch higher I should be blind as well as crippled."

The other laughed. It was a pleasant surprise to find Chilcote amiable under discomfort. He looked round again in slight curiosity.

Loder felt the scrutiny. To create a diversion he looked out along the corridor. "I believe we are waiting for something," he exclaimed. "What's this?" Then quite abruptly be ceased to speak.

"Anything interesting?" Eve touched his arm.

He said nothing; he made no effort to look round. His thought as well as his speech was suddenly suspended.

The man in front of him let his eye-glass fall from his eye, then screwed it in again.

"Jove!" he exclaimed. "Here comes our sorceress. It's like the progress of a fairy princess. I believe this is the meaning of our getting penned in here," he chuckled delightedly.

Loder said nothing. He stared straight on over the other's head.

Along the corridor, agreeably conscious of the hum of admiration she aroused, came Lillian Astrupp, surrounded by a little court. Her delicate face was lit up; her eyes shone under the faint gleam of her hair; her gown of gold embroidery swept round her gracefully. She was radiant and triumphant, but she was also excited. The excitement was evident in her laugh, in her gestures, in her eyes, as they turned quickly in one direction and then another.

Loder, gazing in stupefaction over the other man's head, saw it—felt and understood it with a mind that leaped back over a space of years. As in a shifting panorama he saw a night of disturbance and confusion in a far-off Italian valley—a confusion from which one face shone out with something of the pale, alluring radiance that filtered over the hillside from the crescent moon. It passed across his consciousness slowly but with a slow completeness; and in its light the incidents of the past hour stood out in a new aspect. The echo of recollection stirred by Lady Bramfell's voice, the re-echo of it in the sister's tones; his own blindness, his own egregious assurance—all struck across his mind.

Meanwhile the party about Lillian drew nearer. He felt with instinctive certainty that the supper-room was its destination, but he remained motionless, held by a species of fatalism. He watched her draw near with an unmoved face, but in the brief space that passed while she traversed the corridor he gauged to the full the hold that the new atmosphere, the new existence, had gained over his mind. With an unlooked-for rush of feeling he realized how dearly he would part with it.

As Lillian came closer, the meaning of her manner became clearer to him. She talked incessantly, laughing now and then, but her eyes were never quiet. These skimmed the length of the corridor, then glanced over the heads crowded in the door-way.

"I'll have something quite sweet, Geoffrey," she was saying to the man beside her, as she came within hearing. "You know what I like—a sort of snowflake wrapped up in sugar." As she said the words her glance wandered. Loder saw it rest uninterestedly on a boy a yard or two in front of him, then move to the man over whose head he gazed, then lift itself inevitably to his face.

The glance was quick and direct. He saw the look of recognition spring across it; he saw her move forward suddenly as the crowd in the corridor parted to let her pass. Then he saw what seemed to him a miracle.

Her whole expression altered, her lips parted, and she colored with annoyance. She looked like a spoiled child who, seeing a bonbon-box, opens it—to find it empty.

As the press about the door-way melted to give her passage, the red-haired man in front of Loder was the first to take advantage of the space. "Jove! Lillian," he said, moving forward, "you look as if you expected Chilcote to be somebody else, and are disappointed to find he's only himself!" He laughed delightedly at his own joke.

The words were exactly the tonic that Lillian needed. She smiled her usual undisturbed smile as she turned her eyes upon him.

"My dear Leonard, you're using your eye-glass; when that happens you're never responsible for what you see." Her words came more slowly and with a touch of languid amusement. Her composure was suddenly restored.

Then for the first time Loder changed his position. Moved by an impulse he made no effort to dissect, he stepped back to Eve's side and slipped his arm through hers—successfully concealing his left hand.

The warmth of her skin through her long glove thrilled him unexpectedly. His impulse had been one of self-defence, but the result was of a different character. At the quick contact the wish to fight for—to hold and defend—the position that had grown so dear woke in renewed force. With a new determination he turned again towards Lillian.

"I caught the same impression—without an eyeglass," he said. "Why did you look like that?" He asked the question steadily and with apparent carelessness, though, through it all, his reason stood aghast—his common-sense cried aloud that it was impossible for the eyes that had seen his face in admiration, in love, in contempt, to fail now in recognition. The air seemed breathless while he spoke and waited. His impression of Lillian was a mere shimmering of gold dress and gold hair; all that he was really conscious of was the pressure of his hand on Eve's arm and the warmth of her skin through the soft glove. Then, abruptly, the mist lifted. He saw Lillian's eyes—indifferent, amused, slightly contemptuous; and a second later he heard her voice.

"My dear Jack," she said, sweetly, "how absurd of you! It was simply the contrast of your eyes peering over Leonard's hair It was like a gorgeous sunset with a black cloud overhead." She laughed. "Do you see what I mean, Eve?" She affected to see Eve for the first time.

Eve had been looking calmly ahead. She turned now and smiled serenely. Loder felt no vibration of the arm he held, yet by an instant intuition he knew that the two women were antagonistic. He experienced it with the divination that follows upon a moment of acute suspense. He understood it, as he had understood Lillian's look of recognition when his forehead, eyes, and nose had shown him to be himself; her blank surprise when his close-shaven lip and chin had proclaimed him Chilcote.

He felt like a man who has looked into an abyss and stepped back from the edge, outwardly calm but mentally shaken. The commonplaces of life seemed for the moment to hold deeper meanings. He did not hear Eve's answer, he paid no heed to Lillian's next remark. He saw her smile and turn to the red-haired man; finally he saw her move on into the supper-room, followed by her little court. Then he pressed the arm he was still holding. He felt an urgent need of companionship—of a human expression to the crisis he had passed.

"Shall we get out of this?" he asked again.

Eve looked up. "Out of the room?" she said.

He looked down at her, compelling her gaze. "Out of the room —and the house," he answered. "Let us go-home."

XVII

The necessary formalities of departure were speedily got through. The passing of the corridors, the gaining of the carriage, seemed to Loder to be marvellously simple proceedings. Then, as he sat by Eve's side and again felt the forward movement of the horses, he had leisure for the first time to wonder whether the time that had passed since last he occupied that position had actually been lived through.

Only that night he had unconsciously compared one incident in his life to a sketch in which the lights and shadows have been obliterated and lost. Now that picture rose before him, startlingly and incredibly intact. He saw the sunlit houses of Santasalare, backgrounded by the sunlit hills—saw them as plainly as when he himself had sketched them on his memory. Every detail of the scene remained the same, even to the central figure; only the eye and the hand of the artist had changed.

At this point Eve broke in upon his thoughts. Her first words were curiously coincidental.

"What did you think of Lillian Astrupp to-night?" she asked. "Wasn't her gown perfect?"

Loder lifted his head with an almost guilty start. Then he answered straight from his thoughts.

"I—I didn't notice it," he said; "but her eyes reminded me of a cat's eyes—and she walks like a cat. I never seemed to see it—until to-night."

Eve changed her position. "She was very artistic," she said, tentatively. "Don't you think the gold gown was beautiful with her pale-colored hair?"

Loder felt surprised. He was convinced that Eve disliked the other and he was not sufficiently versed in women to understand her praise. "I thought—" he began. Then he wisely stopped. "I didn't see the gown," he substituted.

Eve looked out of the window. "How unappreciative men are!" she said. But her tone was strangely free from censure.

After this there was silence until Grosvenor Square was reached. Having left the carriage and passed into the house, Eve paused for a moment at the foot of the stairs to give an order to Crapham, who was still in attendance in the hall; and again Loder had an opportunity of studying her. As he looked, a sharp comparison rose to his mind.

"A fairy princess!" he had heard the red-haired man say as Lillian Astrupp came into view along the Bramfells' corridor, and the simile had seemed particularly apt. With her grace, her delicacy, her subtle attraction, she might well be the outcome of imagination. But with Eve it was different. She also was graceful and attractive—but it was grace and attraction of a different order. One was beautiful with the beauty of the white rose that springs from the hot-house and withers at the first touch of cold; the other with the beauty of the wild rose on the cliffs above the sea, that keeps its petals fine and transparent in face of salt spray and wet mist. Eve, too, had her realm, but it was the realm of real things. A great confidence, a feeling that here one might rely even if all other faiths were shaken, touched him suddenly. For a moment he stood irresolute, watching her mount the stairs with her easy, assured step. Then a determination came to him. Fate favored him to-night; he was in luck tonight. He would put his fortune to one more test. He swung across the hall and ran up the stairs.

His face was keen with interest as he reached her side. The hard outline of his features and the hard grayness of his eyes were softened as when he had paused to talk with Lakely. Action was the breath of his life, and his face changed under it as another's might change under the influence of stirring music or good wine.

Eve saw the look and again the uneasy expression of surprise crossed her eyes. She paused, her hand resting on the banister.

Loder looked at her directly. "Will you come into the study —as you came that other night? There's something I want to say." He spoke quietly. He felt master of himself and of her.

She hesitated, glanced at him, and then glanced away.

"Will you come?" he said again. And as he said it his eyes rested on the sweep of her thick eyelashes, the curve of the black hair.

At last her lashes lifted, and the perplexity and doubt in her blue eyes stirred him. Without waiting for her answer, he leaned forward.

"Say yes!" he urged. "I don't often ask for favors."

Still she hesitated; then her decision was made for her. With a new boldness he touched her arm, drawing her forward gently but decisively towards Chilcote's rooms.

In the study a fire burned brightly, the desk was laden with papers, the lights were nicely adjusted; even the chairs were in their accustomed places. Loder's senses responded to each suggestion. It seemed but a day since he had seen it last. It was precisely as he had left it—the niche needing but the man.

To hide his emotion he crossed the floor quickly and drew a chair forward. In less than six hours he had run up and down the scale of emotions. He had looked despair in the face, till the sudden sight of Chilcote had lifted him to the skies; since then, surprise had assailed him in its strongest form; he had known the full meaning of the word "risk"; and from every contingency he had come out conqueror. He bent over the chair as he pulled it forward, to hide the expression in his eyes.

"Sit down," he said, gently.

Eve moved towards him. She moved slowly, as if half afraid. Many emotions stirred her—distrust, uncertainty, and a curious half-dominant, half-suppressed questioning that it was difficult to define. Loder remembered her shrinking coldness, her reluctant tolerance on the night of his first coming, and his individuality, his certainty of power, kindled afresh. Never had he been so vehemently himself; never had Chilcote seemed so complete a shadow.

As Eve seated herself, he moved forward and leaned over the back of her chair. The impulse that had filled him in his interview with Renwick, that had goaded him as he drove to the reception, was dominant again.

"I tried to say something as we drove to the Bramfells' to-night," he began. Like many men who possess eloquence for an impersonal cause, he was brusque, even blunt, in the stating of his own case. "May I hark back, and go on from where I broke off?"

Eve half turned. Her face was still puzzled and questioning. "Of course." She sat forward again, clasping her hands.

He looked thoughtfully at the back of her head, at the slim outline of her shoulders, the glitter of the diamonds about her neck.

"Do you remember the day, three weeks ago, that we talked together in this room? The day a great many things seemed possible?"

This time she did not look round. She kept her gaze upon the fire.

"Do you remember?" he persisted, quietly. In his college days men who heard that tone of quiet persistence had been wont to lose heart. Eve heard it now for the first time, and, without being aware, answered to it.

"Yes, I remember," she said.

"On that day you believed in me—" In his earnestness he no longer simulated Chilcote; he spoke with his own steady reliance. He saw Eve stir, unclasp and clasp her hands, but he went steadily on. "On that day you saw me in a new light. You acknowledged me." He emphasized the slightly peculiar word. "But since that day"—his voice quickened "since that day your feelings have changed—your faith in me has fallen away." He watched her closely; but she made no sign, save to lean still nearer to the fire. He crossed his arms over the back of her chair. "You were justified," he said, suddenly. "I've not been— myself since that day." As he said the words his coolness forsook him slightly. He loathed the necessary lie, yet his egotism clamored for vindication. "All men have their lapses," he went on; "there are times—there are days and weeks when I—when my—" The word "nerves" touched his tongue, hung upon it, then died away unspoken.

Very quietly, almost without a sound, Eve had risen and turned towards him. She was standing very straight, her face a little pale, the hand that rested on the arm of her chair trembling slightly.

"John," she said, quickly, "don't say that word? Don't say that hideous word `nerves'! I don't feel that I can bear it to-night—not just to-night. Can you understand?"

Loder stepped back. Without comprehending, he felt suddenly and strangely at a loss. Something in her face struck him silent and perplexed. It seemed that without preparation he had stepped upon dangerous ground. With an undefined apprehension he waited, looking at her.

"I can't explain it," she went on with nervous haste, "I can't give any reasons, but quite suddenly the—the farce has grown unbearable. I used not to think— used not even to care—but suddenly things have changed—or I have changed." She paused, confused and distressed. "Why should it be? Why should things change?" She asked the question sharp. ly, as if in appeal against her own incredulity.

Loder turned aside. He was afraid of the triumph, volcanic and irrepressible, that her admission roused.

"Why?" she said again.

He turned slowly back. "You forget that I'm not a magician," he said, gently. "I hardly know what you are speaking of."

For a moment she was silent, but in that moment her eyes spoke. Pain, distress, pride, all strove for expression; then at last her lips parted.

"Do you say that in seriousness?" she asked.

It was no moment for fencing, and Loder knew it. "In seriousness," he replied, shortly.

"Then I shall speak seriously, too." Her voice shook slightly and the color came back into her face, but the hand on the arm of the chair ceased to tremble. "For more than four years I have known that you take drugs—for more than four years I have acquiesced in your deceptions—in your meannesses—"

There was an instant's silence. Then Loder stepped forward.

"You knew—for four years?" he said, very slowly. For the first time that night he remembered Chilcote and forgot himself.

Eve lifted her head with a quick gesture—as if, in flinging off discretion and silence, she appreciated to the full the new relief of speech.

"Yes, I knew. Perhaps I should have spoken when I first surprised the secret, but it's all so past that it's useless to speculate now. It was fate, I suppose. I was very young, you were very unapproachable, and—and we had no love to make the way easy." For a second her glance faltered and she looked away. "A woman's—a girl's—disillusioning is a very sad comedy—it should never have an audience." She laughed a little bitterly as she looked back again. "I saw all the deceits, all the subterfuges, all the—lies." She said the word deliberately, meeting his eyes.

Again he thought of Chilcote, but his face paled.

"I saw it all. I lived with it all till I grew hard and indifferent—till I acquiesced in your 'nerves' as readily as the rest of the world that hadn't suspected and didn't know." Again she laughed nervously. "And I thought the indifference would last forever. If one lives in a groove for years, one gets frozen up; I never felt more frozen than on the night Mr. Fraide spoke to me of you—asked me to use my influence; then, on that night—"

"Yes. On that night?" Loder's voice was tense.

But her excitement had suddenly fallen. Whether his glance had quelled it or whether the force of her feelings had worked itself out it was impossible to say, but her eyes had lost their resolution. She stood hesitating for a moment, then she turned and moved to the mantel-piece.

"That night you found me—changed?" Loder was insistent.

"Changed—and yet not changed." She spoke reluctantly, with averted head.

"And what did you think?"

Again she was silent; then again a faint excitement tinged her cheeks.

"I thought—" she began. "It seemed—" Once more she paused, hampered by her own uncertainty, her own sense of puzzling incongruity. "I don't know why I speak like this," she went on at last, as if in justification of herself, "or why I want to speak. But a feeling—an extraordinary, incomprehensible feeling seems to urge me on. The same feeling that came to me on the day we had tea together—the feeling that made me—that almost made me believe—"

"Believe what?" The words escaped him without volition.

At sound of his voice she turned. "Believe that a miracle had happened," she said—"that you had found strength—had freed yourself."

"From morphia?"

"From morphia."

In the silence that followed, Loder lived through a century of suggestion and indecision. His first feeling was for himself, but his first clear thought was for Chilcote and their compact. He stood, metaphorically, on a stone in the middle of a stream, balancing on one foot, then the other; looking to the right bank, then to the left. At last, as it always did, inspiration came to him slowly. He realized that by one plunge he might save both Chilcote and himself!

He crossed quickly to the fireplace and stood by Eve. "You were right in your belief," he said. "For all that time from the night you spoke to me of Fraide to the day you had tea in this room—I never touched a drug."

She moved suddenly, and he saw her face. "John," she said, unsteadily, "you—I—I have known you to lie to me—about other things."

With a hasty movement he averted his head. The doubt, the appeal in her words shocked him. The whole isolation of her life seemed summed up in the one short sentence. For the instant he forgot Chilcote. With a reaction of feeling he turned to her again.

"Look at me!" he said, brusquely.

She raised her eyes.

"Do you believe I'm speaking the truth?"

She searched his eyes intently, the doubt and hesitancy still struggling in her face.

"But the last three weeks?" she said, reluctantly. "How can you ask me to believe?"

He had expected this, and he met it steadily enough; nevertheless his courage faltered. To deceive this woman, even to justify himself, had in the last halfhour become something sacrilegious.

"The last three weeks must be buried," he said, hurriedly. "No man could free himself suddenly from—from a vice." He broke off abruptly. He hated Chilcote; he hated himself. Then Eve's face, raised in distressed appeal, overshadowed all scruples. "You have been silent and patient for years," he said, suddenly. "Can you be patient and silent a little longer?" He spoke without consideration. He was conscious of no selfishness beneath his words. In the first exercise of conscious strength the primitive desire to reduce all elements to his own sovereignty submerged every other emotion. "I can't enter into the thing," he said; "like you, I give no explanations. I can only tell you that on the day we talked together in this room I was myself—in the full possession of my reason, the full knowledge of my own capacities. The man you have known in the last three weeks, the man you have imagined in the last four years, is a shadow, an unreality—a weakness in human form. There is a new Chilcote—if you will only see him."

Ewe was trembling as he ceased; her face was flushed; there was a strange brightness in her eyes She was moved beyond herself.

"But the other you—the old you?"

"You must be patient." He looked down into the fire. "Times like the last three weeks will come again—must come again; they are inevitable. When they do come, you must shut your eyes—you must blind yourself. You must ignore them—and me. Is it a compact?" He still avoided her eyes.

She turned to him quietly. "Yes—if you wish it," she said, below her breath.

He was conscious of her glance, but he dared not meet it. He felt sick at the part he was playing, yet he held to it tenaciously.

"I wonder if you could do what few men and fewer women are capable of?" he asked, at last. "I wonder if you could learn to live in the present?" He lifted his head slowly and met her eyes. "This is an—an experiment," he went on. "And, like all experiments, it has good phases and bad. When the bad phases come round I—I want you to tell yourself that you are not altogether alone in your unhappiness—that I am suffering too—in another way."

There was silence when he had spoken, and for a space it seemed that Eve would make no response. Then the last surprise in a day of surprises came to him. With a slight stir, a slight, quick rustle of skirts, she stepped forward and laid her hand in his.

The gesture was simple and very sweet; her eyes were soft and full of light as she raised her face to his, her lips parted in unconscious appeal.

There is no surrender so seductive as the surrender of a proud woman. Loder's blood stirred, the undeniable suggestion of the moment thrilled and disconcerted him in a tumult of thought. Honor, duty, principle rose in a triple barrier; but honor, duty, and principle are but words to a headstrong man. Tho full significance of his position came to him as it had never come before. His hand closed on hers; he bent towards her, his pulses beating unevenly.

"Eve!" he said. Then at sound of his voice he suddenly hesitated. It was the voice of a man who has forgotten everything but his own existence.

For an instant he stayed motionless; then very quietly he drew away from her, releasing her hands.

"No," he said. "No—I haven't got the right,"

XVIII

That night, for almost the first time since he had adopted his dual role, Loder slept ill. He was not a man over whom imagination held any powerful sway—his doubts and misgivings seldom ran to speculation, upon future possibilities; nevertheless, the fact that, consciously or unconsciously, he had adopted a new attitude towards Eve came home to him with unpleasant force during the hours of darkness; and long before the first hint of daylight had slipped through the heavy window-curtains he had arranged a plan of action—a plan wherein, by the simple method of altogether avoiding her, he might soothe his own conscience and safeguard Chilcote's domestic interests.

It was a satisfactory if a somewhat negative arrangement, and he rose next morning with a feeling that things had begun to shape themselves. But chance sometimes has a disconcerting knack of forestalling even our best-planned schemes. He dressed slowly, and descended to his solitary breakfast with the pleasant sensation of having put last night out of consideration by the turning over of a new leaf; but scarcely had he opened Chilcote's letters, scarcely had he taken a cursory glance at the morning's newspaper, than it was borne in upon him that not only a new leaf, but a whole sheaf of new leaves, had been turned in his prospects—by a hand infinitely more powerful and arbitrary than his own. He realized within the space of a few moments that the leisure Eve might have claimed, the leisure he might have been tempted to devote to her, was no longer his to dispose of—being already demanded of him from a quarter that allowed of no refusal.

For the first rumbling of the political earthquake that was to shake the country made itself audible beyond denial on that morning of March 27th, when the news spread through England that, in view of the disorganized state of the Persian army and the Shah's consequent inability to suppress the open insurrection of the border tribes in the north-eastern districts of Meshed, Russia, with a great show of magnanimity, had come to the rescue by despatching a large armed force from her military station at Merv across the Persian frontier to the seat of the disturbance.

To many hundreds of Englishmen who read their papers on that morning this announcement conveyed bat little. That there is such a country as Persia we all know, that English interests predominate in the south and Russian interests in the north we have all superficially understood from childhood; but in this knowledge, coupled with the fact that Persia is comfortably far away, we are apt to rest content. It is only to the eyes that see through long-distance glasses, the minds that regard the present as nothing more nor less than an inevitable link joining the future to the past, that this distant, debatable land stands out in its true political significance.

To the average reader of news the statement of Russia's move seemed scarcely more important than had the first report of the border risings in January, but to the men who had watched the growth of the disturbance it came charged with portentous meaning. Through the entire ranks of the opposition, from Fraide himself downward, it caused a thrill of expectation —that peculiar prophetic sensation that every politician has experienced at some moment of his career.

In no member of his party did this feeling strike deeper root than in Loder. Imbued with a lifelong interest in the Eastern question, specially equipped by personal knowledge to hold and proclaim an opinion upon Persian affairs, he read the signs and portents with instinctive insight. Seated at Chilcote's table, surrounded by Chilcote's letters and papers, he forgot the breakfast that was slowly growing cold, forgot the interests and dangers, personal or pleasurable, of the night before, while his mental eyes persistently conjured up the map of Persia, travelling with steady deliberation from Merv to Meshed, from Meshed to Herat, from Herat to the empire of India! For it was not the fact that the Hazaras had risen against the Shah that occupied the thinking mind, nor was it the fact that Russian and not Persian troops were destined to subdue them, but the deeply important consideration that an armed Russian force had crossed the frontier and was encamped within twenty miles of Meshed-Meshed, upon which covetous Russian eyes have rested ever since the days of Peter the Great.

So Loder's thoughts ran as he read and reread the news from the varying political stand-points, and so they continued to run when, some hours later, an urgent telephone message from the 'St. George's Gazette' asked him to call at Lakely's office.

The message was interesting as well as imperative, and he made an instant response. The thought of Lakely's keen eyes and shrewd enthusiasms always possessed strong attractions for his own slower temperament, but even had this impetus been lacking, the knowledge that at the 'St. George's' offices, if anywhere, the true feelings of the party were invariably voiced would have drawn him without hesitation.

It was scarcely twelve o'clock when he turned the corner of the tall building, but already the keen spirit that Lakely everywhere diffused was making itself felt. Loder smiled to himself as his eyes fell on the day's placards with their uncompromising headings, and passed onward from the string of gayly painted carts drawn up to receive their first consignment of the paper to the troop of eager newsboys passing in and out of the big swing-doors with their piled-up bundles of the early edition; and with a renewed thrill of anticipation and energy he passed through the doorway and ran up-stairs.

Passing unchallenged through the long corridor that led to Lakely's office, he caught a fresh impression of action and vitality from the click of the tape machines in the subeditors' office, and a glimpse through the open door of the subeditors themselves, each occupied with his particular task; then without time for further observation he found himself at Lakely's door. Without waiting to knock, as he had felt compelled to do on the one or two previous occasions that business had brought him there, he immediately turned the handle and entered the room.

Editors' offices differ but little in general effect.

Lakely's surroundings were rather more elaborate than is usual, as became the dignity of the oldest Tory evening paper, but the atmosphere was unmistakable. As Loder entered he glanced up from the desk at which he was sitting, but instantly returned to his task of looking through and marking the pile of early evening editions that were spread around him. His coat was off and hung on the chair behind him, axed he pulled vigorously on a long cigar.

"Hullo! That's right," he said, laconically. "Make yourself comfortable half a second, while I skim the 'St. Stephen's'."

His salutation pleased Loder. With a nod of acquiescence he crossed the office to the brisk fire that burned in, the grate.

For a minute or two Lakely worked steadily, occasionally breaking the quiet by an unintelligible remark or a vigorous stroke of his pencil. At last he dropped the paper with a gesture of satisfaction and leaned back in his chair.

"Well," he said, "what d'you think of this? How's this for a complication?"

Loder turned round. "I think," he said, quietly, "that we can't overestimate it."

Lakely laughed and took a long pull at his cigar. "And we mustn't be afraid to let the Sefborough crowd know it, eh?" He waved his hand to the poster of the first edition that hung before his desk.

Loder, following his glance, smiled.

Lakely laughed again. "They might have known it all along, if they'd cared to deduce," he said. "Did they really believe that Russia was going to sit calmly looking across the Heri-Rud while the Shah played at mobilizing? But what became of you last night? We had a regular prophesying of the whole business at Bramfell's; the great Fraide looked in for five minutes. I went on with him to the club afterwards and was there when the news came in. 'Twas a great night!"

Loder's face lighted up. "I can imagine it," he said, with an unusual touch of warmth.

Lakely watched him intently for a moment. Then with a quick action he leaned forward and rested his elbows on the desk.

"It's going to be something more than imagination for you, Chilcote," he said, impressively. "It's going to be solid earnest!" He spoke rapidly and with rather more than his usual shrewd decisiveness; then he paused to see the effect of his announcement.

Loder was still studying the flaring poster. At the other's words he turned sharply. Something in Lakely's voice, something in his manner, arrested him. A tinge of color crossed his face.

"Reality?" he said. "What do you mean?"

For a further space his companion watched him; then with a rapid movement he tilted back his chair.

"Yes," he said. "Yes; old Fraide's instincts are never far out. He's quite right. You're the man!"

Still quietly, but with a strange underglow of excitement, Loder left the fire, and, coming forward, took a chair at Lakely's desk.

"Do you mind telling me what you're driving at?" he asked, in his old, laconic voice.

Lakely still scrutinized him with an air of brisk satisfaction; then with a gesture of finality he tossed his cigar away.

"My dear chap," he said, "there's going to be a breach somewhere—and Fraide says you're the man to step in and fill it! You see, five years ago, when things looked lively on the Gulf and the Bundar Abbas business came to light, you did some promising work; and a reputation like that sticks to a man —even when he turns slacker! I won't deny that you've slacked abominably," he added, as Loder made an uneasy movement, "but slacking has different effects. Some men run to seed, others mature. I had almost put you down on the black list, but I've altered my mind in the last two months."

Again Loder stirred in his seat. A host of emotions were stirring in his mind. Every word wrung from Lakely was another stimulus to pride, another subtle tribute to the curious force of personality.

"Well?" he said. "Well?"

Lakely smiled. "We all know that Sefborough's ministry is —well, top-heavy," he said. "Sefborough is building his card house just a story too high. It's a toss-up what 'll upset the balance. It might be the army, of course, or it might be education; but it might quite as well be a matter of foreign policy!"

They looked at each other in comprehensive silence.

"You know as well as I that it's not the question of whether Russia comes into Persia, but the question of whether Russia goes out of Persia when these Hazaras are subdued! I'll lay you what you like, Chilcote, that within one week we hear that the risings are suppressed, but that Russia, instead of retiring, has advanced those tempting twenty miles and comfortably ensconced herself at Meshed—as she ensconced herself on the island of Ashurada. Lakely's nervous, energetic figure was braced, his light-blue eyes brightened, by the intensity of his interest.

"If this news comes before the Easter recess," he went on, "the first nail can be hammered in on the motion for adjournment. And if the right man does it in the right way, I'll lay my life 'twill be a nail in Sefborough's coffin."

Loder sat very still. Overwhelming possibilities had suddenly opened before him. In a moment the unreality of the past months had become real; a tangible justification of himself and his imposture was suddenly made possible. In the stress of understanding he, too, leaned forward, and, resting his elbows on the desk, took his face between his hands.

For a space Lakely made no remark. To him man and man's moods came second in interest to his paper and his party politics. That Chilcote should be conscious of the glories he had opened up seemed only natural; that he should show that consciousness in a becoming gravity seemed only right. For some seconds he made no attempt to disturb him; but at last his own irrepressible activity made silence unendurable. He caught up his pencil and tapped impatiently on the desk.

"Chilcote," he said, quickly and with a gleam of sudden anxiety, "you're not by any chance doubtful of yourself?"

At sound of his voice Loder lifted his face; it was quite pale again, but the energy and resolution that had come into it when Lakely first spoke were still to be seen.

"No, Lakely," he said, very slowly, "it's not the sort of moment in which a man doubts himself,"

XIX

And so it came about that Loder was freed from one responsibility to undertake another. From the morning of March 27th, when Lakely had expounded the political programme in the offices of the 'St. George's Gazette', to the afternoon of April 1st he found himself a central figure in the whirlpool of activity that formed itself in Conservative circles.

With the acumen for which he was noted, Lakely had touched the key-stone of the situation on that morning; and succeeding events, each fraught with its own importance, had established the precision of his forecast.

Minutely watchful of Russia's attitude, Fraide quietly organized his forces and strengthened his position with a statesmanlike grasp of opportunity; and to Loder the attributes displayed by his leader during those trying days formed an endless and absorbing study. Setting the thought of Chilcote aside, ignoring his own position and the risks he daily ran, he had fully yielded to the glamour of the moment, and in the first freedom of a loose rein he had given unreservedly all that he possessed of activity, capacity, and determination to the cause that had claimed him.

Singularly privileged in a constant, personal contact with Fraide, he learned many valuable lessons of tact and organization in those five vital days during which the tactics of a whole party hung upon one item of news from a country thousands of miles away. For should Russia subdue the insurgent Hazaras and, laden with the honors of the peacemaker, retire across the frontier, then the political arena would remain undisturbed; but should the all-important movement predicted by Lakely become an accepted fact before Parliament rose for the Easter recess, then the first blow in the fight that would rage during the succeeding session must inevitably be struck. In the mean time it was Fraide's difficult position to wait and watch and yet preserve his dignity.

It was early in the afternoon of March 29th that Loder, in response to a long-standing invitation, lunched quietly with the Fraides. Being delayed by some communications from Wark, he was a few minutes late in keeping his appointment, and on being shown into the drawing-room found the little group of three that was to make up the party already assembled—Fraide, Lady Sarah—and Eve. As he entered the room they ceased to speak, and all three turned in his direction.

In the first moment he had a vague impression of responding suitably to Lady Sarah's cordial greeting; but he knew that immediately and unconsciously his eyes turned to Eve, while a quick sense of surprise and satisfaction passed through him at sight of her. For an instant he wondered how she would mark his avoidance of her since their last eventful interview; then instantly he blamed himself for the passing doubt. For, before all things, he knew her to be a woman of the world.

He took Fraide's outstretched hand; and again he looked towards Eve, waiting for her to speak.

She met his glance, but said nothing. Instead of speaking she smiled at him—a smile that was far more reassuring than any words, a smile that in a single second conveyed forgiveness, approbation, and a warm, almost tender sense of sympathy and comprehension. The remembrance of that smile stayed with him long after they were seated at table; and far into the future the remembrance of the lunch itself, with its pleasant private sense of satisfaction, was destined to return to him in retrospective moments. The delightful atmosphere of the Fraides' home life had always been a wonder and an enigma to him; but on this day he seemed to grasp its meaning by a new light, as he watched Eve soften under its influence and felt himself drawn imperceptibly from the position of a speculative outsider to that of an intimate. It was a fresh side to the complex, fascinating life of which Fraide was the master spirit.

These reflections had grown agreeably familiar to his mind; the talk, momentarily diverted into social channels, was quietly drifting back to the inevitable question of the "situation" that in private moments was never far from their lips, when the event that was to mark and separate that day from those that had preceded it was unceremoniously thrust upon them.

Without announcement or apology, the door was suddenly flung open and Lakely entered the room.

His face was brimming with excitement, and his eyes flashed. In the first haste of the entry he failed to see that there were ladies in the room, And, crossing instantly to Fraide, laid an open telegram before him.

"This is official, sir," he said. Then at last he glanced round the table.

"Lady Sarah!" he exclaimed. "Can you forgive me? But I'd have given a hundred pounds to be the first with this!" He glanced back at Fraide.

Lady Sarah rose and stretched out her hand. "Mr. Lakely," she said, "I more than understand!" There was a thrill in her warm, cordial voice, and her eyes also turned towards her husband.

Of the whole party, Fraide alone was perfectly calm. He sat very still, his small, thin figure erect and dignified, as his eyes scanned the message that meant so much.

Eve, who had sprung from her seat and passed round the table at sound of Lakely's news, was leaning over his shoulder, reading the telegram with him. At the last word she lifted her head, her face flushed with excitement.

"How splendid it must be to be a man!" she exclaimed. And without premeditation her eyes and Loder's met.

In this manner came the news from Persia, and with it Loder's definite call. In the momentary stress of action it was impossible that any thought of Chilcote could obtrude itself. Events had followed each other too rapidly, decisive action had been too much thrust upon him, to allow of hesitation; and it was in this spirit, under this vigorous pressure, that he made his attack upon the government on the day that followed Fraide's luncheon party.

That indefinable attentiveness, that alert sensation of impending storm. that is so strong an index of the parliamentary atmosphere was very keen on that memorable first of April. It was obvious in the crowded benches on both sides of the House—in the oneness of purpose that insensibly made itself felt through the ranks of the Opposition, and found definite expression in Fraide's stiff figure and tightly shut lips—in the unmistakable uneasiness that lay upon the ministerial benches.

But notwithstanding these indications of battle, the early portion of the proceedings was unmarked by excitement, being tinged with the purposeless lack of vitality that had of late marked all affairs of the Sefborough Ministry; and it was not until the adjournment of the House for the Easter recess had at last been moved that the spirit of activity hovering in the air descended and galvanized the assembly into life. It was then, amid a stir of interest, that Loder slowly rose.

Many curious incidents have marked the speech-making annals of the House of Commons, but it is doubtful whether it has ever been the lot of a member to hear his own voice raised for the first time on a subject of vital interest to his party, having been denied all initial assistance of minor questions asked or unimportant amendments made. Of all those gathered together in the great building on that day, only one man appreciated the difficulty of Loder's position —and that man was Loder himself.

He rose slowly and stood silent for a couple of seconds, his body braced, his fingers touching the sheaf of notes that lay in front of him. To the waiting House the silence was effective. It might mean over-assurance, or it might mean a failure of nerve at a critical moment. Either possibility had a tinge of piquancy. Moved by the same impulse, fifty pairs o eyes turned upon him with new interest; but up in the Ladies' Gallery Eve clasped her hands in sudden apprehension; and Fraide, sitting stiffly in his seat, turned and shot one swift glance at the man on whom, against prudence and precedent, he had pinned his faith. The glance was swift but very searching, and with a characteristic movement of his wiry shoulders he resumed his position and his usual grave, attentive attitude. At the same moment Loder lifted his head and began to speak.

Here at the outset his inexperience met him. His voice, pitched too low, only reached those directly near him. It was a moment of great strain. Eve, listening intently, drew a long breath of suspense and let her fingers drop apart; the sceptical, watchful eyes that faced him, line upon line, seemed to flash and brighten with critical interest; only Fraide made no change of expression. He sat placid, serious, attentive, with the shadow of a smile behind his eyes.

Again Loder paused, but this time the pause was shorter. The ordeal he had dreaded and waited for was passed and he saw his way clearly. With the old movement of the shoulders he straightened himself and once more began to speak. This time his voice rang quietly true and commanding across the floor of the House.

No first step can be really great; it must of necessity possess more of prophecy than of achievement; nevertheless it is by the first step that a man marks the value, not only of his cause, but of himself. Following broadly on the lines that tradition has laid down for the Conservative orator, Loder disguised rather than displayed the vein of strong, persuasive eloquence that was his natural gift. The occasion that might possibly justify such a display of individuality might lie with the future, but it had no application to the present. For the moment his duty was to voice his party sentiments with as much lucidity, as much logic, and as much calm conviction as lay within his capacity.

Standing quietly in Chilcote's place, he was conscious with a deep sense of gravity of the peculiarity of his position; and perhaps it was this unconscious and unstudied seriousness that lent him the tone of weight and judgment so essential to the cause he had in hand. It has always been difficult to arouse the interest of the House on matters of British policy in Persia. Once aroused, it may, it is true, reach fever heat with remarkable rapidity, but the introductory stages offer that worst danger to the earnest speaker—the dread of an apathetic audience. But from this consideration Loder, by his sharp consciousness of personal difficulties, was given immunity.

Pitching his voice in that quietly masterful tone that beyond all others compels attention, he took up his subject and dealt with it with dispassionate force. With great skill he touched on the steady southward advance of Russia into Persian territory from the distant days when, by a curious irony of fate, Russian and British enterprise combined to make entry into the country under the sanction of the Grand-Duke of Moscovy, to the present hour, when this great power of Russia —long since alienated by interests and desires from her former co-operator—had taken a step which in the eyes of every thinking man must possess a deep significance. With quiet persistence he pointed out the peculiar position of Meshed in the distant province of Khorasan; its vast distance from the Persian Gulf, round which British interests and influence centre, and the consequently alarming position of hundreds of traders who, in the security of British sovereignty, are fighting their way upward from India, from Afghanistan, even from England herself.

Following up his point, he dilated on these subjects of the British crown who, cut off from adequate assistance, can only turn in personal or commercial peril to the protective power of the nearest consulate. Then, quietly demanding the attention of his hearers, he marshalled fact after fact to demonstrate the isolation and inadequacy of a consulate so situated; the all but arbitrary power of Russia, who in her new occupation of Meshed had only two considerations to withhold her from open aggression—the knowledge of England as a very considerable but also a very distant power; the knowledge of Persia as an imminent but wholly impotent factor in the case.

Having stated his opinions, he reverted to the motive of his speech—his desire to put forward a strong protest against the adjournment of the House without an assurance from the government that immediate measures would be taken to safeguard British interests in Meshed and throughout the province of Khorasan.

The immediate outcome of Loder's speech was all that his party had desired. The effect on the House had been marked; and when, no satisfactory response coming to his demand, he had in still more resolute and insistent terms called for a division on the motion for adjournment, the result had been an appreciable fall in the government majority.

To Loder himself, the realization that he had at last vindicated and justified himself by individual action had a peculiar effect. His position had been altered in one remarkable particular. Before this day he alone had known himself to be strong; now the knowledge was shared by others and he was human enough to be susceptible to the change.

The first appreciation of it came immediately after the excitement of the division, when Fraide, singling him out, took his arm and pressed it affectionately.

"My dear Chilcote," he said, "we are all proud of you!" Then, looking up into his face, he added, in a graver tone, "But keep your mind upon the future; never be blinded by the present—however bright it seems."

At the touch of his hand, at the spontaneous approval of his first words, Loder's pride thrilled, and in a vehement rush of ambition his senses answered to the praise. Then, as Fraide in all unconsciousness added his second sentence, the hot glow of feeling suddenly chilled. In a sweep of intuitive reaction the meaning and the danger of his falsely real position extinguished his excitement and turned his triumph cold. With an involuntary gesture he withdrew his arm.

"You're very good, sir," he said. "And you're very right. We never should forget that there is—a future."

The old man glanced up, surprised by the tone.

"Quite so, Chilcote," he said, kindly. "But we only advise those in whom we believe to look towards it. Shall we find my wife? I know she will want to bear you home with us."

But Loder's joy in himself and his achievement had dropped from him. He shrank suddenly from Lady Sarah's congratulations and Eve's warm, silent approbation.

"Thanks, sir," he said, "but I don't feel fit for society. A touch of my—nerves, I suppose." He laughed shortly. "But do you mind saying to Eve that I hope I have—satisfied her?" he added this as if in half-reluctant after-thought. Then, with a short pressure of Fraide's hand, he turned, evading the many groups that waited to claim him, and passed out of the House alone.

Hailing a cab, he drove to Grosvenor Square. All the exaltation of an hour ago had turned to ashes. His excitement had found its culmination in a sense of futility and premonition.

He met no one in the hall or on the stairs of Chilcote's house, and on entering the study he found that also deserted. Greening had been among the most absorbed of those who had listened to his speech. Passing at once into the room, he crossed as if by instinct to the desk, and there halted. On the top of some unopened letters lay the significant yellow envelope of a telegram—the telegram that in an unformed, subconscious way had sprung to his expectation on the moment of Fraide's congratulation.

Very quietly he picked it up, opened and read it, and, with the automatic caution that had become habitual, carried it across the room and dropped it in the fire. This done, he returned to the desk, read the letters that awaited Chilcote, and, scribbling the necessary notes upon the margins, left them in readiness for Greening. Then, moving with the same quiet suppression, he passed from the room, down the stairs, and out into the street by the way he had come.

XX

On the fifth day after the momentous 1st of April on which he had recalled Loder and resumed his own life Chilcote left his house and walked towards Bond Street. Though the morning was clear and the air almost warm for the time of year, he was buttoned into a long overcoat and was wearing a muffler and a pair of doeskin gloves. As he passed along the street he kept close to the house fronts to avoid the sun that was everywhere stirring the winterbound town, like a suffusion of young blood through old veins. He avoided the warmth because in this instance warmth meant light, but as he moved he shivered slightly from time to time with the haunting, permeating cold that of late had become his persistent shadow.

He was ill at ease as he hurried forward. With each succeeding day of the old life the new annoyances, the new obligations became more hampering. Before his compact with Loder this old life had been a net about his feet; now the meshes seemed to have narrowed, the net itself to have spread till it smothered his whole being. His own household—his own rooms, even—offered no sanctuary. The presence of another personality tinged the atmosphere. It was preposterous, but it was undeniable. The lay figure that he had set in his place had proved to be flesh and blood—had usurped his life, his position, his very personality, by sheer right of strength. As he walked along Bond Street in the first sunshine of the year, jostled by the well-dressed crowd, he felt a pariah.

He revolted at the new order of things, but the revolt was a silent one—the iron of expediency had entered into his soul. He dared not jeopardize Loder's position, because he dared not dispense with Loder. The door that guarded his vice drew him more resistlessly with every indulgence, and Loder's was the voice that called the "Open Sesame!"

He walked on aimlessly. He had been but five days at home, and already the quiet, grass-grown court of Clifford's Inn, the bare staircase, the comfortless privacy of Loder's rooms seemed a haven of refuge. The speed with which this hunger had returned frightened him.

He walked forward rapidly and without encountering a check. Then, suddenly, the spell was broken. From the slowly moving, brilliantly dressed throng of people some one called him by his name; and turning he saw Lillian Astrupp.

She was stepping from the door of a jeweller's, and as he turned she paused, holding out her hand.

"The very person I would have wished to see!" she exclaimed. "Where have you been these hundred years? I've heard of nobody but you since you've turned politician and ceased to be a mere member of Parliament!" She laughed softly. The laugh suited the light spring air, as she herself suited the pleasant, superficial scene.

He took her hand and held it, while his eyes travelled from her delicate face to her pale cloth gown, from her soft furs to the bunch of roses fastened in her muff. The sight of her was a curious relief. Her cool, slim fingers were so casual, yet so clinging, her voice and her presence were so redolent of easy, artificial things.

"How well you look!" he said, involuntarily.

Again she laughed. "That's my prerogative," she responded, lightly. "But I was serious in being glad to see you. Sarcastic people are always so intuitive. I'm looking for some one with intuition."

Chilcote glanced up. "Extravagant again?" he said, dryly.

She smiled at him sweetly. "Jack!" she murmured with slow reproach.

Chilcote laughed quickly. "I understand. You've changed your Minister of Finance. I'm wanted in some other direction."

This time her reproach was expressed by a glance. "You are always wanted," she said.

The words seemed to rouse him again to the shadowy self-distrust that the sight of her had lifted.

"It's—it's delightful to meet you like this," he began, "and I wish the meeting wasn't momentary. But I'm—I'm rather pressed for time. You must let me come round one afternoon —or evening, when you're alone." He fumbled for a moment with the collar of his coat, and glanced furtively upward towards Oxford Street.

But again Lillian smiled—this time to herself. If she understood anything on earth it was Chilcote and his moods.

"If one may be careless of anything, Jack," she said, lightly, "surely it's of time. I can imagine being pressed for anything else in the world. If it's an appointment you're worrying about, a motor goes ever so much faster than a cab—" She looked at him tentatively, her head slightly on one side, her muff raised till the roses and some of the soft fur touched her cheek.

She looked very charming and very persuasive as Chilcote glanced back. Again she seemed to represent a respite —something graceful and subtle in a world of oppressive obligations. His eyes strayed from her figure to the smart motor-car drawn up beside the curb.

She saw the glance. "Ever so much quicker," she insinuated; and, smiling again, she stepped forward from the door of the shop. After a second's indecision Chilcote followed her.

The waiting car had three seats—one in front for the chauffeur, two vis-a-vis at the back, offering pleasant possibilities of a tete-a-tete.

"The Park—and drive slowly," Lillian ordered, as she stepped inside, motioning Chilcote to the seat opposite.

They moved up Bond Street smoothly and rapidly. Lillian was absorbed in the passing traffic until the Marble Arch was reached; then, as they glided through the big gates, she looked across at her companion. He had turned up the collar of his coat, though the wind was scarcely perceptible, and buried, himself in it to the ears.

"It is extraordinary!" she exclaimed, suddenly, as her eyes rested on his face. It was seldom that she felt drawn to exclamation. She was usually too indolent to show surprise. But now the feeling was called forth before she was aware.

Chilcote looked up. "What's extraordinary?" he said, sensitively.

She leaned forward for an instant and touched his hand.

"Bear!" she said, teasingly. "Did I rub your fur the wrong way?" Then, seeing his expression, she tactfully changed her tone. "I'll explain. It was the same thing that struck me the night of Blanche's party—when you looked at me over Leonard Kaine's head. You remember?" She glanced away from him across the Park to where the grass was already showing greener.

Chilcote felt ill at ease. Again he put his hand to his coat collar.

"Oh yes," he said, hastily—"yes." He wished now that he had questioned Loder more closely on the proceedings of that party. It seemed to him, on looking back, that Loder had mentioned nothing on the day of their last exchange but the political complications that absorbed his mind.

"I couldn't explain then," Lillian went on. "I couldn't explain before a crowd of people that it wasn't your dark head showing over Leonard's red one that surprised me, but the most wonderful, the most extraordinary likeness—" She paused.

The car was moving slower; there was a delight in the easy motion through the fresh, early air. But Chilcote's uneasiness had been aroused. He no longer felt soothed.

"What likeness?" he asked, sharply.

She turned to him easily. "Oh, a likeness I have noticed before," she said. "A likeness that always seemed strange, but that suddenly became incredible at Blanche's party."

He moved quickly. "Likenesses are an illusion," he said, "a mere imagination of the brain!" His manner was short; his annoyance seemingly out of all proportion to its cause. Lillian looked at him afresh in slightly interested surprise.

"Yet not so very long ago, you yourself—" she began.

"Nonsense!" he broke in. "I've always denied likenesses. Such things don't really exist. Likeness-seeing is purely an individual matter—a preconception." He spoke fast; he was uneasy under the cool scrutiny of her green eyes. And with a sharp attempt at self-control and reassurance he altered his voice. "After all, we're being very stupid!" he exclaimed. "We're worrying over something that doesn't exist."

Lillian was still lazily interested. To her own belief, she had seen Chilcote last on the night of her sister's reception. Then she had been too preoccupied to notice either his manner or his health, though superficially it had lingered in her mind that he had seemed unusually reliant, unusually well on that night. A remembrance of the impression came to her now as she studied his face, upon which imperceptibly and yet relentlessly his vice was setting its mark—in the dull restlessness of eye, the unhealthy sallowness of skin.

Some shred of her thought, some suggestion of the comparison running through her mind, must have shown in her face, for Chilcote altered his position with a touch of uneasiness. He glanced away across the long sweep of tan-covered drive stretching between the trees; then he glanced furtively back.

"By-the-way," he said, quickly, "you wanted me for something?" The memory of her earlier suggestion came as a sudden boon.

She lifted her muff again and smelled her roses thoughtfully. "Oh, it was nothing, really," she said. "You sarcastic people give very shrewd suggestions sometimes, and I've been rather wanting a suggestion on an—an adventure that I've had." She looked down at her flowers with a charmingly attentive air.

But Chilcote's restlessness had increased. Looking up, she suddenly caught the expression, and her own face changed.

"My dear Jack," she said, softly, "what a bore I am! Let's forget tedious things—and enjoy ourselves." She leaned towards him caressingly with an air of concern and reproach.

The action was not without effect. Her soothing voice, her smile, her almost affectionate gesture, each carried weight. With a swift return of assurance he responded to her tone.

"Right!" he said. "Right! We will enjoy ourselves!" He laughed quickly, and again with a conscious movement lifted his hand to his muffler.

"Then we'll postpone the advice?" Lillian laughed, too.

"Yes. Right! We'll postpone it." The word pleased him and he caught at it. "We won't bother about it now, but we won't shelve it altogether. We'll postpone it."

"Exactly." She settled herself more comfortably. "You'll dine with me one night—and we can talk it out then. I see so little of you nowadays," she added, in a lower voice.

"My dear girl, you're unfair!" Chilcote's spirits had risen; he spoke rapidly, almost pleasantly. "It isn't I who keep away—it's the stupid affairs of the world that keep me. I'd be with you every hour of the twelve if I had my way."

She looked up at the bare trees. Her expression was a delightful mixture of amusement, satisfaction, and scepticism. "Then you will dine?" she said at last.

"Certainly." His reaction to high spirits carried him forward.

"How nice! Shall we fix a day?"

"A day? Yes. Yes—if you like." He hesitated for an instant, then again the impulse of the previous moment dominated his other feeling. "Yes," he said, quickly. "Yes. After all, why not fix it now?" With a sudden inclination towards amiability he opened his overcoat, thrust his hand into an inner pocket, and drew out his engagement-book—the same long, narrow book fitted with two pencils that Loder had scanned so interestedly on his first morning at Grosvenor Square. He opened it, turning the pages rapidly. "What day shall it be? Thursday's full—and Friday—and Saturday. What a bore!" He still talked fast.

Lillian leaned across. "What a sweet book!" she said. "But why the blue crosses?" She touched one of the pages with her gloved finger.

Chilcote jerked the book, then laughed with a touch of embarrassment. "Oh, the crosses? Merely to remind me that certain 'appointments must be kept. You know my beastly memory! But what about the day? Shall we fix the day?" His voice was in control, but mentally her trivial question had disturbed and jarred him. "What day shall we say?" he repeated. "Monday in next week?"

Lillian glanced up with a faint exclamation of disappointment. "How horribly faraway!" She spoke with engaging petulance, and, leaning forward afresh, drew the book from Chilcote's hand. "What about to-morrow?" she exclaimed, turning back a page. "Why not to-morrow? I knew I saw a blank space."

"To-morrow! Oh, I—I—" He stopped.   i

"Jack!" Her voice dropped. It was true that she desired Chilcote's opinion on her adventure, for Chilcote's opinion on men and manners had a certain bitter shrewdness; but the exercise of her own power added a point to the desire. If the matter had ended with the gain or loss of a tete-a-tete with him, it is probable that, whatever its utility, she would not have pressed it, but the underlying motive was the stronger. Chilcote had been a satellite for years, and it was unpleasant that any satellite should drop away into space.

"Jack!" she said again, in a lower and still more effective tone; and, lifting her muff, she buried her face in her flowers. "I suppose I shall have to dine and go to a music-hall with Leonard—or stay at home by myself," she murmured, looking out across the trees.

Again Chilcote glanced over the long, tan-strewn ride. They had made the full circuit of the park.

"It's tiresome being by one's self," she murmured.

For a while he was irresponsive, then slowly his eyes returned to her face. He watched her for a second, and, leaning quickly towards her, he took his book and scribbled something in the vacant space.

She watched him interestedly; her face lighted up, and she laid aside her muff.

"Dear Jack!" she said. "How very sweet of you!"

Then, as he held the book towards her, her face fell. "Dine 33 Cadogan Gardens, 8 o'c. Talk with L.," she read. "Why, you've forgotten the essential thing!"

He looked up. "The essential thing?"

She smiled. "The blue cross," she said. "Isn't it worth even a little one?"

The tone was very soft. Chilcote yielded.

"You have the blue pencil," he said, in sudden response to her mood.

She glanced up in quiet pleasure at her Success, and, with a charming affectation of seriousness, marked the engagement with a big cross. At the same moment the car slackened speed, as the chauffeur waited for further orders.

Lillian shut the engagement-book and handed it back. "Where can I drop you?" she asked. "At the club?"

The question recalled him to a sense of present things. He thrust the book into his pocket and glanced about him.

They had paused by Hyde Park corner. The crowd of horses and carriages had thinned as the hour of lunch drew near, and the wide roadway of the park had an air of added space. The suggested loneliness affected him. The tall trees, still bereft of leaves, and the colossal gateway incomprehensively stirred the sense of mental panic that sometimes seized him in face of vastness of space or of architecture. In one moment, Lillian, the appointment he had just made, the manner of its making—all left him. The world was filled with his own personality, his own immediate inclinations.

"Don't bother about me!" he said, quickly. "I can get out here. You've been very good. It's been a delightful morning." With a hurried pressure of her fingers he rose and stepped from the car.

Reaching the ground, he paused for a moment and raised his hat; then, without a second glance, he turned and walked rapidly away.

Lillian sat watching him meditatively. She saw him pass through the gateway, saw him hail a hansom, then she remembered the waiting chauffeur.

XXI

On the same day that Chilcote had parted with Lillian—but at three o'clock in the afternoon—Loder, dressed in Chilcote's clothes and with Chilcote's heavy overcoat slung over his arm, walked from Fleet Street to Grosvenor Square. He walked steadily, neither slowly nor yet fast. The elation of his last journey over the same ground was tempered by feelings he could not satisfactorily bracket even to himself. There was less of vehement elation and more of matured determination in his gait and bearing than there had been on that night, though the incidents of which they were the outcome were very complex.

On reaching Chilcote's house he passed up-stairs; but, still following the routine of his previous return, he did not halt at Chilcote's door, but moved onward towards Eve's sitting-room and there paused.

In that pause his numberless irregular thoughts fused into one.

He had the same undefined sense of standing upon sacred ground that had touched him on the previous occasion, but the outcome of the sensation was different. This time he raised his hand almost immediately and tapped on the door.

He waited, but no voice responded to his knock. With a sense of disappointment he knocked again; then, pressing his determination still further, he turned the handle and entered the room.

No private room is without meaning—whether trivial or the reverse. In a room, perhaps more even than in speech, in look, or in work, does the impress of the individual make itself felt. There, on the wax of outer things, the inner self imprints its seal-enforces its fleeting claim to separate individuality. This thought, with its arresting interest, made Loder walk slowly, almost seriously, half-way across the room and then pause to study his surroundings.

The room was of medium size—not too large for comfort and not too small for ample space. At a first impression it struck him as unlike any anticipation of a woman's sanctum. The walls panelled in dark wood; the richly bound books; the beautifully designed bronze ornaments; even the flowers, deep crimson and violet-blue in tone, had an air of sombre harmony that was scarcely feminine. With a strangely pleasant impression he realized this, and, following his habitual impulse, moved slowly forward towards the fireplace and there paused, his elbow resting on the mantel-piece.

He had scarcely settled comfortably into his position, scarcely entered on his second and more comprehensive study of the place, than the arrangement of his mind was altered by the turning of the handle and the opening of the door.

The new-comer was Eve herself. She was dressed in outdoor clothes, and walked into the room quickly; then, as Loder had done, she too paused.

The gesture, so natural and spontaneous, had a peculiar attraction; as she glanced up at him, her face alight with inquiry, she seemed extraordinarily much the owner and designer of her surroundings. She was framed by them as naturally and effectively as her eyes and her face were framed by her black hair. For one moment he forgot that his presence demanded explanation; the next she had made explanation needless. She had been looking at him intently; now she came forward slowly.

"John?" she said, half in appeal, half in question.

He took a step towards her. "Look at me," he said, quietly and involuntarily. In the sharp desire to establish himself in her regard he forgot that her eyes had never left his face.

But the incongruity of the words did not strike her. "Oh!" she exclaimed, "I—I believe I *knew*, directly I saw you here." The quick ring of life vibrating in her tone surprised him. But he had other thoughts more urgent than surprise.

In the five days of banishment just lived through, the need for a readjustment of his position with regard to her had come to him forcibly. The memory of the night when weakness and he had been at perilously close quarters had returned to him persistently and uncomfortably, spoiling the remembrance of his triumph. It had been well enough to smother the thought of that night in days of work. But had the ignoring of it blotted out the weakness? Had it not rather thrown it into bolder relief? A man strong in his own strength does not turn his back upon temptation; he faces and quells it. In the solitary days in Clifford's Inn, in the solitary night-hours spent in tramping the city streets, this had been the conviction that had recurred again and again, this the problem to which, after much consideration, he had found a solution — satisfactory at least to himself. When next Chilcote called him—It was notable that he had used the word "when" and not "if." When next Chilcote called him he would make a new departure. He would no longer avoid Eve; he would successfully prove to himself that one interest and one alone filled his mind— the pursuance of Chilcote's political career. So does man satisfactorily convince himself against himself. He had this intention fully in mind as he came forward now.

"Well," he said, slowly, "has it been very hard to have faith —these last five days?" It was not precisely the tone he had meant to adopt; but one must begin.

Eve turned at his words. Her eyes were brimming with life, her cheeks still touched to a deep, soft color by the keenness of the wintry air.

"No," she answered, with a shy, responsive touch of confidence. "I seemed to keep on believing. You know converts make the best devotees." She laughed with slight embarrassment, and glanced up at him. Something in the blue of her eyes reminded him unexpectedly of spring skies—full of youth and promise.

He moved abruptly, and crossed the room towards the window. "Eve," he said, without looking round, "I want your help."

He heard the faint rustling of her dress as she turned towards him, and he knew that he had struck the right chord. All true women respond to an appeal for aid as steel answers to the magnet. He could feel her expectancy in the silence.

"You know—we all know—that the present moment is very vital. That it's impossible to deny the crisis in the air. Nobody feels it more than I do—nobody is more exorbitantly keen to have a share—a part, when the real fight comes—" He stopped; then he turned slowly and their eyes met. "If a man is to succeed in such a desire," he went on, deliberately, "he must exclude all others—he must have one purpose, one interest, one thought. He must forget that—"

Eve lifted her head quickly. "—that he has a wife," she finished, gently. "I think I understand."

There was no annoyance in her face or voice, no suggestion of selfishness or of hurt vanity. She had read his meaning with disconcerting clearness, and responded with disconcerting generosity. A sudden and very human dissatisfaction with his readjustment scheme fell upon Loder. Opposition is the whip to action; a too-ready acquiescence the slackened rein.

"Did I say that?" he asked, quickly. The tone was almost Chilcote's.

She glanced up; then a sudden, incomprehensible smile lighted up her face.

"You didn't say, but you thought," she answered, gravely. "Thoughts are the same as words to a woman. That's why we are so unreasonable." Again she smiled. Some idea, baffling and incomprehensible to Loder, was stirring in her mind.

Conscious of the impression, he moved still nearer. "You jump to conclusions," he said, abruptly. "What I meant to imply—"

"—was precisely what I've understood." Again she finished his sentence. Then she laughed softly. "How very wise, but how very, very foolish men are! You come to the conclusion that because a woman is—is interested in you she is going to hamper you in some direction, and after infinite pains you summon all your tact and you set about saving the situation."

There was interest, even a touch of amusement, in her tone, her eyes were still fixed upon his in an indefinable glance. "You think you are being very diplomatic," she went on, quietly, "but in reality you are being very transparent. The woman reads the whole of your meaning in your very first sentence—if she hasn't known it before you began to speak."

Again Loder made an interruption, but again she checked him. "No," she said, still smiling. "You should never attempt such a task. Shall I tell you why?"

He stood silent, puzzled and interested.

"Because," she said, quickly, "when a woman really is —interested, the man's career ranks infinitely higher in her eyes than any personal desire for power."

For a moment their eyes met, then abruptly Loder looked away. She had gauged his intentions incorrectly, yet with disconcerting insight. Again the suggestion of an unusual personality below the serenity of her manner recurred to his imagination.

With an impulse altogether foreign to him he lifted his head and again met her glance. Then at last he spoke, but only two words. "Forgive me!" he said, with simple, direct sincerity.

XXII

After his interview with Eve, Loder retired to the study and spent the remaining hours of the day and the whole span of the evening in work. At one o'clock, still feeling fresh in mind and body, he dismissed Greening and passed into Chilcote's bedroom. The interview with Eve, though widely different from the one he had anticipated, had left him stimulated and alert. In the hours that followed it there had been an added anxiety to put his mind into harness, an added gratification in finding it answer to the rein.

A pleasant sense of retrospection settled upon him as he slowly undressed; and a pleasant sense of interest touched him as, crossing to the dressing-table, he caught sight of Chilcote's engagement-book—taken with other things from the suit he had changed at dinner-time and carefully laid aside by Renwick.

He picked it up and slowly turned the pages. It always held the suggestion of a lottery—this dipping into another man's engagements and drawing a prize or a blank. It was a sensation that even custom had not dulled.

At first he turned the pages slowly, then by degrees his fingers quickened. Beyond the fact that this present evening was free, he knew nothing of his promised movements. The abruptness of Chilcote's arrival at Clifford's Inn in the afternoon had left no time for superfluous questions. He skimmed the writing with a touch of interested haste, then all at once he paused and smiled.

"Big enough for a tombstone!" he said below his breath as his eyes rested on a large blue cross. Then he smiled again and held the book to the light.

"Dine 33 Cadogan Gardens, 8 o'c. Talk with L," he read, still speaking softly to himself.

He stood for a moment pondering on the entry, then once more his glance reverted to the cross.

"Evidently meant it to be seen," he mused; "but why the deuce isn't he more explicit?" As he spoke, a look of comprehension suddenly crossed his face and the puzzled frown between his eyebrows cleared away.

With a feeling of satisfaction he remembered Lakely's frequent and pressing suggestion that he should dine with him at Cadogan Gardens and discuss the political outlook.

Lakely must have written during his absence, and Chilcote, having marked the engagement, felt no further responsibility. The invitation could scarcely have been verbal, as Chilcote, he knew, had lain very low in the five days of his return home.

So he argued, as he stood with the book still open in his hands, the blue cross staring imperatively from the white paper. And from the argument rose thoughts and suggestions that seethed in his mind long after the lights had been switched off, long after the fire had died down and he had been left wrapped in darkness in the great canopied bed.

And so it came about that he took his second false step. Once during the press of the next morning's work it crossed his mind to verify his convictions by a glance at the directory. But for once the strong wish that evolves a thought conquered his caution. His work was absorbing; the need of verification seemed very small. He let the suggestion pass.

At seven o'clock he dressed carefully. His mind was full of Lakely and of the possibilities the night might hold; for more than once before, the weight of the 'St. George's Gazette', with Lakely at its back, had turned the political scales. To be marked by him as a coming man was at any time a favorable portent; to be singled out by him at the present juncture was momentous. A thrill of expectancy, almost of excitement, passed through him as he surveyed his appearance preparatory to leaving the house.

Passing down-stairs, he moved at once to the hall door; but almost as his hand touched it he halted, attracted by a movement on the landing above him. Turning, he saw Eve.

She was standing quite still, looking down upon him as she had looked once before. As their eyes met, she changed her position hastily.

"You are going out?" she asked. And it struck Loder quickly that there was a suggestion, a shadow of disappointment in the tone of her voice. Moved by the impression, he responded with unusual promptness.

"Yes," he said. "I'm dining out—dining with Lakely."

She watched him intently while he spoke; then, as the meaning of his words reached her, her whole face brightened.

"With Mr. Lakely?" she said. "Oh, I'm glad—very glad. It is quite—quite another step." She smiled with a warm, impulsive touch of sympathy.

Loder, looking up at her, felt his senses stir. At sound of her words his secret craving for success quickened to stronger life. The man whose sole incentive lies within may go forward coldly and successfully; but the man who grasps a double inspiration, who, even unconsciously, is impelled by another force, has a stronger impetus for attack, a surer, more vital hewing power. Still watching her, he answered instinctively—

"Yes," he said, slowly, "a long step." And, with a smile of farewell, he turned, opened the door, and passed into the road.

The thrill of that one moment was still warm as he reached Cadogan Gardens and mounted the steps of No. 33—so vitally warm that he paused for an instant before pressing the electric bell. Then at last, dominated by anticipation, he turned and raised his hand.

The action was abrupt, and it was only as his fingers pressed the bell that a certain unexpectedness, a certain want of suitability in the aspect of the house, struck him. The door was white, the handle and knocker were of massive silver. The first seemed a disappointing index of Lakely's private taste, the second a ridiculous temptation to needy humanity. He looked again at the number of the house, but it stared back at him convincingly. Then the door opened.

So keen was his sense of unfitness that, still trying to fuse his impression of Lakely with the idea of silver door-fittings, he stepped into the hall without the usual preliminary question. Suddenly realizing the necessity, he turned to the servant; but the man forestalled him:

"Will you come to the white room, sir? And may I take your coat?"

The smooth certainty of the man's manner surprised him. It held another savor of disappointment—seeming as little in keeping with the keen, business-like Lakely as did the house. Still struggling with his impression, he allowed himself to be relieved of his hat and coat and in silence ushered up the shallow staircase.

As the last step was reached it came to him again to mention his host's name; but simultaneously with the suggestion the servant stepped forward with a quick, silent movement and threw open a door.

"Mr. Chilcote!" he announced, in a subdued, discreet voice.

Loder's first impression was of a room that seemed unusually luxurious, soft, and shadowed. Then all impression of inanimate things left him suddenly.

For the fraction of a second he stood in the door-way, while the room seemed emptied of everything, except a figure that rose slowly from a couch before the fire at sound of Chilcote's name; then, with a calmness that to himself seemed incredible, he moved forward into the room.

He might, of course, have beaten a retreat and obviated many things; but life is full of might-have-beens, and retreat never presents itself agreeably to a strong man. His impulse was to face the difficulty, and he acted on the impulse.

Lillian had risen slowly; and as he neared her she held out her hand.

"Jack!" she exclaimed, softly. "How sweet of you to remember!"

The voice and words came to him with great distinctness, and as they came one uncertainty passed forever from his mind —the question as to what relation she and Chilcote held to each other. With the realization came the thought of Eve, and in the midst of his own difficulty his face hardened.

Lillian ignored the coldness. Taking his hand, she smiled. "You're unusually punctual," she said. "But your hands are cold. Come closer to the fire."

Loder was not sensible that his hands were cold, but he suffered himself to be drawn forward.

One end of the couch was in firelight, the other in shadow. By a fortunate arrangement of chance Lillian selected the brighter end for herself and offered the other to her guest. With a quick sense of respite he accepted it. At least he could sit secure from detection while he temporized with fate.

For a moment they sat silent, then Lillian stirred. "Won't you smoke?" she asked.

Everything in the room seemed soft and enervating—the subdued glow of the fire, the smell of roses that hung about the air, and, last of all, Lillian's slow, soothing voice. With a sense of oppression he stiffened his shoulders and sat straighter in his place.

"No," he said, "I don't think I shall smoke."

She moved nearer to him. "Dear Jack," she said, pleadingly, "don't say you're in a bad mood. Don't say you want to postpone again." She looked up at him and laughed a little in mock consternation.

Loder was at a loss.

Another silence followed, while Lillian waited; then she frowned suddenly and rose from the couch. Like many indolent people, she possessed a touch of obstinacy; and now that her triumph over Chilcote was obtained, now that she had vindicated her right to command him, her original purpose came uppermost again. Cold or interested, indifferent or attentive, she intended to make use of him.

She moved to the fire and stood looking down into it.

"Jack," she began, gently, "a really amazing thing has happened to me. I do so want you to throw some light."

Loder said nothing.

There was a fresh pause while she softly smoothed the silk embroidery that edged her gown. Then once more she looked up at him.

"Did I ever tell you," she began, "that I was once in a railway accident on a funny little Italian railway, centuries before I met you?" She laughed softly; and with a pretty air of confidence turned from the fire and resumed her seat.

"Astrupp had caught a fever in Florence, and I was rushing away for fear of the infection, when our stupid little train ran off the rails near Pistoria and smashed itself up. Fortunately we were within half a mile of a village, so we weren't quite bereft. The village was impossibly like a toy village, and the accommodation what one would expect in a Noah's Ark, but it was all absolutely picturesque. I put up at the little inn with my maid and Ko Ko—Ko Ko was such a sweet dog—a white poodle. I was tremendously keen on poodles that year." She stopped and looked thoughtfully towards the fire.

"But to come to the point of the story, Jack, the toy village had a boy doll!" She laughed again. "He was an Englishman —and the first person to come to my rescue on the night of the smash-up. He was staying at the Noah's Ark inn; and after that first night I—he—we—Oh, Jack, haven't you any imagination?" Her voice sounded petulant and sharp. The man who is indifferent to the recital of an old love affair implies the worst kind of listener. "I believe you aren't interested," she added, in another and more reproachful tone.

He leaned forward. "You're wrong there," he said, slowly. "I'm deeply interested."

She glanced at him again. His tone reassured her, but his words left her uncertain; Chilcote was rarely emphatic. With a touch of hesitation she went on with her tale:

"As I told you, he was the first to find us—to find me, I should say, for my stupid maid was having hysterics farther up the line, and Ko Ko was lost. I remember the first thing I did was to send him in search of Ko Ko—"

Notwithstanding his position, Loder found occasion to smile. "Did he succeed?" he said, dryly.

"Succeed? Oh yes, he succeeded." She also smiled involuntarily. "Poor Ko Ko was stowed away under the luggage-van; and after quite a lot of trouble he pulled him out. When it was all done the dog was quite unhurt and livelier than ever, but the Englishman had his finger almost bitten through. Ko Ko was a dear, but his teeth and his temper were both very sharp!" She laughed once more in soft amusement.

Loder was silent for a second, then he too laughed—Chilcote's short, sarcastic laugh. "And you tied up the wound, I suppose?"

She glanced up, half displeased. "We were both staying at the little inn," she said, as though no further explanation could be needed. Then again her manner changed. She moved imperceptibly nearer and touched his right hand. His left, which was farther away from her, was well in the shadow of the cushions.

"Jack," she said, caressingly, "it isn't to tell you this stupid old story that I've brought you here; it's really to tell you a sort of sequel." She stroked his hand gently once or twice. "As I say, I met this man and we—we had an affair. You understand? Then we quarrelled—quarrelled quite badly —and I came away. I've remembered him rather longer than I remember most people—he was one of those dogged individuals who stick in one's mind. But he has stayed in mine for another reason—" Again she looked up. "He has stayed because you helped to keep him there. You know how I have sometimes put my hands over your mouth and told you that your eyes reminded me of some one else? Well, that some one else was my Englishman. But you mustn't be jealous; he was a horrid, obstinate person, and you—well, you know what I think of you—" She pressed his hand. "But to come to the end of the story, I never saw this man since that long-ago time, until—until the night of Blanche's party !" She spoke slowly, to give full effect to her words; then she waited for his surprise.

But the result was not what she expected. He said nothing; and, with an abrupt movement, he drew his hand from between hers.

"Aren't you surprised?" she asked at last, with a delicate note of reproof.

He started slightly, as if recalled to the necessity of the moment. "Surprised?" he said. "Why should I be surprised? One person more or less at a big party isn't astonishing. Besides, you expect a man to turn up sooner or later in his own country. Why should I be surprised?"

She lay back luxuriously. "Because, my dear boy," she said, softly, "it's a mystery! It's one of those fascinating mysteries that come once in a lifetime."

Loder made no movement. "You must explain," he said, very quietly.

Lillian smiled. "That's just what I want to do. When I was in my tent on the night of Blanche's party, a man came to be gazed for. He came just like anybody else, and laid his hands upon the table. He had strong, thin hands like—well, rather like yours But he wore two rings on the third finger of his left hand—a heavy signet-ring and a plain gold one."

Loder moved his hand imperceptibly till the cushion covered it. Lillian's words caused him no surprise, scarcely even any trepidation. He felt now that he had expected them, even waited for them, all along.

"I asked him to, take off his rings," she went on, "and just for a second he hesitated—I could feel him hesitate; then he seemed to make up his mind, for he drew them off. He drew them off, Jack, and guess what I saw! Do guess!"

For the first time Loder involuntarily drew back into his corner of the couch. "I never guess," he said, brusquely.

"Then I'll tell you. His hands were the hands of my Englishman! The rings covered the scar made by Ko Ko's teeth. I knew it instantly—the second my eyes rested on it. It was the same scar that I had bound up dozens of times—that I had seen healed before I left Santasalare."

"And you? What did you do?" Loder felt it singularly difficult and unpleasant to speak.

"Ah, that's the point. That's where I was stupid and made my mistake. I should have spoken to him on the moment, but I didn't. You know how one sometimes hesitates. Afterwards it was too late."

"But you saw him afterwards—in the rooms?" Loder spoke unwillingly.

"No, I didn't—that's the other point. I didn't see him in the rooms, and I haven't seen him since. Directly he was gone, I left the tent—I pretended to be hungry and bored; but, though I went through every room, he was nowhere to be found. Once—" she hesitated and laughed again—" once I thought I had found him, but it was only you—you, as you stood in that door-way with your mouth and chin hidden by Leonard Kaine's head. Wasn't it a quaint mistake?"

There was an uncertain pause. Then Loder, feeling the need of speech, broke the silence suddenly. "Where do I come in?" he asked abruptly. "What am I wanted for?"

"To help to throw light on the mystery! I've seen Blanche's list of people, and there wasn't a man I couldn't place—no outsider ever squeezes through Blanche's door. I have questioned Bobby Blessington, but he can't remember who came to the tent last. And Bobby was supposed to have kept count!" She spoke in deep scorn; but almost immediately the scorn faded and she smiled again. "Now that I've explain ed, Jack," she added, "what do you suggest?"

Then for the first time Loder knew what his presence in the room really meant; and at best the knowledge was disconcerting. It is not every day that a man is called upon to unearth himself.

"Suggest?" he repeated, blankly.

"Yes. I'd rather have your idea of the affair than anybody else's. You are so dear and sarcastic and keen that you can't help getting straight at the middle of a fact."

When Lillian wanted anything she could be very sweet. She suddenly dropped her half-petulant tone; she suddenly ceased to be a spoiled child. With a perfectly graceful movement she drew quite close to Loder and slid gently to her knees.

This is an attitude that few women can safely assume; it requires all the attributes of youth, suppleness, and a certain buoyant ease. But Lillian never acted without justification, and as she leaned towards Loder her face lifted, her slight figure and pale hair softened by the firelight, she made a picture that it would have been difficult to criticise.

But the person who should have appreciated it stared steadily beyond it to the fire. His mind was absorbed by one question —the question of how he might reasonably leave the house before discovery became assured.

Lillian, attentively watchful of him, saw the uneasy look, and her own face fell. But, as she looked, an inspiration came to her—a remembrance of many interviews with Chilcote smoothed and facilitated by the timely use of tobacco.

"Jack," she said, softly, "before you say another word I insist on your lighting a cigarette." She leaned forward. resting against his knee.

At her words Loder's eyes left the fire. His attention was suddenly needed for a new and more imminent difficulty. "Thanks!" he said, quickly. "I have no wish to smoke."

"It isn't a matter of what you wish but of what I say." She smiled. She knew that Chilcote with a cigarette between his lips was infinitely more tractable than Chilcote sitting idle, and she had no intention of ignoring the knowledge.

But Loder caught at her words. "Before you ordered me to smoke," he said, "you told me to give you some advice. Your first command must have prior claim." He grasped unhesitatingly at the less risky theme.

She looked up at him. "You're always nicer when you smoke," she persisted, caressingly. "Light a cigarette—and give me one."

Loder's mouth became set. "No," he said, "we'll stick to this advice business. It interests me."

"Yes—afterwards."

"No, now. You want to find out why this Englishman from Italy was at your sister's party, and why he disappeared?"

There are times when a malignant obstinacy seems to affect certain people. The only answer Lillian made was to pass her hand over Loder's waistcoat, and, feeling his cigarette-case, to draw it from the pocket.

He affected not to see it. "Do you think he recognized you in that tent?" he insisted, desperately.

She held out the case. "Here are your cigarettes. You know we're always more social when we smoke."

In the short interval while she looked up into his face several ideas passed through Loder's mind. He thought of standing up suddenly and so regaining his advantage; he wondered quickly whether one hand could possibly suffice for the taking out and lighting of two cigarettes. Then all need for speculation was pushed suddenly aside.

Lillian, looking into his face, saw his fresh look of disturbance, and from long experience again changed her tactics. Laying the cigarette-case on the couch, she put one hand on his shoulder, the other on his left arm. Hundreds of times this caressing touch had quieted Chilcote.

"Dear old boy!" she said, soothingly, her hand moving slowly down his arm.

In a flash of understanding the consequences of this position came to him. Action was imperative, at whatever risk. With an abrupt gesture he rose.

The movement was awkward. He got to his feet precipitately; Lillian drew back, surprised and startled, catching involuntarily at his left hand to steady her position.

Her fingers grasped at, then held his. He made no effort to release them. With a dogged acknowledgment, he admitted himself worsted.

How long she stayed immovable, holding his hand, neither of them knew. The process of a woman's instinct is so subtle, so obscure, that it would be futile to apply to it the commonplace test of time. She kept her hold tenaciously, as though his fingers possessed some peculiar virtue; then at last she spoke.

"Rings, Jack?" she said, very slowly. And under the two short words a whole world of incredulity and surmise made itself felt.

Loder laughed.

At the sound she dropped his hand and rose from her knees. What her suspicions, what her instincts were she could not have clearly defined, but her action was unhesitating. Without a moment's uncertainty she turned to the fireplace, pressed the electric button, and flooded the room with light.

There is no force so demoralizing as unexpected light. Loder took a step backward, his hand hanging unguarded by his side; and Lillian, stepping forward, caught it again before he could protest. Lifting it quickly, she looked scrutinizingly at the two rings.

All women jump to conclusions, and it is extraordinary how seldom they jump short. Seeing only what Lillian saw, knowing only what she knew, no man would have staked a definite opinion; but the other sex takes a different view. As she stood gazing at the rings her thoughts and her conclusions sped through her mind like arrows—all aimed and all tending towards one point. She remembered the day when she and Chilcote had talked of doubles, her scepticism and his vehement defence of the idea; his sudden interest in the book 'Other Men's Shoes', and his anathema against life and its irksome round of duties. She remembered her own first convinced recognition of the eyes that had looked at her in the doorway of her sister's house; and, last of all, she remembered Chilcote's unaccountable avoidance of the same subject of likenesses when she had mentioned it yesterday driving through the Park—and with it his unnecessarily curt repudiation of his former opinions. She reviewed each item, then she raised her head slowly and looked at Loder.

He was prepared for the glance and met it steadily.

In the long moment that her eyes searched his face it was she and not he who changed color. She was the first to speak. "You were the man whose hands I saw in the tent," she said. She made the statement in her usual soft tones, but a slight tremor of excitement underran her voice. Poodles, Persian kittens, even crystal gazing-balls, seemed very far away in face of this tangible, fabulous, present interest. "You are not Jack Chilcote," she said, very slowly. "You are wearing his clothes, and speaking in his voice but you are not Jack Chilcote." Her tone quickened with a touch of excitement. "You needn't keep silent and look at me," she said. "I know quite well what I am saying—though I don't understand it, though I have no real proof—" She paused, momentarily disconcerted by her companion's silent and steady gaze, and in the pause a curious and unexpected thing occurred.

Loder laughed suddenly—a full, confident, reassured laugh. All the web that the past half-hour had spun about him, all the intolerable sense of an impending crash, lifted suddenly. He saw his way clearly—and it was Lillian who had opened his eyes.

Still looking at her, he smiled—a smile of reliant determination, such as Chilcote had never worn in his life. And with a calm gesture he released his hand.

"The greatest charm of woman is her imagination," he said, quietly. "Without it there would be no color in life; we would come into and drop out of it with the same uninteresting tone of drab reality." He paused and smiled again.

At his smile, Lillian involuntarily drew back, the color deepening in her cheeks. "Why do you say that?" she asked.

He lifted his head. With each moment he felt more certain of himself. "Because that is my attitude," he said. "As a man I admire your imagination, but as a man I fail to follow your reasoning."

The words and the tone both stung her. "Do you realize the position?" she asked, sharply. "Do you realize that, whatever your plans are, I can spoil them?"

Loder still met her eyes. "I realize nothing of the sort," he said.

"Then you admit that you are not Jack Chilcote?"

"I neither deny nor admit. My identity is obvious. I can get twenty men to swear to it at any moment that you like. The fact that I haven't worn rings till now will scarcely interest them."

"But you do admit—to me, that you are not Jack?"

"I deny nothing—and admit nothing. I still offer my congratulations."

"Upon what?"

"The same possession—your imagination."

Lillian stamped her foot. Then, by a quick effort, she conquered her temper. "Prove me to be wrong!" she said, with a fresh touch of excitement. "Take off your rings and let me see your hand."

With a deliberate gesture Loder put his hand behind his back. "I never gratify childish curiosity," he said, with another smile.

Again a flash of temper crossed her eyes. "Are you sure," she said, "that it's quite wise to talk like that?"

Loder laughed again. "Is that a threat?"

"Perhaps."

"Then it's an empty one."

"Why?"

Before replying he waited a moment, looking down at her.

"I conclude," he began, quietly, "that your idea is to spread this wild, improbable story—to ask people to believe that John Chilcote, whom they see before them, is not John Chilcote, but somebody else. Now you'll find that a harder task than you imagine. This is a sceptical world, and people are absurdly fond of their own eyesight. We are all journalists nowadays—we all want facts. The first thing you will be asked for is your proof. And what does your proof consist of? The circumstance that John Chilcote, who has always despised jewelry, has lately taken to wearing rings! Your own statement, unattended by any witnesses, that with those rings off his finger bears a scar belonging to another man! No; on close examination I scarcely imagine that your case would hold." He stopped, fired by his own logic. The future might be Chilcote's but the present was his; and this present—with its immeasurable possibilities —had been rescued from catastrophe. "No," he said, again. "When you get your proof perhaps we'll have another talk; but till then—"

"Till then?" She looked up quickly; but almost at once her question died away.

The door had opened, and the servant who had admitted Loder stood in the opening.

"Dinner is served!" he announced, in his deferential voice.

XXIII

And Loder dined with Lillian Astrupp. We live in an age when society expects, even exacts, much. He dined, not through bravado and not through cowardice, but because it seemed the obvious, the only thing to do. To him a scene of any description was distasteful; to Lillian it was unknown. In her world people loved or hated, were spiteful or foolish, were even quixotic or dishonorable, but they seldom made scenes. Loder tacitly saw and tacitly accepted this.

Possibly they ate extremely little during the course of the dinner, and talked extraordinarily much on subjects that interested neither; but the main point at least was gained. They dined. The conventionalities were appeased; the silent, watchful servants who waited on them were given no food for comment. The fact that Loder left immediately after dinner, the fact that he paused on the door-step after the hall door had closed behind him, and drew a long, deep breath of relief, held only an individual significance and therefore did not count.

On reaching Chilcote's house he passed at once to the study and dismissed Greening for the night. But scarcely had he taken advantage of his solitude by settling into an arm-chair and lighting a cigar, than Renwick, displaying an unusual amount of haste and importance, entered the room carrying a letter.

Seeing Loder, he came forward at once. "Mr. Fraide's man brought this, sir," he explained. "He was most particular to give it into my hands—making sure 'twould reach you. He's waiting for an answer, sir."

Loder rose and took the letter, a quick thrill of speculation and interest springing across his mind. During his time of banishment he had followed the political situation with feverish attention, insupportably chafed by the desire to share in it, apprehensively chilled at the thought of Chilcote's possible behavior. He knew that in the comparatively short interval since Parliament had risen no act of aggression had marked the Russian occupation of Meshed, but he also knew that Fraide and his followers looked askance at that great power's amiable attitude, and at sight of his leader's message his intuition stirred.

Turning to the nearest lamp, he tore the envelope open and scanned the letter anxiously. It was written in Fraide's own clear, somewhat old-fashioned writing, and opened with a kindly rebuke for his desertion of him since the day of his speech; then immediately, and with characteristic clearness, it opened up the subject nearest the writer's mind.

Very slowly and attentively Loder read the letter; and with the extreme quiet that with him invariably covered emotion, he moved to the desk, wrote a note, and handed it to the waiting servant. As the man turned towards the door he called him.

"Renwick!" he said, sharply, "when you've given that letter to Mr. Fraide's servant, ask Mrs. Chilcote if she can spare me five minutes."

When Renwick had gone and closed the door behind him, Loder paced the room with feverish activity. In one moment the aspect of life had been changed. Five minutes since he had been glorying in the risk of a barely saved situation;

now that situation with its merely social complications had become a matter of small importance.

His long, striding steps had carried him to the fireplace, and his back was towards the door when at last the handle turned. He wheeled round to receive Eve's message; then a look of pleased surprise crossed his face. It was Eve herself who stood in the doorway.

Without hesitation his lips parted. "Eve," he said, abruptly, "I have had great news! Russia has shown her teeth at last. Two caravans belonging to a British trader were yesterday interfered with by a band of Cossacks. The affair occurred a couple of miles outside Meshed; the traders remonstrated, but the Russians made summary use of their advantage. Two Englishmen were wounded and one of them has since died. Fraide has only now received the news—which cannot be overrated. It gives the precise lever necessary for the big move at the reassembling." He spoke with great earnestness and unusual haste. As he finished he took a step forward. "But that's not all!" he added. "Fraide wants the great move set in motion by a great speech—and he has asked me to make it."

For a moment Eve waited. She looked at him in silence; and in that silence he read in her eyes the reflection of his own expression.

"And you?" she asked, in a suppressed voice. "What answer did you give?"

He watched her for an instant, taking a strange pleasure in her flushed face and brilliantly eager eyes; then the joy of conscious strength, the sense of opportunity regained, swept all other considerations out of sight.

"I accepted," he said, quickly. "Could any man who was merely human have done otherwise?"

That was Loder's attitude and action on the night of his jeopardy and his success, and the following day found his mood unchanged. He was one of those rare individuals who never give a promise overnight and regret it in the morning. He was slow to move, but when he did the movement brushed all obstacles aside. In the first days of his usurpation he had gone cautiously, half fascinated, half distrustful; then the reality, the extraordinary tangibility of the position had gripped him when, matching himself for the first time with men of his own caliber, he had learned his real weight on the day of his protest against the Easter adjournment. With that knowledge had been born the dominant factor in his whole scheme—the overwhelming, insistent desire to manifest his power. That desire that is the salvation or the ruin of every strong man who has once realized his strength. Supremacy was the note to which his ambition reached. To trample out Chilcote's footmarks with his own had been his tacit instinct from the first; now it rose paramount. It was the whole theory of creation—the survival of the fittest—the deep, egotistical certainty that he was the better man.

And it was with this conviction that he entered on the vital period of his dual career. The imminent crisis, and his own share in it, absorbed him absolutely.

In the weeks that followed his answer to Fraide's proposal he gave himself ungrudgingly to his work. He wrote, read, and planned with tireless energy; he frequently forgot to eat, and slept only through sheer exhaustion; in the fullest sense of the word he lived for the culminating hour that was to bring him failure or success.

He seldom left Grosvenor Square in the days that followed, except to confer with his party. All his interest, all his relaxation even, lay in his work and what pertained to it. His strength was like a solid wall, his intelligence was sharp and keen as steel. The moment was his; and by sheer mastery of will he put other considerations out of sight. He forgot Chilcote and forgot Lillian—not because they escaped his memory, but because he chose to shut them from it.

Of Eve he saw but little in this time of high pressure. When a man touches the core of his capacities, puts his best into the work that in his eyes stands paramount, there is little place for, and no need of, woman. She comes before— and after. She inspires, compensates, or completes; but the achievement, the creation, is man's alone. And all true women understand and yield to this unspoken precept.

Eve watched the progress of his labor, and in the depth of her own heart the watching came nearer to actual living than any activity she had known. She was an on-looker—but an on-looker who stood, as it were, on the steps of the arena, who, by a single forward movement, could feel the sand under her feet, the breath of the battle on her face; and in this knowledge she rested satisfied.

There were hours when Loder seemed scarcely conscious of her existence; but on those occasions she smiled in her serene way—and went on waiting. She knew that each day, before the afternoon had passed, he would come into her sitting-room, his face thoughtful, his hands full of books or papers, and, dropping into one of the comfortable, studious chairs, would ask laconically for tea. This was her moment of triumph and recompense—for the very unconsciousness of his coming doubled its value. He would sit for half an hour with a preoccupied glance, or with keen, alert eyes fixed on the fire, while his ideas sorted themselves and fell into line. Sometimes he was silent for the whole half-hour, sometimes he commented to himself as he scanned his notes; but on other and rarer occasions he talked, speaking his thoughts and his theories aloud, with the enjoyment of a man who knows himself fully in his depth, while Eve sipped her tea or stitched peacefully at a strip of embroidery.

On these occasions she made a perfect listener. Here and there she encouraged him with an intelligent remark, but she never interrupted. She knew when to be silent and when to speak; when to merge her own individuality and when to make it felt. In these days of stress and preparation he came to her unconsciously for rest; he treated her as he might have treated a younger brother—relying on her discretion, turning to her as by right for sympathy, comprehension, and friendship. Sometimes, as they sat silent in the richly colored, homelike room, Eve would pause over her embroidery and let her thoughts spin momentarily forward—spin towards the point where, the brunt of his ordeal passed, he must, of necessity, seek something beyond mere rest. But there her thoughts would inevitably break off and the blood flame quickly into her cheek.

Meanwhile Loder worked persistently. With each day that brought the crisis of Fraide's scheme nearer, his activity increased—and with it an intensifying of the nervous strain. For if he had his hours of exaltation, he also had his hours of black apprehension. It is all very well to exorcise a ghost by sheer strength of will, but one has also to eliminate the idea that gave it existence. Lillian Astrupp, with her unattested evidence and her ephemeral interest, gave him no real uneasiness; but Chilcote and Chilcote's possible summons were matters of graver consideration; and there were times when they loomed very dark and sinister: What if at the very moment of fulfilment—? But invariably he snapped the thread of the supposition and turned with fiercer ardor to his work of preparation.

And so the last morning of his probation dawned, and for the first time he breathed freely.

He rose early on the day that was to witness his great effort and dressed slowly. It was a splendid morning; the spirit of the spring seemed embodied in the air, in the pale-blue sky, in the shafts of cool sunshine that danced from the mirror to the dressing-table, from the dressing-table to the pictures on the walls of Chilcote's vast room. Inconsequently with its dancing rose a memory of the distant past—a memory of long-forgotten days when, as a child, he had been bidden to watch the same sun perform the same fantastic evolutions. The sight and the thought stirred him curiously with an unlooked-for sense of youth. He drew himself together with an added touch of decision as he passed out into the corridor; and as he walked down-stairs he whistled a bar or two of an inspiriting tune.

In the morning-room Eve was already waiting. She looked up, colored, and smiled as he entered. Her face looked very fresh and young and she wore a gown of the same pale blue that she had worn on his first coming.

She looked up from an open letter as he came into the room, and the sun that fell through the window caught her in a shaft of light, intensifying her blue eyes, her blue gown, and the bunch of violets fastened in her belt. To Loder, still under the influence of early memories, she seemed the embodiment of some youthful ideal—something lost, sought for, and found again. Realization of his feeling for her almost came to him as be stood there looking at her. It hovered about him; it tipped him, as it were, with its wings; then it rose again and soared away. Men like him—men keen to grasp an opening where their careers are concerned, and tenacious to hold it when once grasped—are frequently the last to look into their own hearts. He glanced at Eve, he acknowledged the stir of his feeling, but he made no attempt to define its cause. He could no more have given reason for his sensations than he could have told the precise date upon which, coming down-stairs at eight o'clock, he had first found her waiting breakfast for him. The time when all such incidents were to stand out, each to a nicety in its appointed place, had not yet arrived. For the moment his youth had returned to him; he possessed the knowledge of work done, the sense of present companionship in a world of agreeable things; above all, the steady, quiet conviction of his own capacity. All these things came to him in the moment of his entering the room, greeting Eve, and passing to the breakfast-table; then, while his eyes still rested contentedly on the pleasant array of china and silver, while his senses were still alive to the fresh, earthly scent of Eve's violets, the blow so long dreaded—so slow in coming fell with accumulated force.

XXIV

The letter through which the blow fell was not voluminous. It was written on cheap paper in a disguised hand, and the contents covered only half a page. Loder read it slowly, mentally articulating every word; then he laid it down, and as he did so he caught Eve's eyes raised in concern. Again he saw something of his own feelings reflected in her face, and the shock braced him; he picked up the letter, tearing it into strips.

"I must go out," he said, slowly. "I must go now—at once." His voice was hard.

Eve's surprised, concerned eyes still searched his. "Now —at once?" she repeated. "Now—without breakfast?"

"I'm not hungry." He rose from his seat, and, carrying the slips of paper across the room, dropped them into the fire. He did it, not so much from caution, as from an imperative wish to do something, to move, if only across the room.

Eve's glance followed him. "Is it bad news?" she asked, anxiously. It was unlike her to be insistent, but she was moved to the impulse by the peculiarity of the moment.

"No," he said shortly. "It's—business. This was written yesterday; I should have got it last night."

Her eyes widened. "But nobody does business at eight in the morning—" she began, in astonishment; then she suddenly broke off.

Without apology or farewell, Loder had left the fireplace and walked out of the room.

He passed through the hall hurriedly, picking up a hat as he went; and, reaching the pavement outside, he went straight forward until Grosvenor Square was left behind; then he ran. At the risk of reputation, at the loss of dignity, he ran until he saw a cab. Hailing it, he sprang inside, and, as the cabman whipped up and the horse responded to the call, he realized for the first time the full significance of what had occurred.

Realization, like the need for action, came to him slowly, but when it came it was with terrible lucidity. He did not swear as he leaned back in his seat, mechanically watching the stream of men on their way to business, the belated cars of green produce blocking the way between the Strand and Covent Garden. He had no use for oaths; his feelings lay deeper than mere words. But his mouth was sternly set and his eyes looked cold.

Outside the Law Courts he dismissed his cab and walked forward to Clifford's Inn. As he passed through the familiar entrance a chill fell on him. In the clear, early light it seemed more than ever a place of dead hopes, dead enterprises, dead ambitions. In the onward march of life it had been forgotten. The very air had a breath of unfulfilment.

He crossed the court rapidly, but his mouth set itself afresh as he passed through the door-way of his own house and crossed the bare hall.

As he mounted the well-known stairs, he received his first indication of life in the appearance of a cat from the second-floor rooms. At sight of him, the animal came forward, rubbed demonstratively against his legs, and with affectionate persistence followed him up-stairs.

Outside his door he paused. On the ground stood the usual morning can of milk—evidence that Chilcote was not yet awake or that, like himself, he had no appetite for breakfast. He smiled ironically as the idea struck him, but it was a smile that stiffened rather than relaxed his lips. Then he drew out the duplicate key he always carried, and, inserting it quietly, opened the door. A close, unpleasant smell greeted him as he entered the small passage that divided the bed and sitting rooms—a smell of whiskey mingling with the odor of stale smoke. With a quick gesture he pushed open the bedroom door; then on the threshold he paused, a look of contempt and repulsion passing over his face.

In his first glance he scarcely grasped the details of the scene, for the half-drawn curtains kept the light dim, but as his eyes grew accustomed to the obscurity he gathered their significance.

The room had a sleepless, jaded air—the room that under his own occupation had shown a rigid, almost monastic severity. The plain dressing-table was littered with cigarette ends and marked with black and tawny patches where the tobacco had been left to burn itself out. On one corner of the table a carafe of water and a whiskey-decanter rested one against the other, as if for support, and at the other end an overturned tumbler lay in a pool of liquid. The whole effect was sickly and nauseating. His glance turned involuntarily to the bed, and there halted.

On the hard, narrow mattress, from which the sheets and blankets had fallen in a disordered heap, lay Chilcote. He was fully dressed in a shabby tweed suit of Loder's; his collar was open, his lip and chin unshaven; one hand was limply grasping the pillow, while the other hung out over the side of the bed. His face, pale, almost earthy in hue, might have been a mask, save for the slight convulsive spasms that crossed it from time to time, and corresponded with the faint, shivering starts that passed at intervals over his whole body. To complete his repellent appearance, a lock of hair had fallen loose and lay black and damp across his forehead.

Loder stood for a space shocked and spellbound by the sight. Even in the ghastly disarray, the likeness—the extraordinary, sinister likeness that had become the pivot upon which he himself revolved—struck him like a blow. The man who lay there was himself-bound to him by some subtle, inexplicable tie of similarity. As the idea touched him he turned aside and stepped quickly to the dressing-table; there, with unnecessary energy, he flung back the curtains and threw the window wide; then again he turned towards the bed. He had one dominant impulse—to waken Chilcote, to be free of the repulsive, inert presence that chilled him with so personal a horror. Leaning over the bed, he caught the shoulder nearest to him and shook it. It was not the moment for niceties, and his gesture was rough.

At his first touch Chilcote made no response—his brain, dulled by indulgence in his vice, had become a laggard in conveying sensations; but at last, as the pressure on his shoulder increased, his nervous system seemed suddenly to jar into consciousness. A long shudder shook him; he half lifted himself and then dropped back upon the pillow.

"Oh!" he exclaimed, in a trembling breath. "Oh!" The sound seemed drawn from him by compulsion.

Its uncanny tone chilled Loder anew. "Wake up, man!" he said, suddenly. "Wake up! It's I—Loder."

Again the other shuddered; then he turned quickly and nervously. "Loder?" he said, doubtfully. "Loder?" Then his face changed. "Good God!" he exclaimed, "what a relief!"

The words were so intense, so spontaneous and unexpected, that Loder took a step back.

Chilcote laughed discordantly, and lifted a shaky hand to protect his eyes from the light.

"It's—it's all right, Loder! It's all right! It's only that I—that I had a beastly dream. But, for Heaven's sake, shut that window!" He shivered involuntarily and pushed the lock of damp hair from his forehead with a weak touch of his old irritability.

In silence Loder moved back to the window and shut it. He was affected more than he would own even to himself by the obvious change in Chilcote. He had seen him moody, restless, nervously excited; but never before had he seen him entirely demoralized. With a dull feeling of impotence and disgust he stood by the closed window, looking unseeingly at the roofs of the opposite houses.

But Chilcote had followed his movements restlessly; and now, as he watched him, a flicker of excitement crossed his face. "God! Loder," he said, again, "'twas a relief to see you! I dreamed I was in hell—a horrible hell, worse than the one they preach about."

He laughed to reassure himself, but his voice shook pitiably.

Loder, who had come to fight, stood silent and inert.

"It was horrible—beastly," Chilcote went on. "There was no fire and brimstone, but there was something worse. It was a great ironic scheme of punishment by which every man was chained to his own vice—by which the thing he had gone to pieces over, instead of being denied him, was made compulsory. You can't imagine it." He shivered nervously and his voice rose. "Fancy being satiated beyond the limit of satiety, being driven and dogged by the thing you had run after all your life!"

He paused excitedly, and in the pause Loder found resolution. He shut his ears to the panic in Chilcote's voice, he closed his consciousness to the sight of his shaken face. With a surge of determination he rallied his theories. After all, he had himself and his own interests to claim his thought. At the moment Chilcote was a wreck, with no desire towards rehabilitation; but there was no guarantee that in an hour or two he might not have regained control over himself, and with it the inclination that had prompted his letter of the day before. No; he had himself to look to. The survival of the fittest was the true, the only principle. Chilcote had had intellect, education, opportunity, and Chilcote had deliberately cast them aside. Fortifying himself in the knowledge, he turned from the window and moved slowly back to the bed.

"Look here," he began, "you wrote for me last night—" His voice was hard; he had come to fight.

Chilcote glanced up quickly. His mouth was drawn and there was a new anxiety in his eyes. "Loder!" he exclaimed, quickly. "Loder, come here! Come nearer!"

Reluctantly Loder obeyed. Stepping closer to the side of the bed, he bent down.

The other put up his hand and caught his arm. His fingers trembled and jerked. "I say, Loder," he said, suddenly, "I —I've had such a beastly night—my nerves, you know—"

With a quick, involuntary disgust Loder drew back. "Don't you think we might shove that aside?" he asked.

But Chilcote's gaze had wandered from his face and strayed to the dressing-table; there it moved feverishly from one object to another.

"Loder," he exclaimed, "do you see—can you see if there's a tube of tabloids on the mantel-shelf—or on the dressing-table?" He lifted himself nervously on his elbow and his eyes wandered uneasily about the room. "I—I had a beastly night; my nerves are horribly jarred; and I thought—I think—" He stopped.

With his increasing consciousness his nervous collapse became more marked. At the first moment of waking, the relief of an unexpected presence had surmounted everything else; but now, as one by one his faculties stirred, his wretched condition became patent. With a new sense of perturbation Loder made his next attack.

"Chilcote—" he began, sternly.

But again Chilcote caught his arm, plucking at the coat-sleeve. "Where is it?" he said. "Where is the tube of tabloids—the sedative? I'm—I'm obliged to take something when my nerves go wrong—" In his weakness and nervous tremor he forgot that Loder was the sharer of his secret. Even in his extremity his fear of detection clung to him limply—the lies that had become second nature slipped from him without effort. Then suddenly a fresh panic seized him; his fingers tightened spasmodically, his eyes ceased to rove about the room and settled on his companion's face. "Can you see it, Loder?" he cried. "I can't—the light's in my eyes. Can you see it? Can you see the tube?" He lifted himself higher, an agony of apprehension in his face.

Loder pushed him back upon the pillow. He was striving hard to keep his own mind cool, to steer his own course straight through the chaos that confronted him. "Chilcote," he began once more, "you sent for me last night, and I came the first thing this morning to tell you—" But there he stopped.

With an excitement that lent him strength, Chilcote pushed aside his hands. "God!" he said, suddenly, "suppose 'twas lost—suppose 'twas gone!" The imaginary possibility gripped him. He sat up, his face livid, drops of perspiration showing on his forehead, his whole shattered system trembling before his thought.

At the sight, Loder set his lips. "The tube is on the mantel-shelf," he said, in a cold, abrupt voice.

A groan of relief fell from Chilcote and the muscles of his face relaxed. For a, moment he lay back with closed eyes; then the desire that tortured him stirred afresh. He lifted his eyelids and looked at his companion. "Hand it to me," he said, quickly. "Give it to me. Give it to me, Loder. Quick as you can! There's a glass on the table and some whiskey and water. The tabloids dissolve, you know—" In his new excitement he held out his hand.

But Loder stayed motionless. He had come to fight, to demand, to plead—if need be—for the one hour for which he had lived; the hour that was to satisfy all labor, all endeavor, all ambition. With dogged persistence he made one more essay.

"Chilcote, you wrote last night to recall me—" Once again he paused, checked by a new interruption. Sitting up again, Chilcote struck out suddenly with his left hand in a rush of his old irritability.

"Damn you!" he cried, suddenly, "what are you talking about? Look at me! Get me the stuff. I tell you it's imperative." In his excitement his breath failed and he coughed. At the effort his whole frame was shaken.

Loder walked to the dressing-table, then back to the bed. A deep agitation was at work in his mind.

Again Chilcote's lips parted. "Loder," he said, faintly —"Loder, I must—I must have it. It's imperative." Once more he attempted to lift himself, but the effort was futile.

Again Loder turned away.

"Loder—for God's sake—"

With a fierce gesture the other turned on him. "Good heavens! man—" he began. Then unaccountably his voice changed. The suggestion that had been hovering in his mind took sudden and definite shape. "All right!" he said, in a lower voice. "All right! Stay as you are."

He crossed to where the empty tumbler stood and hastily mixed the whiskey and water; then crossing to the mantel-piece where lay the small glass tube containing the tightly packed tabloids, he paused and glanced once more towards the bed. "How many?" he said, laconically.

Chilcote lifted his head. His face was pitiably drawn, but the feverish brightness in his eyes had increased. "Five," he said, sharply. "Five. Do you hear, Loder?"

"Five?" Involuntarily Loder lowered the hand that held the tube. From previous confidences of Chilcote's he knew the amount of morphia contained in each tabloid, and realized that five tabloids, if not an absolutely dangerous, was at least an excessive dose, even for one accustomed to the drug. For a moment his resolution failed; then the dominant-note of his nature—the unconscious, fundamental egotism on which his character was based—asserted itself beyond denial. It might be reprehensible, it might even be criminal to accede to such a request, made by a man in such a condition of body and mind; yet the laws of the universe demanded self-assertion—prompted every human mind to desire, to grasp, and to hold. With a perception swifter than any he had experienced, he realized the certain respite to be gained by yielding to his impulse. He looked at Chilcote with his haggard, anxious expression, his eager, restless eyes; and a vision of himself followed sharp upon his glance. A vision of the untiring labor of the past ten days, of the slowly kindling ambition, of the supremacy all but gained. Then, as the picture completed itself, he lifted his hand with an abrupt movement and dropped the five tabloids one after another into the glass.

XXV

Having taken a definite step in any direction, it was not in Loder's nature to wish it retraced. His face was set, but set with determination, when he closed the outer door of his own rooms and passed quietly down the stairs and out into the silent court. The thought of Chilcote, his pitiable condition, his sordid environments, were things that required a firm will to drive into the background of the imagination; but a whole inferno of such visions would not have daunted Loder on that morning as, unobserved by any eyes, he left the little court-yard with its grass, its trees, its pavement—all so distastefully familiar—and passed down the Strand towards life and action.

As he walked, his steps increased in speed and vigor. Now, for the first time, he fully appreciated the great mental strain that he had undergone in the past ten days—the unnatural tension; the suppressed, but perpetual, sense of impending recall; the consequently high pressure at which work, and even existence, had been carried on. And as he hurried forward the natural reaction to this state of things came upon him in a flood of security and confidence—a strong realization of the temporary respite and freedom for which no price would have seemed too high. The moment for which he had unconsciously lived ever since Chilcote's first memorable proposition was within reach at last—safeguarded by his own action.

The walk from Clifford's Inn to Grosvenor Square was long enough to dispel any excitement that his interview had aroused; and long before the well-known house came into view he felt sufficiently braced mentally and physically to seek Eve in the morning-room—where he instinctively felt she would still be waiting for him.

Thus he encountered and overpassed the obstacle that had so nearly threatened ruin; and, with the singleness of purpose that always distinguished him, he was able, once having passed it, to dismiss it altogether from his mind. From the moment of his return to Chilcote's house no misgiving as to his own action, no shadow of doubt, rose to trouble his mind. His feelings on the matter were quite simple. He had inordinately desired a certain opportunity; one factor had arisen to debar that opportunity, and he, claiming the right of strength, had set the barrier aside. In the simplicity of the reasoning lay its power to convince; and were a tonic needed to brace him for his task, he was provided with one in the masterful sense of a difficulty set at nought. For the man who has fought and conquered one obstacle feels strong to vanquish a score.

It was on this day, at the reassembling of Parliament, that Fraide's great blow was to be struck. In the ten days since the affair of the caravans had been reported from Persia public feeling had run high, and it was upon the pivot of this incident that Loder's attack was to turn; for, as Lakely was fond of remarking, "In the scales of public opinion, one dead Englishman has more weight than the whole Eastern Question!" It had been arranged that, following the customary procedure, Loder was to rise after questions at the morning sitting and ask leave to move the adjournment of the House on a definite matter of urgent public importance; upon which—leave having been granted by the rising of forty members in his support —the way was to lie open for his definite attack at the evening sitting. And it was with a mind attuned to this plan of action that he retired to the study immediately he had breakfasted, and settled to a final revision of his speech before an early party conference should compel him to leave the house. But here again circumstances were destined to change his programme. Scarcely had he sorted his notes and drawn his chair to Chilcote's desk than Renwick entered the room with the same air of important haste that he had shown on a previous occasion.

"A letter from Mr. Fraide, sir. But there's no answer," he said, with unusual brevity.

Loder waited till he had left the room, then he tore the letter open. He read:

"MY DEAR CHILCOTE,—Lakely is the recipient of special and very vital news from Meshed—unofficial, but none the less alarming. Acts of Russian aggression towards British traders are reported to be rapidly increasing, and it is stated that the authority of the Consulate is treated with contempt. Pending a possible confirmation of this, I would suggest that you keep an open mind on the subject of to-night's speech. By adopting an anticipatory—even an unprepared—attitude you may find your hand materially strengthened. I shall put my opinions before you more explicitly when we meet.

"Yours faithfully, HERBERT FRAIDE."

The letter, worded with Fraide's usual restraint, made a strong impression on its recipient. The thought that his speech might not only express opinions already tacitly held, but voice a situation of intense and national importance, struck him with full force. For many minutes after he had grasped the meaning of Fraide's message he sat neglectful of his notes, his elbows resting on the desk, his face between his hands, stirred by the suggestion that here might lie a greater opportunity than any he had anticipated.

Still moved by this new suggestion, he attended the party conclave that Fraide had convened, and afterwards lunched with and accompanied his leader to the House. They spoke very little as they drove to Westminster, for each was engrossed by his own thoughts. Only once did Fraide allude to the incident that was paramount in both their minds. Then, turning to Loder with a smile of encouragement, he had laid his fingers for an instant on his arm.

"Chilcote," he had said, "when the time comes, remember you have all my confidence."

Looking back upon that day, Loder often wondered at the calmness with which he bore the uncertainty. To sit apparently unmoved, and wait without emotion for news that might change the whole tenor of one's action, would have tried the stoicism of the most experienced; to the novice it was wellnigh unendurable. And it was under these conditions, and fighting against these odds, that he sat through the long afternoon in Chilcote's place, obeying the dictates of his chief. But if the day was fraught with difficulties for him, it was fraught with dulness and disappointment for others; for the undercurrent of interest that had stirred at the Easter adjournment, and risen with added force on this first day of the new session, was gradually but surely threatened with extinction, as hour after hour passed, bringing no suggestion of the battle that had on every side been tacitly expected. Slowly and unmistakably speculation and dissatisfaction crept into the atmosphere of the House, as moment succeeded moment, and the Opposition made no sign. Was Fraide shirking the attack? Or was he playing a waiting game? Again and again the question arose, filling the air with a passing flicker of interest; but each time it sprang up only to die down again, as the ordinary business of the day dragged itself out.

Gradually, as the afternoon wore on, daylight began to fade. Loder, sitting rigidly in Chilcote's place, watched with suppressed inquiry the faces of the men who entered through the constantly swinging doors; but not one face, so eagerly scanned, carried the message for which he waited. Monotonously and mechanically the time passed. The Government, adopting a neutral attitude, carefully skirted all dangerous subjects; while the Opposition, acting under Fraide's suggestion, assisted rather than hindered the programme of postponement. For the moment the, eagerly anticipated reassembling threatened dismal failure; and it was with a universal movement of weariness and relief that at last the House rose to dine.

But there are no possibilities so elastic as those of politics. At half-past seven the House rose in a spirit of boredom and disappointment; and at eight o'clock the lobbies, the dining-room, the entire space of the vast building, was stirred into activity by the arrival of a single telegraphic message.

The new development for which Fraide had waited came indeed, but it came with a force he had little anticipated. With a thrill of awe and consternation men heard and repeated the astounding news that—while personally exercising his authority on behalf of British traders—Sir William Brice-Field, Consul-General at Meshed, had been fired at by a Russian officer and instantly killed.

The interval immediately following the receipt of this news was too confused for detailed remembrance. Two ideas made themselves slowly felt—a deep horror that such an event could obtrude itself upon our high civilization, and a strong personal dismay that so honored, distinguished, and esteemed a representative as Sir William Brice-Field could have been allowed to meet death in so terrible a manner.

It was in the consciousness of this feeling—the consciousness that, in his own person, he might voice, not only the feelings of his party, but those of the whole country—that Loder rose an hour later to make his long-delayed attack.

He stood silent for a moment, as he had done on an earlier occasion; but this time his motive was different. Roused beyond any feeling of self-consciousness, he waited as by right for the full attention of the House; then quietly, but with self-possessed firmness, he moved the motion for adjournment.

Like a match to a train of powder, the words set flame to the excitement that had smouldered for weeks; and in an atmosphere of stirring activity, a scene of such tense and vital concentration as the House has rarely witnessed, he found inspiration for his great achievement.

To give Loder's speech in mere words would be little short of futile. The gift of oratory is too illusive, too much a matter of eye and voice and individuality, to allow of cold reproduction. To those who heard him speak on that night of April 18th the speech will require no recalling; and to those who did not hear him there would be no substitute in bare reproduction.

In the moment of action it mattered nothing to him that his previous preparations were to a great extent rendered useless by this news that had come with such paralyzing effect. In the sweeping consciousness of his own ability, he found added joy in the freedom it opened up. He ceased to consider that by fate he was a Conservative, bound by traditional conventionalities: in that great moment he knew himself sufficiently a man to exercise whatever individuality instinct prompted. He forgot the didactic methods by which he had proposed to show knowledge of his subject—both as a past and a future factor in European politics. With his own strong appreciation of present things, he saw and grasped the vast present interest lying beneath his hand.

For fifty minutes he held the interest of the House, speaking insistently, fearlessly, commandingly on the immediate need of action. He unhesitatingly pointed out that the news which had just reached England was not so much an appalling fact as a sinister warning to those in whose keeping lay the safety of the country's interests. Lastly, with a fine touch of eloquence, he paid tribute to the steadfast fidelity of such men as Sir William Brice-Field, who, whatever political complications arise at home, pursue their duty unswervingly on the outposts of the empire.

At his last words there was silence—the silence that marks a genuine effect—then all at once, with vehement, impressive force, the storm of enthusiasm broke its bounds.

It was one of those stupendous bursts of feeling that no etiquette, no decorum is powerful enough to quell. As he resumed his seat, very pale, but exalted as men are exalted only once or twice in a lifetime, it rose about him—clamorous, spontaneous, undeniable. Near at hand were the faces of his party, excited and triumphant; across the house were the faces of Sefborough and his Ministry, uncomfortable and disturbed.

The tumult swelled, then fell away; and in the partial lull that followed Fraide leaned over the back of his seat. His quiet, dignified expression was unaltered, but his eyes were intensely bright.

"Chilcote," he whispered, "I don't congratulate you—or myself. I congratulate the country on possessing a great man!"

The remaining features of the debate followed quickly one upon the other; the electric atmosphere of the House possessed a strong incentive power. Immediately Loder's ovation had subsided, the Under-Secretary for Foreign Affairs rose and in a careful and non-incriminating reply defended the attitude of the Government.

Next came Fraide, who, in one of his rare and polished speeches, touched with much feeling upon his personal grief at the news reported from Persia, and made emphatic indorsement of Loder's words.

Following Fraide came one or two dissentient Liberals, and then Sefborough himself closed the debate. His speech was masterly and fluent; but though any disquietude he may have felt was well disguised under a tone of reassuring ease, the attempt to rehabilitate his position—already weakened in more than one direction—was a task beyond his strength.

Amid extraordinary excitement the division followed—and with it a Government defeat.

It was not until half an hour after the votes had, been taken that Loder, freed at last from persistent congratulations, found opportunity to look for Eve. In accordance with a promise made that morning, he was to find her waiting outside the Ladies' Gallery at the close of the debate.

Disengaging himself from the group of men who had surrounded and followed him down the lobby, he discarded the lift and ran up the narrow staircase. Reaching the landing, he went forward hurriedly; then with a certain abrupt movement he paused. In the doorway leading to the gallery Eve was waiting for him. The place was not brightly lighted, and she was standing in the shadow; but it needed only a glance to assure his recognition. He could almost have seen in the dark that night, so vivid were his perceptions. He took a step towards her, then again he stopped. In a second glance he realized that her eyes were bright with tears; and it was with the strangest sensation he had ever experienced that the knowledge flashed upon him. Here, also, he had struck the same note —the long-coveted note of supremacy. It had rung out full and clear as he stood in Chilcote's place dominating the House; it had besieged him clamorously as he passed along the lobbies amid a sea of friendly hands and voices; now in the quiet of the deserted gallery it came home to him with deeper meaning from the eyes of Chilcote's wife.

Without a thought he put out his hands and caught hers.

"I couldn't get away," he said. "I'm afraid I'm very late."

With a smile that scattered her tears Eve looked up. "Are you?" she said, laughing a little. "I don't know what the time is. I scarcely know whether it's night or day."

Still holding one of her hands, he drew her down the stairs; but as they reached the last step she released her fingers.

"In the carriage!" she said, with another little laugh of nervous happiness.

At the foot of the stairs they were surrounded. Men whose faces Loder barely knew crowded about him. The intoxication of excitement was still in the air—the instinct that a new force had made itself felt, a new epoch been entered upon, stirred prophetically in every mind.

Passing through the enthusiastic concourse of men, they came unexpectedly upon Fraide and Lady Sarah surrounded by a group of friends. The old statesman came forward instantly, and, taking Loder's arm, walked with him to Chilcote's waiting brougham. He said little as they slowly made their way to the carriage, but the pressure of his fingers was tense and an unwonted color showed in his face. When Eve and Loder had taken their seats he stepped to the edge of the curb. They were alone for the moment, and, leaning close to the carriage, he put his hand through the open window. In silence he took Eve's fingers and held them in a long, affectionate pressure; then he released them and took Loder's hand.

"Good-night, Chilcote," he said. "You have proved yourself worthy of her. Good-night." He turned quickly and rejoined his waiting friends. In another second the horses had wheeled round, and Eve and Loder were carried swiftly forward into the darkness.

In the great moments of man's life woman comes before—and after. Some shadow of this truth was in, Eve's mind as she lay back in her seat with closed eyes, and parted lips. It seemed that life came to her now for the first time— came in the glad, proud, satisfying tide of things accomplished. This was her hour: and the recognition of it brought the blood to her face in a sudden, happy rush. There had been no need to precipitate its coming; it had been ordained from the first. Whether she desired it or no, whether she strove to draw it nearer or strove to ward it off, its coming had been inevitable. She opened her eyes suddenly and looked out into the darkness—the darkness throbbing with multitudes of lives, all awaiting, all desiring fulfilment. She was no longer lonely, no longer aloof; she was kin with all this pitiful, admirable, sinning, loving humanity. Again tears of pride and happiness filled her eyes. Then suddenly the thing she had waited for came to pass.

Loder leaned close to her. She was conscious of his nearer presence, of his strong, masterful personality. With a thrill that caught her breath, she felt his arm. about her shoulder and heard the sound of his voice.

"Eve," he said,—"I love you. Do you understand I love you." And drawing her close to him he bent and kissed her.

With Loder, to do was to do fully. When he gave, he gave generously; when he swept aside a barrier he left no stone standing. He had been slow to recognize his capacities —slower still to recognize his feelings. But now that the knowledge came he received it openly. In this matter of newly comprehended love he gave no thought to either past or future. That they loved and were alone was all he knew or questioned. She was as much Eve—the one woman—as though they were together in the primeval garden; and in that spirit he claimed her.

He neither spoke nor behaved extravagantly in that great moment of comprehension. He acted quietly, with the completeness of purpose that he gave to everything. He had found a new capacity within himself, and he was strong enough to dread no weakness in displaying it.

Holding her close to him, he repeated his declaration again and again, as though repetition ratified it. He found no need to question her feeling for him— he had divined it in a flash of inspiration as she stood waiting in the doorway of the gallery; but his own surrender was a different matter.

As the carriage passed round the corner of Whitehall and dipped into the traffic of Piccadilly he bent down again until her soft hair brushed his face; and the warm personal contact, the slight, fresh smell of violets so suggestive of her presence, stirred' him afresh.

"Eve," he said, vehemently, "do you understand? Do you know that I have loved you always—from the very first?" As he said it he bent still nearer, kissing her lips, her forehead, her hair.

At the same moment the horses slackened speed and then stopped, arrested by one of the temporary blocks that so often occur in the traffic of Piccadilly Circus.

Loder, preoccupied with his own feelings, scarcely noticed the halt, but Eve drew away from him laughing.

"You mustn't!" she said, softly. "Look!"

The carriage had stopped beside one of the small islands that intersect the place; a group of pedestrians were crowded upon it, under the light of the electric lamp—wayfarers who, like themselves, were awaiting a passage. Loder took a cursory glance at them, then turned back to Eve.

"What are they, after all, but men and women?" he said. "They'd understand—every one of them." He laughed in his turn; nevertheless he withdrew his arm. Her feminine thought for conventionalities appealed to him. It was an acknowledgment of dependency.

For a while they sat silent, the light of the street lamp flickering through the glass of the window, the hum of voices and traffic coming to them in a continuous rise and fall of sound. At first the position was interesting; but, as the seconds followed each other, it gradually became irksome. Loder, watching the varying expressions of Eve's face, grew impatient of the delay, grew suddenly eager to be alone again in the fragrant darkness.

Impelled by the desire, he leaned forward and opened the window.

"Let's find the meaning of this," he said. "Is there nobody to regulate the traffic?" As he spoke he half rose and leaned out of the window. There was a touch of imperious annoyance in his manner. Fresh from the realization of power, there was something irksome in this commonplace check to his desires.

"Isn't it possible to get out of this?" Eve heard him call to the coachman. Then she heard no more.

He had leaned out of the carriage with the intention of looking onward towards the cause of the delay; instead, by that magnetic attraction that undoubtedly exists, he looked directly in front of him at the group of people waiting on the little island—at one man who leaned against the lamp-post in an attitude of apathy—a man with a pallid, unshaven face and lustreless eyes, who wore a cap drawn low over his forehead.

He looked at this man, and the man saw and returned his glance. For a space that seemed interminable they held each other's eyes; then very slowly Loder drew back into the carriage.

As he dropped into his seat, Eve glanced at him anxiously.

"John," she said, "has anything happened? You look ill."

He turned to her and tried to smile.

"It's nothing," he said. "Nothing to worry about." He spoke quickly, but his voice had suddenly become flat. All the command, all the domination had dropped away from it.

Eve bent close to him, her face lighting up with anxious tenderness. "It was the excitement," she said, "the strain of tonight."

He looked at her; but he made no attempt to press the fingers that clasped his own.

"Yes," he said, slowly. "Yes. It was the excitement of to-night—and the reaction."

XXVI

The next morning at eight o'clock, and again without breakfast, Loder covered the distance between Grosvenor Square and Clifford's Inn. He left Chilcote's house hastily—with a haste that only an urgent motive could have driven him to adopt. His steps were quick and uneven as he traversed the intervening streets; his shoulders lacked their decisive pose, and his pale face was marked with shadows beneath the eyes —shadows that bore witness to the sleepless night spent in pacing Chilcote's vast and lonely room. By the curious effect of circumstances the likeness between the two men had never been more significantly marked than on that morning of April 19th, when Loder walked along the pavements crowded with early workers and brisk with insistent news-venders already alive to the value of last night's political crisis.

The irony of this last element in the day's concerns came to him fully when one newsboy, more energetic than his fellows, thrust a paper in front of him.

"Sensation in the 'Ouse, sir! Speech by Mr. Chilcote! Government defeat!"

For a moment Loder stopped and his face reddened. The tide of emotions still ran strong. His hand went instinctively to his pocket; then his lips set. He shook his head and walked on.

With the same hard expression about his mouth, he turned into Clifford's Inn, passed through his own doorway, and mounted the stairs.

This time there was no milk-can on the threshold of his rooms and the door yielded to his pressure without the need of a key. With a strange sensation of reluctance he walked into the narrow passage and paused, uncertain which room to enter first. As he stood hesitating a voice from the sitting-room settled the question.

"Who's there?" it called, irritably. "What do you want?"

Without further ceremony the intruder pushed the door open and entered the room. As he did so he drew a quick breath —whether of disappointment or relief it was impossible to say. Whether he had hoped for or dreaded it, Chilcote was conscious.

As Loder entered he was sitting by the cheerless grate, the ashes of yesterday's fire showing charred and dreary where the sun touched them. His back was to the light, and about his shoulders was an old plaid rug. Behind him on the table stood a cup, a teapot, and the can of milk; farther off a kettle was set to boil upon a tiny spirit-stove.

In all strong situations we are more or less commonplace. Loder's first remark as he glanced round the disordered room seemed strangely inefficient.

"Where's Robins?" he asked, in a brusque voice. His mind teemed with big considerations, yet this was his first involuntary question.

Chilcote had started at the entrance of his visitor; now he sat staring at him, his hands holding the arms of his chair.

"Where's Robins?" Loder asked again.

"I don't know. She—I—We didn't hit it off. She's gone —went yesterday." He shivered and drew the rug about him.

"Chilcote—" Loder began, sternly; then he paused. There was something in the other's look and attitude that arrested him. A change of expression passed over his own face; he turned about with an abrupt gesture, pulled off his coat and threw it on a chair; then crossing deliberately to the fireplace, he began to rake the ashes from the grate.

Within a few minutes he had a fire crackling where the bed of dead cinders had been, and, having finished the task, he rose slowly from his knees, wiped his hands, and crossed to the table. On the small spirit-stove the kettle had boiled and the cover was lifting and falling with a tinkling sound. Blowing out the flame, Loder picked up the teapot, and with hands that were evidently accustomed to the task set about making the tea.

During the whole operation he never spoke, though all the while he was fully conscious of Chilcote's puzzled gaze. The tea ready, he poured it into the cup and carried it across the room.

"Drink this!" he said, laconically. "The fire will be up presently."

Chilcote extended a cold and shaky hand. "You see—" he began.

But Loder checked him almost savagely. "I do—as well as though I had followed you from Piccadilly last night! You've been hanging about, God knows where, till the small hours of the morning; then you've come back—slunk back, starving for your damned poison and shivering with cold. You've settled the first part of the business, but the cold has still to be reckoned with. Drink the tea. I've something to say to you." He mastered his vehemence, and, walking to the window, stood looking down into the court. His eyes were blank, his face hard; his ears heard nothing but the faint sound of Chilcote's swallowing, the click of the cup against his teeth.

For a time that seemed interminable he stood motionless; then, when he judged the tea finished, he turned slowly. Chilcote had drawn closer to the fire. He was obviously braced by the warmth; and the apathy that hung about him was to some extent dispelled. Still moving slowly, Loder went towards him, and, relieving him of the empty cup, stood looking down at him.

"Chilcote," he said, very quietly, "I've come to fell you that the thing must end."

After he spoke there was a prolonged pause; then, as if shaken with sudden consciousness, Chilcote rose. The rug dropped from one shoulder and hung down ludicrously; his hand caught the back of the chair for support; his unshaven face looked absurd and repulsive in its sudden expression of scared inquiry. Loder involuntarily turned away.

"I mean it," he said, slowly. "It's over; we've come to the end."

"But why?" Chilcote articulated, blankly. "Why? Why?" In his confusion he could think of no better word.

"Because I throw it up. My side of the bargain's off!"

Again Chilcote's lips parted stammeringly. The apathy caused by physical exhaustion and his recently administered drug was passing from him; the hopelessly shattered condition of mind and body was showing through it like a skeleton through a thin covering of flesh.

"But why?" he said again. "Why?"

Still Loder avoided the frightened surprise of his, eyes. "Because I withdraw," he answered, doggedly.

Then suddenly Chilcote's tongue was loosened. "Loder," he cried, excitedly, "you can't do it! God! man, you can't do it!" To reassure himself he laughed—a painfully thin echo of his old, sarcastic laugh. "If it's a matter of greater opportunity—" he began, "of more money—"

But Loder turned upon him.

"Be quiet!" he said, so menacingly that the other stopped. Then by an effort he conquered himself, "It's not a matter of money, Chilcote," he said, quietly; "it's a matter of necessity." He brought the word out with difficulty.

Chilcote glanced up. "Necessity?" he repeated. "How? Why?"

The reiteration roused Loder. "Because there was a great scene in the House last night," he began, hurriedly; "because when you go back you'll find that Sefborough has smashed up over the assassination of Sir William Brice-Field at Meshed, and that you have made your mark in a big speech; and because —" Abruptly he stopped. The thing he had come to say—the thing he had meant to say—would not be said. Either his tongue or his resolution failed him, and for the instant he stood as silent and almost as ill at ease as his companion. Then all at once inspiration came to him, in the suggestion of a wellnigh forgotten argument by which he might influence Chilcote and save his own self-respect. "It's all over, Chilcote," he said, more quietly; "it has run itself out." And in a dozen sentences he sketched the story of Lillian Astrupp—her past relations with himself, her present suspicions. It was not what he had meant to say; it was not what he had come to say; but it served the purpose—it saved him humiliation.

Chilcote listened to the last word; then, as the other finished, he dropped nervously back into his chair. "Good heavens! man," he said, "why didn't you tell me—why didn't you warn me, instead of filling my mind with your political position? Your political position!" He laughed unsteadily. The long spells of indulgence that had weakened his already maimed faculties showed in the laugh, in the sudden breaking of his voice. "You must do something, Loder!" he added, nervously, checking his amusement; "you must do something!"

Loder looked down at him. "No," he said, decisively. "It's your turn now. It's you who've got to do something."

Chilcote's face turned a shade grayer. "I can't," he said, below his breath.

"Can't? Oh yes, you can. We can all do—anything. It's not too late; there's just sufficient time. Chilcote," he added, suddenly, "don't you see that the thing has been madness all along—has been like playing with the most infernal explosives? You may thank whatever you have faith in that nobody has been smashed up! You are going back. Do you understand me? You are going back— now, to-day, before it's too late." There was a great change in Loder; his strong, imperturbable face was stirred; he was moved in both voice and manner. Time after time he repeated his injunction—reasoning, expostulating, insisting. It almost seemed that he fought some strenuous invisible force rather than the shattered man before him.

Chilcote moved nervously in his seat. It was the first real clash of personalities. He felt it—recognized it by instinct. The sense of domination had fallen on him; he knew himself impotent in the other's hands. Whatever he might attempt in moments of solitude, he possessed no voice in presence of this invincible second self. For a while he struggled—he did not fight, he struggled to resist—then, lifting his eyes, he met Loder's. "And what will you do?" he said, weakly.

Loder returned his questioning gaze; but almost immediately he turned aside. "I?" he said. "Oh, I shall leave London."

XXVII

But Loder did not leave London. And the hour of two on the day following his dismissal of Chilcote found him again in his sitting-room.

He sat at the centre-table surrounded by a cloud of smoke; a pipe was between his lips and the morning's newspapers lay in a heap beside his elbow. To the student of humanity his attitude was intensely interesting. It was the attitude of a man trammelled by the knowledge of his strength. Before him, as he sat smoking, stretched a future of absolute nothingness; and towards this blank future one portion of his consciousness —a struggling and as yet scarcely sentient portion—pushed him inevitably; while another—a vigorous, persistent, human portion—cried to him to pause. So actual, so clamorous was this silent mental combat that had raged unceasingly since the moment of his renunciation that at last in physical response to it he pushed back his chair.

"It's too late!" he said, aloud. "I'm a fool. It's too late!"

Then abruptly, astonishingly, as though in direct response to his spoken thought, the door opened and Chilcote walked into the room.

Slowly Loder rose and stared at him. The feeling he acknowledged to himself was anger; but below the anger a very different sensation ran riotously strong.

And it was in time to this second feeling, this sudden, lawless joy, that his pulses beat as he turned a cold face on the intruder.

"Well?" he said, sternly.

But Chilcote was impervious to sternness. He was mentally shaken and distressed, though outwardly irreproachable, even to the violets in the lapel of his coat—the violets that for a week past had been brought each morning to the door of Loder's rooms by Eve's maid. For one second, as Loder's eyes' rested on the flowers, a sting of ungovernable jealousy shot through him; then as suddenly it died away, superseded by another feeling—a feeling of new, spontaneous joy. Worn by Chilcote or by himself, the flowers were a symbol!

"Well?" he said again, in a gentler voice.

Chilcote had walked to the table and laid down his hat. His face was white and the muscles of his lips twitched nervously as he drew off his gloves.

"Thank Heaven, you're here!" he said, shortly. "Give me something to drink."

In silence Loder brought out the whiskey and set it on the table; then instinctively he turned aside. As plainly as though he saw the action, he mentally figured Chilcote's furtive glance, the furtive movement of his fingers to his waistcoat-pocket, the hasty dropping of the tabloids into the glass. For an instant the sense of his tacit connivance came to him sharply; the next, he flung it from him. The human, inner voice was whispering its old watchword. The strong man has no time to waste over his weaker brother!

When he heard Chilcote lay down his tumbler he looked back again. "Well, what is it?" he said. "What have you come for?" He strove resolutely to keep his voice severe, but, try as he might, he could not quite subdue the eager force that lay behind his words. Once again, as on the night of their second interchange, life had become a phoenix, rising to fresh existence even while he sifted its ashes. "Well?" he said, once again.

Chilcote had set down his glass. He was nervously passing his handkerchief across his lips. There was something in the gesture that attracted Loder. Looking at him more attentively, he saw what his own feelings and the other's conventional dress had blinded him to—the almost piteous panic and excitement in his visitor's eyes.

"Something's gone wrong!" he said, with abrupt intuition.

Chilcote started. "Yes—no—that is, yes," he stammered.

Loder moved round the table. "Something's gone wrong," he repeated. "And you've come to tell me."

The tone unnerved Chilcote; he suddenly dropped into a chair. "It—it wasn't my fault," he began. "I—I have had a horrible time!"

Loder's lips tightened. "Yes," he said, "yes—I understand."

The other glanced up with a gleam of his old suspicion "'Twas all my nerves, Loder—"

"Of course. Yes, of course." Loder's interruption was curt.

Chilcote eyed him doubtfully. Then recollection took the place of doubt, and a change passed over his expression. "It wasn't my fault," he began, hastily. "On my soul, it wasn't! It was Crapham's beastly fault for showing her into the morning-room—"

Loder kept silent. His curiosity had flared into sudden life at the other's words, but he feared to break the shattered train of thought even by a word.

In the silence Chilcote moved uneasily. "You see," he went on, at last, "when I was here with you I—I felt strong. I —I—" He stopped.

"Yes, yes. When you were here with me you felt strong."

"Yes, that's it. While I was here, I felt I could do the thing. But when I went home—when I went up to my rooms—" Again he paused, passing his handkerchief across his forehead.

"When you went up to your rooms?" Loder strove hard to keep his control.

"To my room—? Oh, I—I forget about that. I forget about the night" He hesitated confusedly. "All I remember is the coming down to breakfast next morning—this morning—at twelve o'clock—"

Loder turned to the table and poured himself out some whiskey. "Yes," he acquiesced, in a very quiet voice.

At the word Chilcote rose from his seat. His disquietude was very evident. "Oh, there was breakfast on the table when I came down-stairs—breakfast with flowers and a horrible, dazzling glare of sun. It was then, Loder, as I stood and looked into the room, that the impossibility of it all came to me—that I knew I couldn't stand it—couldn't go on."

Loder swallowed his whiskey slowly. His sense of overpowering curiosity held him very still; but he made no effort to prompt his companion.

Again Chilcote shifted his position agitatedly. "It, had to be done," he said, disjointedly. "I had to do it—then and there. The things were on the bureau—the pens and ink and telegraph forms. They tempted me."

Loder laid down his glass suddenly. An exclamation rose to his lips, but he checked it.

At the slight sound of the tumbler touching the table Chilcote turned; but there was no expression on the other's face to affright him.

"They tempted me," he repeated, hastily. "They seemed like magnets—they seemed to draw me towards them. I sat at the bureau staring at them for a long time; then a terrible compulsion seized me—something you could never understand —and I caught up the nearest pen and wrote just what was in my mind. It wasn't a telegram, properly speaking—it was more a letter. I wanted you back and I had to make myself plain. The writing of the message seemed to steady me; the mere forming of the words quieted my mind. I was almost cool when I got up from the bureau and pressed the bell—"

"The bell?"

"Yes. I rang for a servant. I had to send the wire myself, so I had to get a cab." His voice rose to irritability. "I pressed the bell several times; but the thing had gone wrong —'twouldn't work. At last I gave it up and went into the corridor to call some one."

"Well?" In the intense suspense of the moment the word escaped Loder.

"Oh, I went out of the room; but there at the door, before I could call anybody, I knocked up against that idiot Greening. He was looking for me—for you, rather—about some beastly Wark affair. I tried to explain that I wasn't in a state for business; I tried to shake him off, but he was worse than Blessington. At last, to be rid of the fellow, I went with him to the study—"

"But the telegram?" Loder began; then again he checked himself. "Yes—yes—I understand," he added, quietly.

"I'm getting to the telegram! I wish you wouldn't jar me with sudden questions. I wasn't in the study more than a minute —more than five or six minutes—" His voice became confused; the strain of the connected recital was telling upon him. With nervous haste he made a rush for the end of his story. "I wasn't more than seven or eight minutes in the study; then, as I came downstairs, Crapham met me in the hall. He told me that Lillian Astrupp had called and wished to see me. And that he had shown her into the morningroom—"

"The morning-room?" Loder suddenly stepped back from the table. "The morning-room? With your telegram lying on the bureau?"

His sudden speech and movement startled Chilcote. The blood rushed to his face, then died out, leaving it ashen. "Don't do that, Loder!" he cried. "I—I can't bear it!"

With an immense effort Loder controlled himself. "Sorry!" he said. "Go on!"

"I'm going on! I tell you I'm going on. I got a horrid shock when Chapham told me. Your story came clattering through my mind. I knew Lillian had come to see you—I knew there was going to be a scene—"

"But the, telegram? The telegram?"

Chilcote paid no heed to the interruption. He was following his own train of ideas. "I knew she had come to see you—I knew there was going to be a scene. When I got to the morning-room my hand was shaking so that I could scarcely turn the handle; then, as the door opened, I could have cried out with relief. Eve was there as well!"

"Eve?"

"Yes. I don't think I was ever so glad to see her in my life." He laughed almost hysterically. "I was quite civil to her, and she was—quite sweet to me—" Again he laughed.

Loder's lips tightened.

"You see, it saved the situation. Even if Lillian wanted to be nasty, she couldn't, while Eve was there. We talked for about ten minutes. We were quite an amiable trio. Then Lillian told me why she'd called. She wanted me to make a fourth in a theatre party at the 'Arcadian' to-night, and I —I was so pleased and so relieved that I said yes!" He paused and laughed again unsteadily.

In his tense anxiety, Loder ground his heel into the floor. "Go on!" he said, fiercely. "Go on!"

"Don't!" Chilcote exclaimed. "I'm going on—I'm going on." He passed his handkerchief across his lips. "We talked for ten minutes or so, and then Lillian left. I went with her to the hall door, but Chapham was there too—so I was still safe. She laughed and chatted and seemed in high spirits as we crossed the hall, and she was still smiling as she waved to me from her motor. But then, Loder— then, as I stood in the hall, it all came to me suddenly. I remembered that Lillian must have been alone in the morning-room before Eve found her! I remembered the telegram! I ran back to the room, meaning to question Eve as to how long Lillian had been alone, but she had left the room. I ran to the bureau —but the telegram wasn't there!"

"Gone?"

"Yes, gone. That's why I've come straight here."

For a moment they confronted each other. Then, moved by a sudden impulse, Loder pushed Chilcote aside and crossed the room. An instant later the opening and shutting of doors, the hasty pulling out of drawers and moving of boxes, came from the bedroom.

Chilcote, shaken and nervous, stood for a minute where his companion had left him; at last, impelled by curiosity, he too crossed the narrow passage and entered the second room.

The full light streamed in through the open window; the keen spring air blew freshly across the house-tops; and on the window-sill a band of grimy, joyous sparrows twittered and preened themselves. In the middle of the room stood Loder. His coat was off, and round him on chairs and floor lay an array of waistcoats, gloves, and ties.

For a space Chilcote stood in the doorway staring at him; then his lips parted and he took a step forward. "Loder—" he said, anxiously. "Loder, what are you going to do?"

Loder turned. His shoulders were stiff, his face alight with energy. "I'm going back," he said, "to unravel the tangle you have made."

XXVIII

Loder's plan of action was arrived at before he reached Trafalgar Square. The facts of the case were simple. Chilcote had left an incriminating telegram on the bureau in the morning-room at Grosvenor Square; by an unlucky chance Lillian Astrupp had been shown up into that room, where she had remained alone until the moment that Eve, either by request or by accident, had found her there. The facts resolved themselves into one question. What use had Lillian made of those solitary moments? Without deviation, Loder's mind turned towards one answer. Lillian was not the woman to lose an opportunity, whether the space at her command were long or short. True, Eve too had been alone in the room, while Chilcote had accompanied Lillian to the door; but of this he made small account. Eve had been there, but Lillian had been there first. Judging by precedent, by personal character, by all human probability, it was not to be supposed that anything would have been left for the second comer.

So convinced was he that, reaching Trafalgar Square, he stopped and hailed a hansom.

"Cadogan Gardens!" he called. "No. 33."

The moments seemed very few before the cab drew up beside the curb and he caught his second glimpse of the enamelled door with its silver fittings. The white and silver gleamed in the sunshine; banks of cream colored hyacinths clustered on the window-sills, filling the clear air with a warm and fragrant scent. With that strange sensation of having lived through the scene before, Loder left the cab and walked up the steps. Instantly he pressed the bell the door was opened by Lillian's discreet, deferential man-servant.

"Is Lady Astrupp at home?" he asked.

The man looked thoughtful. "Her ladyship lunched at home, sir—" he began, cautiously.

But Loder interrupted him. "Ask her to see me," he said, laconically.

The servant expressed no surprise. His only comment was to throw the door wide.

"If you'll wait in the white room, sir," he said, "I'll inform her ladyship." Chilcote was evidently a frequent and a favored visitor.

In this manner Loder for the second time entered the house so unfamiliar— and yet so familiar in all that it suggested. Entering the drawing-room, he had leisure to look about him. It was a beautiful room, large and lofty; luxury was evident on every hand, but it was not the luxury that palls or offends. Each object was graceful, and possessed its own intrinsic value. The atmosphere was too effeminate to appeal to him, but he acknowledged the taste and artistic delicacy it conveyed. Almost at the moment of acknowledgment the door opened to admit Lillian.

She wore the same gown of pale-colored cloth, warmed and softened by rich furs, that she had worn on the day she and Chilcote had driven in the park.

She was drawing on her gloves as she came into the room; and pausing near the door, she looked across at Loder and, laughed in her slow, amused way.

"I thought it would be you," she said, enigmatically.

Loder came forward. "You expected me?" he said, guardedly. A sudden conviction filled him that it was not the evidence of her eyes, but something at once subtler and more definite, that prompted her recognition of him.

She smiled. "Why should I expect you? On the contrary, I'm waiting to know why you're here?"

He was silent for an instant; then he answered in her own light tone. "As far as that goes," he said, "let's make it my duty call-having dined with you. I'm an old-fashioned person."

For a full second she surveyed him amusedly; then at last she spoke. "My dear Jack"—she laid particular stress on the name—" I never imagined you punctilious. I should have thought bohemian would have been more the word."

Loder felt disconcerted and annoyed. Either, like himself, she was fishing for information, or she was deliberately playing with him. In his perplexity he glanced across the room towards the fireplace.

Lillian saw the look. "Won't you sit down?" she said, indicating the couch. "I promise not to make you smoke. I sha'n't even ask you to take off your gloves!"

Loder made no movement. His mind was unpleasantly upset. It was nearly a fortnight since he had seen Lillian, and in the interval her attitude had changed, and the change puzzled him. It might mean the philosophy of a woman who, knowing herself without adequate weapons, withdraws from a combat that has proved fruitless; or it might imply the merely catlike desire to toy with a certainty. He looked quickly at the delicate face, the green eyes somewhat obliquely set, the unreliable mouth; and instantly he inclined to the latter theory. The conviction that she possessed the telegram filled him suddenly, and with it came the desire to put his belief to the test—to know beyond question whether her smiling unconcern meant malice or mere entertainment.

"When you first came into the room," he said, quietly, "you said 'I thought it would be you.' Why did you say that?"

Again she smiled—the smile that might be malicious or might be merely amused. "Oh," she answered at last, "I only meant that though I had been told Jack Chilcote wanted me, it wasn't Jack Chilcote I expected to see!"

After her statement there was a pause. Loder's position was difficult. Instinctively convinced that, strong in the possession of her proof, she was enjoying his tantalized discomfort, he yet craved the actual evidence that should set his suspicions to rest. Acting upon the desire, he made a new beginning.

"Do you know why I came?" he asked.

Lillian looked up innocently. "It's so hard to be certain of anything in this world," she said. "But one is always at liberty to guess."

Again he was perplexed. Her attitude was not quite the attitude of one who controls the game, and yet—He looked at her with a puzzled scrutiny. Women for him had always spelled the incomprehensible; he was at his best, his strongest, his surest in the presence of men. Feeling his disadvantage, yet determined to gain his end, he made a last attempt.

"How did you amuse yourself at Grosvenor Square this morning before Eve came to you?" he asked. The effort was awkwardly blunt, but it was direct.

Lillian was buttoning her glove. She did not raise her head as he spoke, but her fingers paused in their task. For a second she remained motionless, then she looked up slowly.

"Oh," she said, sweetly, "so I was right in my guess? You did come to find out whether I sat in the morning-room with my hands in my lap—or wandered about in search of entertainment?"

Loder colored with annoyance and apprehension. Every look, every tone of Lillian's was distasteful to him. No microscope could have revealed her more fully to him than did his own eyesight. But it was not the moment for personal antipathies; there were other interests than his own at stake. With new resolution he returned her glance.

"Then I must still ask my first question, why did you say, 'I thought it would be you?'" His gaze was direct—so direct that it disconcerted her. She laughed a little uneasily.

"Because I knew."

"How did you know?"

"Because—" she began; then again she laughed. "Because," she added, quickly, as if moved by a fresh impulse, "Jack Chilcote made it very obvious to any one who was in his morning-room at twelve o'clock today that it would be you and not he who would be found filling his place this afternoon! It's all very well to talk about honor, but when one walks into an empty room and sees a telegram as long as a letter open on a bureau—"

But her sentence was never finished. Loder had heard what he came to hear; any confession she might have to offer was of no moment in his eyes.

"My dear girl," he broke in, brusquely, "don't trouble! I should make a most unsatisfactory father confessor." He spoke quickly. His color was still high, but not of annoyance. His suspense was transformed into unpleasant certainty; but the exchange left him surer of himself. His perplexity had dropped to a quiet sense of self-reliance; his paramount desire was for solitude in which to prepare for the task that lay before him; the most congenial task the world possessed— the unravelling of Chilcote's tangled skeins. Looking into Lillian's eyes, he smiled. "Good-bye!" he said, holding out his hand. "I think we've finished—for to-day."

She slowly extended her fingers. Her expression and attitude were slightly puzzled—a puzzlement that was either spontaneous or singularly well assumed. As their hands touched she smiled again.

"Will you drop in at the 'Arcadian' to-night?" she said. "It's the dramatized version of 'Other Men's Shoes!' The temptation to make you see it was too irresistible—as you know."

There was a pause while she waited for his answer—her head inclined to one side, her green eyes gleaming.

Loder, conscious of her regard, hesitated for a moment. Then his face cleared. "Right!" he said, slowly. "'The Arcadian' tonight!"

XXIX

Loder's frame of mind as he left Cadogan Gardens was peculiar. Once more he was living in the present—the forceful, exhilarating present, and the knowledge braced him. Upon one point his mind was satisfied. Lillian Astrupp had found the telegram, and it remained to him to render her find valueless. How he proposed to do this, how he proposed to come out triumphant in face of such a situation, was a matter that as yet was shapeless in his mind; nevertheless, the danger—the sense of impending conflict—had a savor of life after the inaction of the day and night just passed. Chilcote in his weakness and his entanglement had turned to him; and he in his strength and capacity had responded to the appeal.

His step was firm and his bearing assured as he turned into Grosvenor Square and walked towards the familiar house.

The habit of self-deceit is as insidious and tenacious as any vice. For one moment on the night of his great speech, as he leaned out of Chilcote's carriage and met Chilcote's eyes, Loder had seen himself—and under the shock of revelation had taken decisive action. But in the hours subsequent to that action the plausible, inner voice had whispered unceasingly, soothing his wounded self-esteem, rebuilding stone by stone the temple of his egotism; until at last when Chilcote, panic-stricken at his own action, had burst into his rooms ready to plead or to coerce, he had found no need for either coercion or entreaty. By a power more subtle and effective than any at his command, Loder had been prepared for his coming—unconsciously ready with an acquiescence before his appeal had been made. It was the fruit of this preparation, the inevitable outcome of it, that strengthened his step and steadied his hand as he mounted the steps and opened the hall door of Chilcote's house on that eventful afternoon.

The, dignity, the air of quiet solidity, impressed him as it never failed to do, as he crossed the large hall and ascended the stairs—the same stairs that he had passed down almost as an outcast not so many hours before. He was filled with the sense of things regained; belief in his own star lifted him as it had done a hundred times before in these same surroundings.

He quickened his steps as the sensation came to him. Then, reaching the head of the stairs, he turned directly towards Eve's sitting-room, and, gaining the door, knocked. The strength of his eagerness, the quick beating of his pulse as he waited for a response, surprised him. He had told himself many times that his passion, however strong, would never again conquer as it had done two nights ago—and the fact that he had come thus candidly to Eve's room was to his mind a proof that temptation could be dared. Nevertheless there was something disconcerting to a strong man in this merely physical perturbation; and when Eve's voice came to him, giving permission to enter, he paused for an instant to steady himself; then with sudden decision he opened the door and walked into the room.

The blinds were partly drawn, there was a scent of violets in the air, and a fire glowed warmly in the grate. He noted these things carefully, telling himself that a man should always be alertly sensible of his surroundings; then all at once the nice balancing of detail suddenly gave way. He forgot everything but the one circumstance that Eve was standing in the window—her back to the light, her face towards him. With his pulses beating faster and an unsteady sensation in his brain, he moved forward holding out his hand.

"Eve—?" he said below his breath.

But Eve remained motionless. As he came into the room she had glanced at him—a glance of quick, searching question; then with equal suddenness she had averted her eyes. As he drew close to her now, she remained immovable.

"Eve—" he said again. "I wanted to see you—I wanted to explain about yesterday and about this morning." He paused, suddenly disturbed. The full remembrance of the scene in the brougham had surged up at sight of her—had risen a fierce, unquenchable recollection. "Eve—" he began again in a new, abrupt tone.

And then it was that Eve showed herself in a fresh light. From his entrance into the room she had stayed motionless, save for her first glance of acute inquiry; but now her demeanor changed. For almost the first time in Loder's knowledge of her the vitality and force that he had vaguely apprehended below her quiet, serene exterior sprang up like a flame within whose radius things are illuminated. With a quick gesture she turned towards him, her warm color deepening, her eyes suddenly alight.

"I understand," she said, "I understand. Don't try to explain! Can't you see that it's enough to—to see you as you are—?"

Loder was surprised. Remembering their last passionate scene, and the damper Chilcote's subsequent presence must inevitably have cast upon it, he had expected to be doubtfully received; but the reality of the reception left him bewildered. Eve's manner was not that of the ill-used wife; its vehemence, its note of desire and depreciation, were more suggestive of his own ardent seizing of the present, as distinguished from past or future. With an odd sense of confusion he turned to her afresh.

"Then I am forgiven?" he said. And unconsciously, as he moved nearer, he touched her arm.

At his touch she started. All the yielding sweetness, all the submission, that had marked her two nights ago was gone; in its place she was possessed by a curious excitement that stirred while it perplexed.

Loder, moved by the sensation, took another step forward. "Then I am forgiven?" he repeated, more softly.

Her face was averted as he spoke, but he felt hen arm quiver; and when at last she lifted her head, their eyes met. Neither spoke, but in an instant Loder's arms were round her.

For a long, silent space they stood holding each other closely. Then, with a sharp movement, Eve freed Herself. Her color was still high, her eyes still peculiarly bright, but the bunch of violets she had worn in her belt had fallen to the ground.

"John—" she said, quickly; but on the word her breath caught. With a touch of nervousness she stooped to pick up the flowers.

Loder noticed both voice and gesture. "What is it?" he said. "What were you going to say?"

But she made no answer. For a second longer she searched for the violets; then, as he bent to assist her, she stood up quickly and laughed—a short, embarrassed laugh.

"How absurd and nervous I am!" she exclaimed. "Like a schoolgirl instead of a woman of twenty-four. You must help me to be sensible." Her cheeks still burned, her manner was still excited, like one who holds an emotion or an impulse at bay.

Loder looked at her uncertainly. "Eve—" he began afresh with his odd, characteristic perseverance, but she instantly checked him. There was a finality, a faint suggestion of fear, in her protest.

"Don't!" she said. "Don't! I don't want explanations. I want to—to enjoy the moment without having things analyzed or smoothed away. Can't you understand? Can't you see that I'm wonderfully, terribly happy to—to have you—as you are!" Again her voice broke—a break that might have been a laugh or a sob.

The sound was an emotional crisis, as such a sound invariably is. It arrested and steadied her. For a moment she stood absolutely still; then, with something very closely resembling her old repose of manner, she stooped again and quietly picked up the flowers still lying at her feet.

"Now," she said, quietly, "I must say what I've wanted to say all along. How does it feel to be a great man?" Her manner was controlled, she looked at him evenly and directly; save for the faint vibration in her voice there was nothing to indicate the tumult of a moment ago.

But Loder was still uncertain. He caught her hand, his eyes searching hers.

"But Eve—" he began.

Then Eve played the last card in her mysterious game. Laughing quickly and nervously, she freed her hand and laid it over his mouth.

"No!" she said. "Not one word! All this past fortnight has belonged to you; now it's my turn. To-day is mine."

XXX

And so, once again, the woman conquered. Whatever Eve's intentions were, whatever she wished to evade or ward off, she was successful in gaining her end. For more than two hours she kept Loder at her side. There may have been moments in those two hours when the tension was high, when the efforts she made to interest and hold him were somewhat strained. But if this was so, it escaped the notice of the one person concerned; for it was long after tea had been served, long after Eve had offered to do penance for her monopoly of him by driving him to Chilcote's club, that Loder realized with any degree of distinctness that it was she and not he who had taken the lead in their interview; that it was she and not he who had bridged the difficult silences and given a fresh direction to dangerous channels of talk. It was long before he recognized this; but it was still longer before he realized the far more potent fact that, without any coldness, without any lessening of the subtle consideration she always showed him, she had given him no further opportunity of making love.

Talking continuously, elated with the sense of conflict still to come, he drove with her to the club. Considering that drive in the light of after events, his own frame of mind invariably filled him with incredulity.

In the eyes of any sane man his position was not worth an hour's purchase; yet in the blind self-confidence of the moment he would not have changed places with Fraide himself. The great song of Self was sounding in his ears as he drove through the crowded streets, conscious of the cool, crisp air, of Eve's close presence, of the numberless infinitesimal things that went to make up the value of life. It was this acknowledgment of personality that upheld him; the personality, the power that had carried him unswervingly through eleven colorless years; that had impelled him towards this new career when the new career had first been opened to him; that had hewn a way for him in this fresh existence against colossal odds. The indomitable force that had trampled out Chilcote's footmarks in public life, in private life—in love. It was a triumphant paean that clamored in his ears, something persistent and prophetic with an undernote of menace. The cry of the human soul that has dared to stand alone.

His glance was keen and bright as he waited for a moment at the carriage door and took Eve's hand before entering the club.

"You're dining out to-night?" he said. His fingers, always tenacious and masterful, continued to hold hers. The compunction that had driven him temporarily towards sacrifice had passed. His pride, his confidence, and with them his desire, had flowed back in full measure.

Eve, watching him attentively, paled a little. "Yes," she said, "I'm dining with the Bramfells."

"What time will you get home?" He scarcely realized why he put the question. The song of Self still sounded triumphantly, and he responded without reflection.

His eyes held hers, his fingers pressed her hand; the intense mastery of his will passed through her in a sudden sense of fear. Her lips parted in deprecation, but he—closely attentive of her expression—spoke again quickly.

"When can I see you?" he asked, very quietly.

Again she was about to speak. She leaned forward, as if some thought long suppressed trembled on her lips; then her courage or her desire failed her. She leaned back, letting her lashes droop over her eyes. "I shall be home at eleven," she said below her breath.

Loder dined with Lakely at Chilcote's club; and so absorbing were the political interests of the hour—the resignation of Sir Robert Sefborough, the King's summoning of Fraide, the probable features of the new ministry—that it was after nine o'clock when at last he freed himself and drove to the "Arcadian" Theatre.

The sound of music came to him as he entered the theatre —light, measured music suggestive of tiny streams, toy lambs, and painted shepherdesses. It sounded singularly inappropriate to his mood—as inappropriate as the theatre itself with its gay gilding, its pale tones of pink and blue. It was the setting of a different world—a world of laughter, light thoughts, and shallow impulses, in which he had no part. He halted for an instant outside the box to which the attendant had shown him; then, as the door was thrown open, he straightened himself resolutely and stepped forward.

It was the interval between the first and second acts.

The box was in shadow, and Loder's first impression was of voices and rustling skirts, broken in upon by the murmur of frequent, amused laughter; later, as his eyes grew accustomed to the light, he distinguished the occupants— two women and a man. The man was speaking as he entered, and the story he was relating was evidently interesting from the faint exclamations of question and delight that punctuated it in the listeners' higher, softer voices. As the new-comer entered they all three turned and looked at him.

"Ah, here comes the legislator!" exclaimed Leonard Kaine. For it was he who formed the male element in the party.

"The Revolutionary, Lennie!" Lillian corrected, softly. "Bramfell says he has changed the whole face of things—" She laughed softly and meaningly as she closed her fan. "So good of you to come, Jack!" she added. "Let me introduce you to Miss Esseltyn; I don't think you two have met. This is Mr. Chilcote, Mary—the great, new Mr. Chilcote." Again she laughed.

Loder bowed and moved to the front of the box, nodding to Kaine as he passed.

"It's only for an hour," he explained to Lillian. "I have an appointment for eleven." He turned and bowed to the third occupant of the box—a remarkably young and well-dressed girl with wide-awake eyes and a retrousse nose.

"Only an hour! Oh, how unkind! How should I punish him, Lennie?" Lillian looked round at Kaine with a lingering, caressing glance.

He bent towards her in quick response and answered in a whisper.

She laughed and replied in an equally low tone.

Loder, to whom both remarks had been inaudible dropped into the vacant seat beside Mary Esseltyn. He had the unsettled feeling that things were not falling out exactly as he had calculated.

"What is the play like?" he hazarded as he looked towards his companion. At all times social trivialities bored him; to-night they were intolerable. He had come to fight, but all at once it seemed that there was no opponent. Lillian's attitude disturbed him; her careless graciousness, her evident ignoring of him for Kaine, might mean nothing—but also it might mean much.

So he speculated as he put his question and spurred his attention towards the girl's answer; but with the speculation came the resolve to hold his own—to meet his enemy upon whatever ground she chose to appropriate.

The girl looked at him with interest. She, too, had heard of his triumph.

"It is a good play," she responded. "I like it better than the book. You've read the book, of course?"

"No." Loder tried hard to fix his thoughts.

"It's amusing—but far-fetched."

"Indeed?" He picked up the programme lying on the edge of the box. His ears were strained to catch the tone of Lillian's voice as she laughed and whispered with Kaine.

"Yes; men exchanging identities, you know."

He looked up and caught the girl's self-possessed glance. "Oh?" he said. "Indeed?" Then again he looked away. It was intolerable this feeling of being caged up! A sense of anger crept through his mind. It almost seemed that Lillian had brought him there to prove that she had finished with him—had cast him aside, having used him for the day's excitement as she had used her poodles, her Persian cats, her crystal-gazing. All at once the impotency and uncertainty of his position goaded him. Turning swiftly in his seat, he glanced back to where she sat, slowly swaying her fan, her pale, golden hair and her pale-colored gown delicately silhouetted against the background of the box.

"What's your idea of the play, Lillian?" he said, abruptly. To his own ears there was a note of challenge in his voice.

She looked round languidly. "Oh, it's quite amusing," she said. "It makes a delicious farce—absolutely French."

"French?"

"Quite. Don't you think so, Lennie?"

"Oh, quite," Kaine agreed.

"They mean that it's so very light—and yet so very subtle, Mr. Chilcote," Mary Esseltyn explained.

"Indeed?" he said. "Then my imagination was at fault. I thought the piece was serious."

"Serious!" Lillian smiled again. "Why, where's your sense of humor? The motive of the play debars all seriousness."

Loder looked down at the programme still between his hands. "What is the motive?" he asked.

Lillian waved her fan once or twice, then closed it softly. "Love is the motive," she said.

Now the balancing—the adjusting of impression and inspirationis, of all processes in life, the most deli. cately fine. The simple sound of the word "love" coming at that precise juncture changed the whole current of Loder's thought. It fell like a seed; and like a seed in ultra-productive soil, it bore fruit with amazing rapidity.

The word itself was small and the manner in which it was spoken trivial, but Loder's mind was attracted and held by it. The last time it had met his ears his environment had been vastly different; and this echo of it in an uncongenial atmosphere stung him to resentment. The vision of Eve, the thought of Eve, became suddenly dominant.

"Love?" he repeated, coldly. "So love is the motive?"

"Yes." This time it was Kaine who responded in his methodical, contented voice. "The motive of the play is love, as Lillian says. And when was love ever serious in a three-act comedy—on or off the stage?" He leaned forward in his seat, screwed in his eye-glass, and lazily scanned the stalls.

The orchestra was playing a Hungarian dance—its erratic harmonies and wild alternations of expression falling abruptly across the pinks and blues, the gilding and lights of the pretty, conventional theatre. Something in the suggestion of unfitness appealed to Loder. It was the force of the real as opposed to the ideal. With a new expression on his face, he turned again to Kaine.

"And how does it work?" he said. "This treatment that you find so— French?"

His voice as well as his expression had changed. He still spoke quietly, but he spoke with interest. He was no longer conscious of his vague and uneasiness; a fresh chord had been struck in his mind, and his curiosity had responded to it. For the first time it occurred to him that love—the dangerous, mysterious garden whose paths had so suddenly stretched out before his own feet—was a pleasure-ground that possessed many doors—and an infinite number of keys. He was stirred by the desire to peer through another entrance than his own, to see the secret, alluring byways from another stand-point. He waited with interest for the answer to his question.

For a second or two Kaine continued to survey the house; then his eye-glass dropped from his eye and he turned round.

"To understand the thing," he said, pleasantly, "you must have read the book. Have you read the book?"

"No, Mr. Kaine," Mary Esseltyn interrupted, "Mr. Chilcote hasn't read the book."

Lillian laughed. "Outline the story for him, Lennie," she said. "I love to see other people taking pains."

Kaine glanced at her admiringly. "Well, to begin with," he said, amiably, "two men, an artist and a millionaire, exchange lives. See?"

"You may presume that he does see, Lennie."

"Right! Well, then, as I say, these beggars change identities. They're as like as pins; and to all appearances one chap's the other chap—and the other chap's the first chap. See?"

Loder laughed. The newly quickened interest was enhanced by treading on dangerous ground.

"Well, they change for a lark, of course, but there's one fact they both overlook. They're men, you know, and they forget these little things!" He laughed delightedly. "They overlook the fact that one of 'em has got a wife!"

There was a crash of music from the orchestra. Loder sat straighter in his seat; he was conscious that the blood had rushed into his face.

"Oh, indeed?" he said, quickly. "One of them had a wife?"

"Exactly!" Again Kaine chuckled. "And the point of the joke is that the wife is the least larky person under the sun. See?"

A second hot wave passed over Loder's face; a sense of mental disgust filled him. This, then, was the wonderful garden seen from another stand-point! He looked from Lillian, graceful, sceptical, and shallow, to the young girl beside him, so frankly modern in her appreciation of life. This, then, was love as seen by the eyes of the world—the world that accepts, judges, and condemns in a slang phrase or two! Very slowly the blood receded from his face.

"And the end of the story?" he asked, in a strained voice.

"The end? Oh, usual end, of course. Chap makes a mess of things and the bubble bursts."

"And the end of the wife?"

"The end of the wife?" Lillian broke in, with a little laugh. "Why, the end of all stupid people who, instead of going through life with a lot of delightfully human stumbles, come just one big cropper. She naturally ends in the divorce court!"

They all laughed boisterously. Then laughter, story, and denouement were all drowned in a tumultuous crash of music. The orchestra ceased; there was a slight hum of applause; and the curtain rose on the second act of the comedy.

XXXI

A few minutes before the curtain fell on the second act of 'Other Men's Shoes' Loder rose from his seat and made his apologies to Lillian.

At any other moment he might have pondered over her manner of accepting them—the easy indifference with which she let him go. But vastly keener issues were claiming his attention, issues whose results were wide and black.

He left the theatre, and, refusing the overtures of cabmen, set himself to walk to Chilcote's house. His face was hard and emotionless as he hurried forward, but the chaos in his mind found expression in the unevenness of his pace. To a strong man the confronting of difficulties is never alarming and is often fraught with inspiration; but this applies essentially to the difficulties evolved through the weakness, the folly, or the force of another; when they arise from within the matter is of another character. It is in presence of his own soul—and in that presence alone —that a man may truly measure himself.

As Loder walked onward, treading the whole familiar length of traffic-filled street, he realized for the first time that he was standing before that solemn tribunal that the hour had come when he must answer to himself for himself. The longer and deeper an oblivion the more painful the awakening. For months the song of self had beaten about his ears, deadening all other sounds; now abruptly that song had ceased—not considerately, not lingeringly, but with a suddenness that made the succeeding silence very terrible.

He walked onward, keeping his direction unseeingly. He was passing through the fire as surely as though actual flames rose about his feet; and whatever the result, whatever the fibre of the man who emerged from the ordeal, the John Loder who had hewn his way through the past weeks would exist no more. The triumphant egotist—the strong man—who, by his own strength, had kept his eyes upon one point, refusing to see in other directions, had ceased to be.

Keen though it was, his realization of this crisis in his life had come with characteristic slowness. When Lillian Astrupp had given her dictum, when the music of the orchestra had ceased and the curtain risen on the second act of the play, nothing but a sense of stupefaction had filled his mind. In that moment the great song was silenced, not by any portentous episode, not by any incident that could have lent dignity to its end, but—with the full measure of life's irony—by a trivial social commonplace. In the first sensation of blank loss his faculties had been numbed; in the quarter of an hour that followed the rise of the curtain he had sat staring at the stage, seeing nothing, hearing nothing, filled with the enormity of the void that suddenly surrounded him. Then, from habit, from constitutional tendency, he had begun slowly and perseveringly to draw first one thread and then another from the tangle of his thoughts—to forge with doubt and difficulty the chain that was to draw him towards the future.

It was upon this same incomplete and yet tenacious chain that his mind worked as he traversed the familiar streets and at last gained the house he had so easily learned to call home.

As he inserted the latch-key and felt it move smoothly in the lock, a momentary revolt against his own judgment, his own censorship swung him sharply towards reaction. But it is only the blind who can walk without a tremor on the edge of an abyss, and there was no longer a bandage across his eyes. The reaction flared up like a strip of lighted paper; then, like a strip of lighted paper, it dropped back to ashes. He pushed the door open and slowly crossed the hall.

The mounting of a staircase is often the index to a man's state of mind. As Loder ascended the stairs of Chilcote's house his shoulders lacked their stiffness, his head was no longer erect; he moved as though his feet were weighted. He had ceased to be the man of achievement whose smallest opinion compels consideration; in the privacy of solitude he was the mere human flotsam to which he had once compared himself—the flotsam that, dreaming it has found a harbor, wakes to find itself the prey of the incoming tide.

He paused at the head of the stairs to rally his resolutions; then, still walking heavily, he passed down the corridor to Eve's room. It was suggestive of his character that, having made his decision, he did not dally over its performance. Without waiting to knock, he turned the handle and walked into the room.

It looked precisely as it always looked, but to Loder the rich, subdued coloring of books and flowers—the whole air of culture and repose that the place conveyed—seemed to hold a deeper meaning than before; and it was on the instant that his eyes, crossing the inanimate objects, rested on their owner that the true force of his position, the enormity of the task before him, made itself plain. Realization came to him with vivid, overwhelming force; and it must be accounted to his credit, in the summing of his qualities, that then, in that moment of trial, the thought of retreat, the thought of yielding did not present itself.

Eve was standing by the mantel-piece. She wore a beautiful gown, a long string of diamonds was twisted about her neck, and her soft, black hair was coiled high after a foreign fashion, and held in place by a large diamond comb. As he entered she turned hastily, almost nervously, and looked at him with the rapid, searching glance he had learned to expect from her; then, almost directly, her expression changed to one of quick concern. With a faint exclamation of alarm she stepped forward.

"What has happened?" she said. "You look like a ghost."

Loder made no answer. Moving into the room, he paused by the oak table that stood between the fireplace and the door.

They made an unconscious tableau as they stood there—he with his hard, set face, she with her heightened color, her inexplicably bright eyes. They stood completely silent for a space—a space that for Loder held no suggestion of time; then, finding the tension unbearable, Eve spoke again.

"Has anything happened?" she asked. "Is anything wrong?"

Had he been less engrossed the intensity of her concern might have struck him; but in a mind so harassed as his there was only room for one consideration—the consideration of himself. The sense of her question reached him, but its significance left him untouched.

"Is anything wrong?" she reiterated for the second time.

By an effort he raised his eyes. No man, he thought, since the beginning of the world was ever set a task so cruel as his. Painfully and slowly his lips parted.

"Everything in the world is wrong," he said, in a slow, hard voice.

Eve said nothing but her color suddenly deepened.

Again Loder was unobservant. But with the dogged resolution that marked him he forced himself to his task.

"You despise lies," he said, at last. "Tell me what you would think of a man whose whole life was one elaborated lie?" The words were slightly exaggerated, but their utterance, their painfully brusque sincerity, precluded all suggestion of effect. Resolutely holding her gaze he repeated his question.

"Tell me! Answer me! I want to know."

Eve's attitude was difficult to read. She stood twisting the string of diamonds between her fingers.

"Tell me?" he said again.

She continued to look at him for a moment; then, as if some fresh impulse moved her, she turned away from him towards the fire.

"I cannot," she said. "We—I—I could not set myself to judge—any one."

Loder held himself rigidly in hand.

"Eve," he said, quietly, "I was at the `Arcadian' to-night. The play was 'Other Men's Shoes.' I suppose you've read the book 'Other Men's Shoes'?"

She was leaning on the mantel-piece and her face was invisible to him. "Yes, I have read it," she said, without looking round.

"It is the story of an extraordinary likeness between two men. Do you believe such a likeness possible? Do you think such a thing could exist?" He spoke with difficulty; his brain and tongue both felt numb.

Eve let the diamond chain slip from her fingers. "Yes," she said, nervously. "Yes, I do believe it. Such things have been—"

Loder caught at the words. "You're quite right," he said, quickly. "You're quite right. The thing is possible—I've proved it. I know a man so like me that you, even you, could not tell us apart."

Eve was silent, still averting her face.

In dire difficulty he labored on. "Eve," he began once more, "such a likeness is a serious thing—a terrible danger—a terrible temptation. Those who have no experience of it cannot possibly gauge its pitfalls—" Again he paused, but again the silent figure by the fireplace gave him no help.

"Eve," he exclaimed, suddenly, "if you only knew, if you only guessed what I'm trying to say—" The perplexity, the whole harassed suffering of his mind showed in the words. Loder, the strong, the resourceful, the self-contained, was palpably, painfully at a loss. There was almost a note of appeal in the vibration of his voice.

And Eve, standing by the fireplace, heard and understood. In that moment of comprehension all that had held her silent, all the conflicting motives that had forbidden speech, melted away before the unconscious demand for help. Quietly and yet quickly she turned, her whole face transfigured by a light that seemed to shine from within —something singularly soft and tender.

"There's no need to say anything," she said, simply, "because I know."

It came quietly, as most great revelations come. Her voice was low and free from any excitement, her face beautiful in its complete unconsciousness of self. In that supreme moment all her thought, all her sympathy was for the man— and his suffering.

To Loder there was a space of incredulity; then his brain slowly swung to realization. "You know?" he repeated, blankly. "You know?"

Without answering she walked to a cabinet that stood in the window, unlocked a drawer, and drew out several sheets of flimsy white paper, crumpled in places and closely covered with writing. Without a word she carried them back and held them out.

He took them in silence, scanned them, then looked up.

In a long, worthless pause their eyes met. It was as if each looked speechlessly into the other's heart, seeing the passions, the contradictions, the shortcomings that went to the making of both. In that silence they drew closer together than they could have done through a torrent of words. There was no asking of forgiveness, no elaborate confession on either side; in the deep, eloquent pause they mutually saw and mutually understood.

"When I came into the morning-room to-day," Eve said, at last, "and saw Lillian Astrupp reading that telegram, nothing could have seemed further from me than the thought that I should follow her example. It was not until afterwards; not until —he came into the room; until I saw that you, as I believed, had fallen back again from what I respected to what I despised—that I knew how human I really was. As I watched them laugh and talk I felt suddenly that I was alone again —terribly alone. I—I think—I believe I was jealous in that moment—" She hesitated.

"Eve!" he exclaimed.

But she broke in quickly on the word. "I felt different in that moment. I didn't care about honor—or things like honor. After they had gone it seemed to me that I had missed something—something that they possessed. Oh, you don't know what a woman feels when she is jealous!" Again she paused. "It was then that the telegram, and the thought of Lillian's amused smile as she had read it, came to my mind. Feeling as I did—acting on what I felt—I crossed to the bureau and picked it up. In one second I had seen enough to make it impossible to draw back. Oh, it may have been dishonorable, it may have been mean, but I wonder if any woman in the world would have done otherwise! I crumpled up the papers just as they were and carried them to my own room."

From the first to the last word of Eve's story Loder's eyes never left her face. Instantly she had finished his voice broke forth in irrepressible question. In that wonderful space of time he had learned many things. All his deductions, all his apprehensions had been scattered and disproved. He had seen the true meaning of Lillian Astrupp's amused indifference—the indifference of a variable, flippant nature that, robbed of any real weapon for mischief, soon tires of a game that promises to be too arduous. He saw all this and understood it with a rapidity born of the moment; nevertheless, when Eve ceased to speak the question that broke from him was not connected with this great discovery—was not even suggestive of it. It was something quite immaterial to any real issue, but something that overshadowed every consideration in the world.

"Eve," he said, "tell me your first thought? Your first thought after the shock and the surprise—when you remembered me?"

There was a fresh pause, but one of very short duration; then Eve met his glance fearlessly and frankly. The same pride and dignity, the same indescribable tenderness that had responded to his first appeal shone in her face.

"My first thought was a great thankfulness," she said, simply. "A thankfulness that you—that no man—could ever understand."

XXXII

As she finished speaking Eve did not lower her eyes. To her there was no suggestion of shame in her thoughts or her words; but to Loder, watching and listening, there was a perilous meaning contained in both.

"Thankfulness?" he repeated, slowly. From his newly stirred sense of responsibility pity and sympathy were gradually rising. He had never seen Eve as he saw her now, and his vision was all the clearer for the long oblivion. With a poignant sense of compassion and remorse, the knowledge of her youth came to him—the youth that some women preserve in the midst of the world, when circumstances have permitted them to see much but to experience little.

"Thankfulness?" he said again, incredulously.

A slight smile touched her lips. "Yes," she answered, softly. "Thankfulness that my trust had been rightly placed."

She spoke simply and confidently, but the words struck Loder more sharply than any accusation. With a heavy sense of bitterness and renunciation he moved slowly forward.

"Eve," he said, very gently, "you don't know what you say."

She had lowered her eyes as he came towards her; now again she lifted them in a swift, upward glance. For the first time since he had entered the room a slight look of personal doubt and uneasiness showed in her face. "Why?" she said. "I—I don't understand."

For a moment he answered nothing. He had found his first explanation overwhelming; now suddenly it seemed to him that his present difficulty was more impossible to surmount. "I came here to-night to tell you something," he began, at last, "but so far I have only said half—"

"Half?"

"Yes, half." He repeated the word quickly, avoiding the question in her eyes. Then, conscious of the need for explanation, he plunged into rapid speech.

"A fraud like mine," he said, "has only one safeguard, one justification—a boundless audacity. Once shake that audacity and the whole motive power crumbles. It was to make the audacity impossible—to tell you the truth and make it impossible—that I came to-night. The fact that you already knew made the telling easier—but it altered nothing."

Eve raised her head, but he went resolutely on.

"To-night," he said, "I have seen into my own life, into my own mind, and my ideas have been very roughly shaken into new places.

"We never make so colossal a mistake as when we imagine that we know ourselves. Months ago, when your husband first proposed this scheme to me, I was, according to my own conception, a solitary being vastly ill-used by Fate, who, with a fine stoicism, was leading a clean life. That was what I believed; but there, at the very outset, I deceived myself. I was simply a man who shut himself up because he cherished a grudge against life, and who lived honestly because he had a constitutional distaste for vice. My first feeling when I saw your husband was one of self-righteous contempt, and that has been my attitude all along. I have often marvelled at the flood of intolerance that has rushed over me at sight of him—the violent desire that has possessed me to look away from his weakness and banish the knowledge of it; but now I understand.

"I know now what the feeling meant. The knowledge came to me to-night. It meant that I turned away from his weakness because deep within myself something stirred in recognition of it. Humanity is really much simpler than we like to think, and human impulses have an extraordinary fundamental connection. Weakness is egotism—but so is strength. Chilcote has followed his vice; I have followed my ambition. It will take a higher judgment than yours or mine to say which of us has been the more selfish man." He paused and looked at her.

She was watching him intently. Some of the meaning in his face had found a pained, alarmed reflection in her own. But the awe and wonder of the morning's discovery still colored her mind too vividly to allow of other considerations possessing their proper value. The thrill of exultation with which the misgivings born of Chilcote's vice had dropped away from her mental image of Loder was still too absorbing to be easily dominated. She loved, and as if by a miracle her love had been justified! For the moment the justification was all-sufficing. Something of confidence—something of the innocence that comes not from ignorance of evil but from a mind singularly uncontaminated—blinded her to the danger of her position.

Loder, waiting apprehensively for some aid, some expression of opinion, became gradually conscious of this lack of realization. Moved by a fresh impulse, he crossed the small space that divided them and caught her hands.

"Eve," he said, gently, "I have been trying to analyze myself and give you the results; but I sha'n't try any more; I shall be quite plain with you.

"From the first moment I took your husband's place I was ambitious. You unconsciously aroused the feeling when you brought me Fraide's message on the first night. You aroused it by your words—but more strongly, though more obscurely, by your underlying antagonism. On that night, though I did not know it, I took up my position—I made my determination. Do you know what that determination was?"

She shook her head.

"It was the desire to stamp out Chilcote's footmarks with my own—to prove that personality is the great force capable of everything. I forgot to reckon that when we draw largely upon Fate she generally extorts a crushing interest.

"First came the wish for your respect; then the desire to stand well with such men as Fraide—to feel the stir of emulation and competition—to prove myself strong in the one career I knew myself really fitted for. For a time the second ambition overshadowed the first, but the first was bound to reassert itself; and in a moment of egotism I conceived the notion of winning your enthusiasm as well as your respect—"

Eve's face, alert and questioning, suddenly paled as a doubt crossed her mind.

"Then it was only—only to stand well with me?"

"I believed it was only the desire to stand well with you; I believed it until the night of my speech—if you can credit anything so absurd—then on that night, as I came up the stairs to the gallery and saw you standing there, the blindness fell away and I knew that I loved you." As he said the last words he released her hands and turned aside, missing the quick wave of joy and color that crossed her face.

"I knew it, but it made no difference; I was only moved to a higher self-glorification. I touched supremacy that night. But as we drove home I experienced the strangest coincidence of my life. You remember the block in the traffic at Piccadilly?"

Again Eve bent her head.

"Well, when I looked out of the carriage window to discover its cause the first man I saw was—Chilcote."

Eve started slightly. This swift, unexpected linking of Chilcote's name with the most exalted moment of her life stirred her unpleasantly. Some glimmering of Loder's intention in so linking it, broke through the web of disturbed and conflicting thoughts.

"You saw him on that night?"

"Yes; and the sight chilled me. It was a big drop from supremacy to the remembrance of—everything."

Involuntarily she put out her hand.

But Loder shook his head. "No," he said, "don't pity me! The sight of him came just in time. I had a reaction in that moment, and, such as it was, I acted on it. I went to him next morning and told him that the thing must end. But then —even then—I shirked being honest with myself. I had meant to tell him that it must end because I had grown to love you, but my pride rose up and tied my tongue. I could not humiliate myself. I put the case before him in another light. It was a tussle of wills—and I won; but the victory was not what it should have been. That was proved to-day when he returned to tell me of the loss of this telegram. It wasn't the fear that Lady Astrupp had found it; it wasn't to save the position that I jumped at the chance of coming back; it was to feel the joy of living, the joy of seeing you—if only for a day!" For one second he turned towards her, then as abruptly he turned away again.

"I was still thinking of myself," he said. "I was still utterly self-centred when I came to this room today and allowed you to talk to me—when I asked you to see me to-night as we parted at the club. I sha'n't tell you the thoughts that unconsciously were in my mind when I asked that favor. You must understand without explanation.

"I went to the theatre with Lady Astrupp ostensibly to find out how the land lay in her direction—really to heighten my self-esteem. But there Fate—or the power we like to call by that name—was lying in wait for me, ready to claim the first interest in the portion of life I had dared to borrow." He said this slowly, as if measuring each word. He did not glance towards Eve as he had done in his previous pause. His whole manner seemed oppressed by the gravity of what he had still to say.

"I doubt if a man has ever seen more in half an hour than I have to-night," he said. "I'm speaking of mental seeing, of course. In this play, 'Other Men's Shoes,' two men change identities—as Chilcote and I have done—but in doing so they overlook one fact—The fact that one of them has a wife! That's not my way of putting it; it's the way it was put to me by one of Lady Astrupp's party."

Again Eve looked up. The doubt and question in her eyes had grown unmistakably. As he ceased to speak her lips parted quickly.

"John," she said, with sudden conviction, "you're trying to say something—something that's terribly hard."

Without raising his head, Loder answered her. "Yes," he answered, "the hardest thing a man ever said—"

His tone was short, almost brusque, but to ears sharpened by instinct it was eloquent. Without a word Eve took a step forward, and, standing quite close to him, laid both hands on his shoulders.

For a space they stood silent, she with her face lifted, he with averted eyes. Then very gently he raised his hands and tried to unclasp her fingers. There was scarcely any color visible in his face, and by a curious effect of emotion it seemed that lines, never before noticeable, had formed about his mouth.

"What is it?" Eve asked, apprehensively. "What is it?"

By a swift, involuntary movement she had tightened the pressure of her fingers; and, without using force, it was impossible for Loder to unloose them. With his hands pressed irresolutely over hers, he looked down into her face.

"As I sat in the theatre to-night, Eve," he said, slowly, "all the pictures I had formed of life shifted. Without desiring it, without knowing it, my whole point of view was changed. I suddenly saw things by the world's search-light instead of by my own miserable candle. I suddenly saw things for you —instead of for myself."

Eve's eyes widened and darkened, but she said nothing.

"I suddenly saw the unpardonable wrong that I have done you —the imperative duty of cutting it short." He spoke very slowly, in a dull, mechanical voice.

Eve—her eyes still wide, her face pained and alarmed —withdrew her hands from his shoulders. "You mean," she said, with difficulty, "that it is going to end? That you are going away? That you are giving everything up? Oh, but you can't! You can't!" she exclaimed, with sudden excitement, her fears suddenly overmastering her incredulity. "You can't! You mustn't! The only proof that could have interfered—"

"I wasn't thinking of the proof."

"Then of what? Of what?"

Loder was silent for a moment. "Of our love," he said, steadily.

She colored deeply. "But why?" she stammered; "why? We have done no wrong. We need do no wrong. We would be friends—nothing more; and I—oh, I so need a friend!"

For almost the first time in Loder's knowledge of her, her voice broke, her control deserted her. She stood before him in all the pathos of her lonely girlhood—her empty life.

The revelation touched him with sudden poignancy; the real strength that lay beneath his faults, the chivalry buried under years of callousness, stirred at the birth of a new emotion. The resolution preserved at such a cost, the sacrifice that had seemed wellnigh impossible, all at once took on a different shape. What before had been a barren duty became suddenly a sacred right. Holding out his arms, he drew her to him as if she had been a child.

"Eve," he said, gently, "I have learned to-night how fully a woman's life is at the mercy of the world—and how scanty that mercy is. If circumstances had been different, I believe—I am convinced—I would have made you a good husband—would have used my right to protect you as well as a man could use it. And now that things are different, I want—I should like—" He hesitated a very little. "Now that I have no right to protect you—except the right my love gives—I want to guard you as closely from all that is sordid as any husband could guard his wife.

"In life there are really only two broad issues—right and wrong. Whatever we may say, whatever we may profess to believe, we know that our action is always a choice between right and wrong. A month ago—a week ago—I would have despised a man who could talk like this—and have thought myself strong for despising him. Now I know that strength is something more than the trampling of others into the dust that we ourselves may have a clear road; that it is something much harder and much less triumphant than that—that it is standing aside to let somebody else pass on. Eve," he exclaimed, suddenly, "I'm trying to do this for you. Don't you see? Don't you understand? The easy course, the happy course, would be to let things drift. Every instinct is calling to me to take that course—to go on as I have gone, trading on Chilcote's weakness and your generosity. But I won't do it! I can't do it!" With a swift impulse he loosed his arms and held her away from him. "Eve, it's the first time I have put another human being before myself!"

Eve kept her head bent. Painful, inaudible sobs were shaking her from head to foot.

"It's something in you—something unconscious—something high and fine, that holds me back—that literally bars the way. Eve, can't you see that I'm fighting—fighting hard?"

After he had spoken there was silence—a long, painful silence—during which Eve waged the battle that so many of her sex have waged before; the battle in which words are useless and tears of no account. She looked very slight, very young, very forlorn, as she stood there. Then, in the oppressive sense of waiting that filled the whole room, she looked up at him.

Her face was stained with tears, her thick, black lashes were still wet with them; but her expression, as her eyes met Loder's, was a strange example of the courage, the firmness, the power of sacrifice that may be hidden in a fragile vessel.

She said nothing, for in such a moment words do not come easily, but with the simplest, most submissive, most eloquent gesture in the world she set his perplexity to rest.

Taking his hand between hers, she lifted it and for a long, silent space held it against her lips.

XXXIII

For a while there was silence; then Loder, bitterly aware that he had conquered, poignantly conscious of the appeal that Eve's attitude made, found further endurance impossible. Gently freeing his hand, he moved away from her to the fireplace, taking up the position that she had first occupied.

"Eve," he said, slowly, "I haven't finished yet. I haven't said everything. I'm going to tax your courage further."

With a touch of pained alarm, Eve lifted her head. "Further?" she said.

Loder shrank from the expression on her face. "Yes," he said, with difficulty. "There's still another point to be faced. The matter doesn't end with my going back. To have the situation fully saved, Chilcote must return—Chilcote must be brought to realize his responsibilities."

Eve's lips parted in dumb dismay.

"It must be done," he went on hurriedly, "and we have got to do it—you and I." He turned and looked at her.

"I? I could do nothing. What could I do?" Her voice failed.

"Everything," he said, "you could do everything. He is morally weak, but he has one sensitive point—the fear of a public exposure. Once make it plain to him that you know his secret, and you can compel him to whatever course of action you select. It was to ask you to do this—to beg you to do this—that I came to you to-night. I know that it's demanding more than a woman's resolution—more than a woman's strength. But you are like no woman in the world!

"Eve!" he cried, with sudden vehemence, "can't you see that it's imperative—the one thing to save us both?"

He stopped abruptly as he had begun, and again a painful silence filled the room. Then, as before, Eve moved instinctively towards him, but this time her steps were slow and uncertain. Nearing his side, she put out her hand as if for comfort and support; and, feeling his fingers tighten round it, stood for a moment resting in the contact.

"I understand," she said at last, very slowly. "I understand. When will you take me to him?"

For a moment Loder said nothing, not daring to trust his voice; then he answered, low and abruptly. "Now!" he said. "Now, at once! Now, this moment, if I may. And—and remember that I know what it costs you." As if imbued with fear that his courage might fail him, he suddenly released her hand, and, crossing the room to where a long, dark cloak lay as she had thrown it on her return home, he picked it up, walked to her side, and silently wrapped it about her. Then, still acting automatically, he moved to the door, opened it, and stood aside while she passed out into the corridor.

In complete silence they descended the stairs and passed to the hall door. There Crapham, who had returned to his duties since Loder's entrance, came quickly forward with an offer of service.

But Loder dismissed him curtly; and with something of the confusion bred of Chilcote's regime, the man drew back towards the staircase.

With a hasty movement Loder stepped forward, and, opening the door, admitted a breath of chill air. Then on the threshold he paused. It was his first sign of hesitation —the one instant in which nature rebelled against the conscience so tardily awakened. He stood motionless for a moment, and it is doubtful whether even Eve fully fathomed the bitterness of his renunciation— the blackness of the night that stretched before his eyes.

Behind him was everything; before him, nothing. The everything symbolized by the luxurious house, the eagerly attentive servants, the pleasant atmosphere of responsibility; the nothing represented by the broad public thoroughfare, the passing figures, each unconscious of and uninterested in his existence. As an interloper he had entered this house; as an interloper—a masquerader—he had played his part, lived his hour, proved himself; as an interloper he was now passing back into the dim world of unrealized hopes and unachieved ambitions.

He stood rigidly quiet, his strong figure silhouetted against the lighted hall, his face cold and set; then, with a touch of fatality, Chance cut short his struggle.

An empty hansom wheeled round the corner of the square; the cabman, seeing him, raised his whip in query, and involuntarily he nodded an acquiescence. A moment later he had helped Eve into the cab.

"Middle Temple Lane!" he directed, pausing on the step.

"Middle Temple Lane is opposite to Clifford's Inn," he explained as he took his place beside her. "When we get out there we have only to cross Fleet Street."

Eve bent her head in token that she understood, and the cab moved out into the roadway.

Within a few minutes the neighborhood of Grosvenor Square was exchanged for the noisier and more crowded one of Piccadilly, but either the cabman was overcautious or the horse was below the average, for they made but slow progress through the more crowded streets. To the two sitting in silence the pace was wellnigh unbearable. With every added movement the tension grew. The methodical care with which they moved seemed like the tightening of a string already strained to breaking-point, yet neither spoke—because neither had the courage necessary for words.

Once or twice as they traversed the Strand, Loder made a movement as if to break the silence, but nothing followed it. He continued to lean forward with a certain dogged stiffness, his clasped hands resting on the doors of the cab, his eyes staring straight ahead. Not once, as they threaded their way, did he dare to glance at Eve, though every movement, every stir of her garments, was forced upon his consciousness by his acutely awakened senses.

When at last they drew up before the dark archway of Middle Temple Lane, he descended hastily. And as he mechanically turned to protect Eve's dress from the wheel, he looked at her fully for the first time since their enterprise had been undertaken. As he looked he felt his heart sink. He had expected to see the marks of suffering on her face, but the expression he saw suggested something more than mere mental pain.

All the rich color that usually deepened and softened the charm of her beauty had been erased as if by a long illness; and against the new pallor of her skin her blue eyes, her black hair and eyebrows, seemed startlingly dark. A chill colder than remorse, a chill that bordered upon actual fear, touched Loder in that moment. With the first impulsive gesture he had allowed himself, he touched her arm.

"Eve—" he began, unsteadily; then the word died off his lips.

Without a sound, almost without a movement, she returned his glance, and something in her eyes checked what he might have said. In that one expressive look he understood all she had desired, all she had renounced—the full extent of the ordeal she had consented to, and the motive that had compelled her consent. He drew back with the heavy sense that repentance and pity were equally futile—equally out of place.

Still in silence she stepped to the pavement and stood aside while Loder dismissed the cab. To both there was something symbolic, something prophetic, in the dismissal. Without intention and almost unconsciously they drew closer together as the horse turned, its hoofs clattering on the roadway, its harness jingling; and, still without realization, they looked after the vehicle as it moved away down the long, shadowed thoroughfare towards the lights and the crowds that they had left. At last involuntarily they turned towards each other.

"Come!" Loder said, abruptly. "It's only across the road."

Fleet Street is generally very quiet, once midnight is passed; and Eve had no need of guidance or protection as they crossed the pavement, shining like ice in the lamplight. They crossed it slowly, walking apart; for the dread of physical contact that had possessed them in the cab seemed to have fallen on them again.

Inquisitiveness has little place in the region of the city, and they gained the opposite footpath unnoticed by the casual passer-by. Then, still holding apart, they reached and entered Clifford's Inn.

Inside the entrance they paused, and Eve shivered involuntarily. "How gray it is!" she said, faintly. "And how cold! Like a graveyard."

Loder turned to her. For one moment control seemed shaken; his blood surged, his vision clouded; the sense that life and love were still within his reach filled him overwhelmingly. He turned towards Eve; he half extended his hands. Then, stirred by what impulse, moved by what instinct, it was impossible to say, he let them drop to his sides again.

"Come!" he said. "Come! This is the way. Keep close to me. Put your hand on my arm."

He spoke quietly, but his eyes were resolutely averted from her face as they crossed the dim, silent court.

Entering the gloomy door-way that led to his own rooms, he felt her fingers tremble on his arm, then tighten in their pressure as the bare passage and cheerless stairs met her view; but he set his lips.

"Come!" he repeated, in the same strained voice. "Come! It isn't far—three or four flights."

With a white face and a curious expression in her eyes, Eve moved forward. She had released Loder's arm as they crossed the hall; and now, reaching the stairs, she put out her hand gropingly and caught the banister. She had a pained, numb sense of submission—of suffering that had sunk to apathy. Moving forward without resistance, she began to mount the stairs.

The ascent was made in silence. Loder went first, his shoulders braced, his head held erect; Eve, mechanically watchful of all his movements, followed a step or two behind. With weary monotony one flight of stairs succeeded another; each, to her unaccustomed eyes, seeming more colorless, more solitary, more desolate than the preceding one.

Then at last, with a sinking sense of apprehension, she realized that their goal was reached.

The knowledge broke sharply through her dulled senses; and, confronted by the closeness of her ordeal, she paused, her head lifted, her hand still nervously grasping the banister. Her lips parted as if in sudden demand for aid; but in the nervous expectation, the pained apprehension, of the moment no sound escaped them. Loder, resolutely crossing the landing, knew nothing of the silent appeal.

For a second she stood hesitating; then her own weakness, her own shrinking dismay, were submerged in the interest of his movements. Slowly mounting the remaining steps, she followed him as if fascinated towards the door that showed dingily conspicuous in the light of an unshaded gas-jet.

Almost at the moment that she reached his side he extended his hand towards the door. The action was decisive and hurried, as though he feared to trust himself.

For a space he fumbled with the lock. And Eve, standing close behind him, heard the handle creak and turn under his pressure. Then he shook the door.

At last, slowly, almost reluctantly, he turned round. "I'm afraid things aren't quite quite right," he said, in a low voice. "The door is locked and I can see no light."

She raised her eyes quickly. "But you have a key?" she whispered. "Haven't you got a key?" It was obvious that, to both, the unexpected check to their designs was fraught with danger.

"Yes, but—" He looked towards the door. "Yes—I have a key. Yes, you're right!" he added, quickly. "I'll use it. Wait, while I go inside."

Filled with a new nervousness, oppressed by the loneliness, the silence about her, Eve drew back obediently. The sense of mystery conveyed by the closed door weighed upon her. Her susceptibilities were tensely alert as she watched Loder search for his key and insert it in the lock. With mingled dread and curiosity she saw the door yield, and gape open like a black gash in the dingy wall; and with a sudden sense of desertion she saw him pass through the aperture and heard him strike a match.

The wait that followed seemed extraordinarily long. Listening intently, she heard him move softly from one room to the other. And at last, to her acutely nervous susceptibilities, it seemed that he paused in absolute silence. In the intensity of listening, she heard her own faint, irregular breathing, and the sound filled her with panic. The quiet, the solitude, the vague, instinctive apprehension, became suddenly unendurable. Then all at once the tension was relieved.. Loder reappeared.

He paused for a second in the shadowy door-way; then he turned unsteadily, drew the door to, and locked; it.

Eve stepped forward. Her glimpse of him had been momentary —and she had not heard his voice—yet the consciousness of his bearing filled her with instinctive alarm. Abruptly, and without reason, their hands turned cold, her heart began to beat violently. "John—" she said below her breath.

For answer, he moved towards her. His face was bereft of color; there was a look of consternation in his eyes. "Come!" he said. "Come at once! I must take you home." He spoke in a shaken, uneven voice.

Eve, looking up at him, caught his hand. "Why? Why?" she questioned. Her tone was low and scared.

Without replying, he drew her imperatively towards the stairs. "Go very softly," he commanded. "No one must see you here."

In the first moment she obeyed him instinctively; then, reaching the head of the stairs, she stopped. With one hand still clasping his, the other clinging nervously to the banister, she refused to descend. "John," she whispered, "I'm not a child. What is it? What has happened? I must know."

For a moment Loder looked at her uncertainly; then, reading the expression in her eyes, he yielded to her demand.

"He's dead," he said, in a very low voice. "Chilcote is dead,"

XXXIV

To fully appreciate a great announcement we must have time at our disposal. At the moment of Loder's disclosure time was denied to Eve; for scarcely had the words left his lips before the thought that dominated him asserted its prior claim. Blind to the incredulity in her eyes, he drew her swiftly forward, and—half impelling, half supporting her—forced her to descend the stairs.

Never in after-life could he obliterate the remembrance of that descent. Fear, such as he could never experience in his own concerns, possessed him. One desire overrode all others —the desire that Eve's reputation, which he himself had so nearly imperilled, should remain unimperilled. In the shadow of that urgent duty, the despair of the past hours, the appalling fact so lately realized, the future with its possible trials, became dark to his imagination. In his new victory over self, the question of her protection predominated.

Moving under this compulsion, he guided her hastily and silently down the deserted stairs, drawing a breath of deep relief as, one after another, the landings were successively passed; and still actuated by the suppressed need of haste, he passed through the door-way that they had entered under such different conditions only a few minutes before.

To leave the quiet court, to gain the Strand, to hail a belated hansom was the work of a moment. By an odd contrivance of circumstance, the luck that had attended every phase of his dual life was again exerted in his behalf. No one had noticed their entry into Clifford's Inn; no one was moved to curiosity by their exit. With an involuntary thrill of feeling he gave expression to his relief.

"Thank God, it's over!" he said, as a cab drew up. "You don't know what the strain has been."

Moving as if in a dream, Eve stepped into the cab. As yet the terrible denouement to their enterprise had made no clear impression upon her mind. For the moment all that she was conscious of, all that she instinctively acknowledged, was the fact that Loder was still beside her.

In quiet obedience she took her place, drawing aside her skirts to make room for him; and in the same subdued manner, he stepped into the vehicle. Then, with the strange sensation of reliving their earlier drive, they were aware of the tightened rein and of the horse's first forward movement.

For several seconds neither spoke. Eve, shutting out all other thoughts, sat close to Loder, clinging tenaciously to the momentary comforting sense of protection; Loder, striving to marshal his ideas, hesitated before the ordeal of speech. At last, realizing his responsibility, he turned to her slowly.

"Eve," he said, in a low voice and with some hesitation, "I want you to know that in all this—from the moment I saw him —from the moment I understood—I have had you in my thoughts —you and no one else."

She raised her eyes to his face.

"Do you realize—?" he began afresh. "Do you know what this —this thing means?"

Still she remained silent.

"It means that after to-night there will be no such person in London as John Loder. To-morrow the man who was known by that name will be found in his rooms; his body will be removed, and at the post-modern examination it will be stated that he died of an overdose of morphia. His charwoman will identify him as a solitary man who lived respectably for years and then suddenly went down-hill with remarkable speed. It will be quite a common case. Nothing of interest will be found in his rooms; no relation will claim his body; after the usual time he will be given the usual burial of his class. These details are horrible; but there are times when we must look at the horrible side of life—because life is incomplete without it.

"These things I speak of are the things that will meet the casual eye; but in our sight they will have a very different meaning.

"Eve," he said, more vehemently, "a whole chapter in my life has been closed to-night, and my first instinct is to shut the book and throw it away. But I'm thinking of you. Remember, I'm thinking of you! Whatever the trial, whatever the difficulty, no harm shall come to you. You have my word for that!

"I'll return with you now to Grosvenor Square; I'll remain there till a reasonable excuse can be given for Chilcote's going abroad; I will avoid Fraide, I will cut politics —whatever the cost; then, at the first reasonable moment, I will do what I would do now, to-night if it were possible. I'll go away, start afresh; do in another country what I have done in this."

There was a long silence; then Eve turned to him. The apathy of a moment before had left her face. "In another country?" she repeated. "In another country?"

"Yes; a fresh career in a fresh country. Something clean to offer you. I'm not too old to do what other men have done."

He paused, and for a moment Eve looked ahead at the gleaming chain of lamps; then, still very slowly, she brought her glance back again. "No," she said very slowly. "You are not too old. But there are times when age—and things like age—are not the real consideration. It seems to me that your own inclination, your own individual sense of right and wrong, has nothing to do with the present moment. The question is whether you are justified in going away"—she paused, her eyes fixed steadily upon his—"whether you are free to go away, and make a new life—whether it is ever justifiable to follow a phantom light when—when there's a lantern waiting to be carried." Her breath caught; she drew away from him, frightened and elated by her own words.

Loder turned to her sharply. "Eve!" he exclaimed; then his tone changed. "You don't know what you're saying," he added, quickly; "you don't understand what you're saying."

Eve leaned forward again. "Yes," she said, slowly, "I do understand." Her voice was controlled, her manner convinced. She was no longer the girl conquered by strength greater than her own: she was the woman strenuously demanding her right to individual happiness.

"I understand it all," she repeated. "I understand every point. It was not Chance that made you change your identity, that made you care for me, that brought about—his death. I don't believe it was Chance; I believe it was something much higher. You are not meant to go away!"

As Loder watched her the remembrance of his first days as Chilcote rose again; the remembrance of how he had been dimly filled with the belief that below her self-possession lay a strength—a depth—uncommon in woman. As he studied her now, the instinctive belief flamed into conviction. "Eve!" he said involuntarily.

With a quick gesture she raised her head. "No!" she exclaimed. "No; don't say anything! You are going to see things as I see them—you must do so—you have no choice. No real man ever casts away the substance for the shadow!" Her eyes shone—the color, the glow, the vitality, rushed back into her face.

"John," she said, softly, "I love you—and I need you—but there is something with a greater claim—a greater need than mine. Don't you know what it is?"

He said nothing; he made no gesture.

"It is the party—the country. You may put love aside, but duty is different. You have pledged yourself. You are not meant to draw back."

Loder's lips parted.

"Don't!" she said again. "Don't say anything! I know all that is in your mind. But, when we sift things right through, it isn't my love—or our happinees—that's really in the balance. It is your future!"

Her voice thrilled. "You are going to be a great man, and a great man is the property of his country. He has no right to individual action."

Again Loder made an effort to speak, but again she checked him.

"Wait!" she exclaimed. "Wait! You believe you have acted wrongly, and you are desperately afraid of acting wrongly again. But is it really truer, more loyal for us to work out a long probation in grooves that are already overfilled than to marry quietly abroad and fill the places that have need of us? That is the question I want you to answer. Is it really truer and nobler? Oh, I see the doubt that is in your mind! You think it finer to go away and make a new life than to live the life that is waiting you—because one is independent and the other means the use of another man's name and another man's money—that is the thought in your mind. But what is it that prompts that thought?" Again her voice caught, but her eyes did not falter. "I will tell you. It is not self-sacrifice — but pride!" She said the word fearlessly.

A flush crossed Loder's face. "A man requires pride," he said in a low voice.

"Yes, at the right time. But is this the right time? Is it ever right to throw away the substance for the shadow? You say that I don't understand—don't realize. I realize more to-night than I have realized in all my life. I know that you have an opportunity that can never come again—and that it's terribly possible to let it slip—"

She paused. Loder, his hands resting on the closed doors of the cab, sat very silent, with averted eyes and bent head.

"Only to-night," she went on, "you told me that everything was crying to you to take the easy, pleasant way. Then it was strong to turn aside; but now it is not strong. It is far nobler to fill an empty niche than to carve one for yourself. John—" She suddenly leaned forward, laying her hands over his. "Mr. Fraide told me to-night that in his new ministry my—my husband was to be Under Secretary for Foreign Affairs!"

The words fell softly. So softly that to ears less comprehending than Loder's their significance might have been lost—as his rigid attitude and unresponsive manner might have conveyed lack of understanding to any eyes less observant than Eve's.

For a long space there was no word spoken. At last, with a very gentle pressure, her fingers tightened over his hands.

"John—" she began, gently. But the word died away. She drew back into her seat, as the cab stopped before Chilcote's house.

Simultaneously as they descended, the hall door was opened and a flood of warm light poured out reassuringly into the darkness.

"I thought it was your cab, sir," Crapham explained deferentially as they passed into the hall. "Mr. Fraide has been waiting to see you this half-hour. I showed him into the study." He closed the door; softly and retired.

Then, in the warm light, amid the gravely dignified surroundings that had marked his first entry into this hazardous second existence, Eve turned to Loder for the verdict upon which the future hung.

As she turned, his face was still hidden from her, and his attitude betrayed nothing.

"John," she said, slowly, "you know why he is here.' You know that he has come to personally offer you this place; to personally receive your refusal—or consent."

She ceased to speak; there was a moment of suspense; then Loder turned. His face was still pale and grave with the gravity of a man who has but recently been close to death, but beneath the gravity was another look—the old expression of strength and self-reliance, tempered, raised, and dignified by a new humility.

Moving forward, he held out his hands.

"My consent or refusal," he said, very quietly, "lies with —my wife."

Echo Library
www.echo-library.com

Echo Library uses advanced digital print-on-demand technology to build and preserve an exciting world class collection of rare and out-of-print books, making them readily available for everyone to enjoy.

Situated just yards from Teddington Lock on the River Thames, Echo Library was founded in 2005 by Tom Cherrington, a specialist dealer in rare and antiquarian books with a passion for literature.

Please visit our website for a complete catalogue of our books, which includes foreign language titles.

The Right to Read

Echo Library actively supports the Royal National Institute for the Blind's Right to Read initiative by publishing a comprehensive range of Large Print (16 point Tiresias font as recommended by the RNIB) and Clear Print (13 point Tiresias font) titles for those who find standard print difficult to read.

Customer Service

If there is a serious error in the text or layout please send details to feedback@echo-library.com and we will supply a corrected copy. If there is a printing fault or the book is damaged please refer to your supplier.